The Blu[e]

A Jonah Penn[...]

Keith Nixon

THE BLUE CODE
Published by Gladius Press 2023
Copyright © Keith Nixon 2023
First Edition
Keith Nixon has asserted his right under the Copyright, Designs and Patents Act 1998 to be identified as the author of this work.
CONDITIONS OF SALE
All rights reserved. No part of this publication may be reproduced, stored in a retrieval system, or transmitted in any form or by any means, electronic, mechanical, photocopying, scanning, recording or otherwise, without the prior permission of the publisher.
This book has been sold subject to the condition that it shall not, by way of trade or otherwise, be lent, resold, hired out, or otherwise circulated without the publisher's prior consent in any form of binding or cover other than that in which it is published and without a similar condition including this condition being imposed on the subsequent purchaser.

Other Novels By Keith Nixon

The Solomon Gray Series
Dig Two Graves
Burn The Evidence
Beg For Mercy
Bury The Bodies
Pity The Dead
The Silent Dead
Betray Them All
The Jonah Pennance Series
Blood Sentence
Dead Money
The Blue Code
The Konstantin Series
Russian Roulette
My Middle Name Is Misery
Dark Heart, Heavy Soul
I'm Dead Again
The Fix
The Harry Vaughan Series
The Nudge Man
The DI Granger Series
The Corpse Role
The Caradoc Series
The Eagle's Shadow
The Eagle's Blood

One

Logan Elliott reached out once more, touched the hard, plastic shell of the security case in the footwell, reassuring himself the secured bag was still there. A steel chain united Elliott and the consignment – The Blue Code. He returned to drumming his fingers on the leather upholstery of the rear seat. Deliberately irritating, although Matt Ferrensby, Elliott's driver, didn't complain. He was paid not to.

Elliott glanced yet again towards the supermarket entrance. Even through the heavily blacked-out windows of the Mercedes, the sunlight reflecting off parked cars was vividly intense. Like God's brilliance irradiating the Earth, but in here Elliott went untouched.

A shimmer of heat rose off the tarmac, corrupting Elliott's observation of the shoppers wandering back and forth on an unseasonably warm Friday afternoon.

Outside, a person could lean right up to the car, nose touching the glass, and detect nothing more than indistinct shadows inside. To passers-by he could be a pop star, a footballer, a pimp. They could only speculate. Even so, Elliott shifted in his seat, feeling exposed. He was taking a risk transporting the package.

Elliott removed his aviator sunglasses, squeezed the bridge of his nose between two fingers. "Where the bloody hell is she?"

"I'm sure she won't be long." Ferrensby's eyes, sunk deep in his drawn face, flickered towards Elliott in the rear-view mirror.

THE BLUE CODE

Elliott checked his watch then his mobile, increasingly annoyed at himself for allowing Olivia to persuade him it would be a good idea to host a barbecue this evening – even though he saw the sense in the pretence of normality. Life carries on, despite the data in his case which hypothesised otherwise.

"There she is." Ferrensby flipped a digit the circumference of a spindly twig towards the large glass doors of the supermarket exit. A brunette in an unfeasibly short skirt tottered out, her usually high centre of gravity, resulting from long legs and high heels, cancelled out by the bulging plastic bags in each hand.

Ferrensby's phone bleeped as Elliott was about to wonder aloud what the hell his girlfriend had bought. Ferrensby checked the screen and then reached for the door handle.

"Don't bother." Elliott curled a lip. "She can manage."

Olivia lowered the carriers to the ground, fished around in the leather handbag slung over her shoulder (which Elliott had purchased) and pulled out a cigarette packet. She clearly intended to squeeze in a smoke.

It was then Elliott realised a car was drawing up beside them, hauling his attention away from Olivia.

He blinked.

A silver Audi had halted inches away from the Merc. The driver, low in the front seat, stared forward, hands gripping the steering wheel, knuckles white. Elliott couldn't see his face or even his hair.

Because the driver wore a black balaclava.

Elliott registered movement; a guy stepping from the passenger side, sporting identical headgear to his colleague. Slowly, almost nonchalantly, like he was off for a stroll, the second guy ambled round the rear of the Merc, forcing Elliott to crane his neck to keep sight of him.

"Shit." Elliott zoned in on the large, black metallic machine gun the guy held in gloved hands, revealed as he emerged from behind the Audi. Elliott's heart blasted into overdrive, his chest tightening, while everything else around him went slo-mo.

However, something was very wrong. The Merc was stationary.

Ferrensby should have been whipping them away from danger, engine screaming, tyres burning rubber, leaving Olivia to fend for herself. Yet the Merc's engine died as Ferrensby withdrew the keys. His gaze met Elliott's once more in the rear-view. "Sorry, boss." Then Ferrensby was moving away quickly, sliding into the rear of the adjacent car as the gunman neared Elliott.

Get out. He had to get out.

But Elliott couldn't open his door more than an inch, the hitman's vehicle was simply too close. He slid over to the other side, bringing the case with him, his palm damp and slippery. A faint hope that maybe he'd exit, use the Merc as a shield. However, the handle flapped uselessly.

His soon-to-be-murderer finally took up a stance. Feet spread apart, shoulders relaxed, just a couple of yards away. The gunman lowered the muzzle until it almost touched the darkened glass while, outside the supermarket, Olivia struggled with a lighter, spinning the wheel again and again.

THE BLUE CODE

The gunman tapped on the window. A grin revealed brilliant white teeth and, bizarrely, both upper canines in gold, like a vampire flaunting his wealth.

Then ... nothing.

Elliott breathed in, out. He felt utterly, shockingly calm. Elliott removed his sunglasses, dropped them, while Olivia shook her lighter and finally got a flame.

Then ... the rapid BAA-DAA!! of bullets zinging out of the barrel at hundreds of feet per second. The window dissolved, there one moment, destroyed the next, scattering glass like brutal confetti. The projectiles thudded into Elliott, tossing him backwards, as if he was being punched unfeasibly hard all over his body by an unseen, lightning-quick hand. Everywhere Elliott was struck, a hot agony sliced through him.

Then ... silence.

Elliott lay sprawled on the backseat. He blinked, a metallic taste in his mouth, remembered sucking a dirty coin when he was a kid and being told off by his mother. He noticed a red haze splattered on the cream interior, like someone had shaken a ketchup bottle with the lid off. Elliott frowned, puzzled by the mess. Until he realised it was blood and it must be his own.

From outside, the sound of screams just about reached him; yet they felt distant and receding.

The car door opened, the suspension tipping before someone leant over him, their features blurred. "Olivia?" His eyesight partially cleared. *No, not Olivia.*

The person hefted a pair of bolt cutters and severed the chain, disconnecting Elliott from the case. Then they felt around in Elliott's pocket before holding his mobile up. An electronic click as the facial recognition system made a match and unlocked Elliot's phone. Without a word they were gone, the suspension tilting again, and Elliott was alone once more.

He was drifting off; his hold on life loosening like a lost helium balloon, floating away from him. He couldn't be bothered fighting. What the hell had it all been for, in the end? All the time away from home. The anger, the upset, and for what?

The sirens in the distance didn't matter. They weren't his saviours. Elliott released his grip and he stepped onto a helter-skelter which stretched out forever beneath him, and from where there would be no return.

Two

"Really, Vance?" Detective Inspector Jonah Pennance of the National Crime Agency, hands on hips and shoulders hunched, surveyed the chaos and destruction that had occurred while he'd been out of the office for just a few, short hours. "It's as if an army of sandwiches had a bareknuckle fight and shredded each other in the process."

Flakes of bread and crust were strewn across the surface of his desk and around the surrounding floor area. Two coke cans pushed into a corner, one crushed and lying on its side, leaking brown fluid, probably eating into the laminated wood right now. The plastic food wrappers tossed towards the bin and not quite made it, sprawled on the grey carpet like the culinary victims of a serial killer.

Detective Sergeant Vance Hoskins leaned around his quadruple monitors and raised an eyebrow before he joined Pennance. Hoskins ate constantly, yet remained rail thin. "Ah, there it is." Hoskins reached out, removed his porkpie hat from where it hung over the corner of one of Pennance's own screens, and plonked it atop his wavy dark hair. "I was working on something for Meacham and I needed two computers."

Pennance considered that for a moment. "So, you know my password?"

"I didn't." Hoskins gave a quick shrug. "But I do now."

"Bloody hell."

"Needs must, mate."

Pennance bent, picked up the bin, which proved to be totally empty, and deposited the wrappers inside before he swept the crumbs off the desk. The scrunched-up can followed.

"Whoa, whoa!" Hoskins waved both hands like he was signalling extreme danger as Pennance reached out for the second coke. "That might still have some inside." Hoskins lifted the container, tentatively shook it. The slosh of liquid was unmistakable. "No point being profligate. And at least *I* turned your computer off. Don't want to waste electricity. Got to be ecological, don't you know?"

As Hoskins retreated to his desk Pennance opened his mouth to tell him the drink was likely flat, then decided not to bother. Hoskins wouldn't care and demonstrated so by taking a swig and eliciting a satisfied lament.

Pennance retrieved his chair from no man's land, halfway across the office he shared with Hoskins and three other National Crime Agency colleagues, two of whom were, as usual, studiously ignoring the exchange. Pennance shrugged off his coat, hung it over the back of his seat and sat down, finally ready to get back to work.

"For God's sake." Pennance shook his keyboard over the bin. Crumbs showered out like rice thrown at a wedding.

"Disgusting, isn't it, ma'am?" said Hoskins. Pennance rotated in his chair. Hoskins rolled his eyes and tutted as Crime Team Manager Stephanie Meacham leaned a hip against Hoskins' desk, arms folded across her chest, attention focused on Pennance, eyes enlarged in the lenses of her rimless glasses. Meacham had recently cut her hair very short, maybe as a time saving device – no styling required.

THE BLUE CODE

Pennance and Hoskins reported to Meacham who ran MCIS, the Major Crime Investigative Support Unit, although Hoskins tended to operate largely by his own rules, seemingly without fear of recourse. Hoskins continued, "You should give him a stern talking to for treating police property so shabbily."

"It'll have to wait for now." Meacham spoke with a soft Scottish burr.

"Shame."

"I need you, Jonah." Meacham bared her teeth, revealing a gap between the front incisors wide enough to produce a shrill whistle, should she so wish. "Right now." She crooked a finger before making for the exit.

Pennance, ignoring Hoskins' pursed-mouth, Kenneth Williams' impersonation, tipped Hoskins' hat off his head as he passed by. "I'll deal with you later."

"You too, Vance," said Meacham over her shoulder.

"Ah, crap." Hoskins scooped his cap off the floor.

In the corridor, Meacham held open a door which led into the small meeting room opposite Pennance's office with obvious intent.

The lights were already on, revealing a standard round table with four chairs – one of which was occupied – a phone and a ridiculously oversized TV screen, like barely fit through the door scale, fixed to a wall.

"Hey, Ava." Hoskins touched two fingers to his temple in a jaunty greeting.

Ava McAleney, the best and the brightest of the NCA's resident digital forensic specialists, grinned at Hoskins. She wore her customary dungarees with high turn-ups. Her t-shirt was tie-dyed – a swirl of purples and blues. The tips of her black hair were telephone-box red. Last week they'd been pink.

"What's going on, ma'am?" Pennance sat. Hoskins lowered himself into the seat adjacent to McAleney.

Meacham pulled the handset towards her as the door closed on a spring. "All in due course, Jonah." She tapped a handful of numbers onto the keypad. A single ring before being answered.

"Director Quant."

The NCA possessed a strategic role to work across the UK, with divisions to tackle organised crime, the trafficking of people, drugs and weapons, cyber-crime and economic corruption. Strictly, the NCA could be tasked to investigate any wrongdoing, and Director Quant ran the whole shebang.

"Ma'am." Meacham addressed her boss. "I have Jonah Pennance with me." Pennance made to reply until Meacham gave a short, sharp shake of the head. Pennance had never suffered any direct contact with Quant, only receiving the occasional forwarded email missive from on high. "Along with Ava McAleney, and Vance Hoskins."

Hoskins leant forward towards the phone. "How are you, Esmie?"

"Fine, thank you, Vance." Quant's accent was Northeast, Newcastle way.

"It's been a while." Hoskins chuckled, like they shared a secret.

Meacham arched a brow at Pennance. News to him, too.

THE BLUE CODE

"I'd love to catch up, but unfortunately now isn't the time."

"Maybe later, then." Hoskins sat back.

"Less than thirty minutes ago," began Quant, "one Logan Elliott was gunned down very publicly outside a supermarket – shot multiple times by a masked gunman. I'm sending all three of you north, to Huntingdon. It's a market town in Cambridgeshire. Middle of the Fens, basically another name for a giant bog. Jonah, I want you on the ground, investigating, soon as, for as long as. I need to know who murdered Elliott and why."

"What's my involvement in all this?" asked Hoskins. "Other than being the good looking sidekick?"

McAlaney put a hand over her face.

"You'll be Jonah's liaison in the Huntingdon station." Quant sounded unfazed. "I don't want the locals having the slightest opportunity to become obstructive."

"Sure, I can manage that." Hoskins lightly punched Pennance on the arm. "Batman and Robin, all over again. Me being the caped crusader, of course."

"And Ava," continued Quant. "You'll be there to provide any IT or systems support."

"Understood."

"Ma'am," said Pennance. "Why the urgency?"

Meacham's gaze met Pennance's. *She knows already.*

"The dead man," said Quant. "He was one of our own."

"A cop?"

Meacham pressed her palms together. "NCA."

That would do it.

Three

"Elliott resigned from the NCA two years ago to take a position as Chief Operations Officer at a Huntingdon based company called Obsidian," said Quant.

"What's Obsidian?" asked Pennance.

"It's a stone formed at the edge of lava flows as they cool," said Hoskins. "Intensely sharp and deep black in colour, obsidian is said to be able to pierce darkness, revealing the truth. Mayan prophets used polished obsidian as mirrors to foretell the future."

"Thank you for the education, Vance," said Quant. "But in this case Obsidian is a company involved in big data analysis."

"I don't know what big data is either," said Pennance.

"It's a huge collection of complex material which grows exponentially with time," said McAlaney. "Potentially highly useful to an organisation, although very difficult to effectively analyse."

"It's like taking The Bible and mixing up all the words into a random mess," said Quant. "Then trying to figure out the story."

"And some," said McAlaney. "For example, over 500 terabytes of data is uploaded into Facebook *every day*. And there are thousands upon thousands of companies all around the world constantly generating a mass of tangled information. Organisations interested in understanding the narrative, to take Director Quant's analogy, have all these

THE BLUE CODE

records analysed by specialist external companies like Obsidian because most aren't capable themselves."

"Why? What would they be looking for?" asked Pennance.

"It depends, Jonah. Oil companies assess drilling data to more easily find new pockets of fossil fuels – otherwise it's largely highly expensive guesswork. Financial businesses analyse trading information in real time looking for developing trends – what to buy or sell ahead of the herd. Governments might use it for optimising transportation systems, or reducing the threat of cybercrime, maybe even for crime prediction."

Hoskins frowned. "Surely criminality is a random event? People and their motivations can't be predicted."

"We haven't the time for a philosophical debate. Let's get back on track," said Quant. "Cambridgeshire Constabulary is under the very real threat of entering special measures. During a routine inspection last year, HMICFRS uncovered issues with the way Huntingdon CID were assessing and reporting some crimes."

Hoskins leaned into Pennance. "Her Majesty's Inspectorate of Constabulary and Fire and Rescue Services is an independent body with the power to assess the effectiveness and efficiency of each force's performance."

"I know who they are," said Pennance.

Meacham aimed a school ma'am grade glare at them both.

Quant continued, "This means external organisations, like us, can send independent people in to support the constabulary until they sort themselves out. That's the pretext you'll operate under if anyone asks, Jonah. I yanked some strings with Superintendent Malik to get you onto the investigating CID team. He wasn't happy, but tough."

The authority in Quant's tone was unmistakable. In her role she could instruct the chief officer of any given police force, making Quant one of the most powerful law enforcement officers in the UK, operating a structure that created envy and loathing across her peers. "You're there under my orders. If anyone gets too pissy, refer them to Malik or come to me. I'm more than happy to step in and pull rank. Bringing out the big guns usually works a treat with anyone being awkward.

"Jonah, I'm expecting you'll work directly in the field with the local DCI while Vance and Ava, you'll be located at Huntingdon police station to help and support where needed. Stephanie is your day-to-day liaison." McAleney and Hoskins nodded "All of you remember, this is a critical assignment. So, I really don't care if you upset people. How you get me answers is down to you."

"Understood, ma'am," said Pennance.

"I'd wish you luck, Jonah, though I suspect fortune is irrelevant. Stephanie tells me you're an excellent, if a little unorthodox, investigator." Quant disconnected before Pennance could respond.

Meacham stabbed a button on the phone, cutting off the speaker, then pushed herself to her feet like her limbs were of stone. "There's a car waiting for you at reception, Jonah. Vance and Ava will follow on shortly afterwards. You'll have the chance to gather any kit you need, but be quick." Meacham headed for the door. "Come on." In the corridor,

THE BLUE CODE

Meacham got fast walking, her heels a rapid staccato on the floor, heading in the direction of the front entrance.

"We'll see you shortly." Hoskins gave Pennance a shove. "Shift your arse."

Pennance trotted to catch up with his boss. When he drew alongside Meacham said, "I've told the SIO, DCI Crosse, to hold the body in-situ." Meacham meant Senior Investigating Officer; the person everyone would look to for answers regarding the crime, whatever their rank. He was the spider in the web. It was on Crosse to run the investigation, make all the key decisions and, ultimately, find the killer and bring them to justice. "So there'll be no changes to the crime scene until you've had chance to look it over. As for clothes, find a shop when you're up there."

"It's quite hard getting trousers and shirts in my size, ma'am. Long limbs." Pennance held out an arm to illustrate.

Meacham seemed to remember Pennance's height then – taller than the average British male, shorter than a regular basketball player, meaning he loomed over most people. Including Meacham. "Of course. Stupid of me. I'll get some stuff sent up with Vance and Ava."

"Simone has a key for my flat." A recent change in their relationship status.

"Simone?"

"Smithson."

"Your friend in City of London police?"

"Pretty much." Partner would be a more accurate description.

"I was going to send Vance round."

"Please, no."

Pennance moved to one side, allowing a colleague past while Meacham maintained her path. Then she paused, blocking access to a door.

"There's one other fact you should be aware of, Jonah. Elliott used to work for Quant, back in the day. They were close. Something happened between them which contributed to his leaving. I've no idea what and I don't want to know. Just be careful, this is personal for her, as well as professional. I've never seen her so agitated."

"Thanks for the heads up."

"Well, I can't have yours rolling." Meacham held the door. "Or, more importantly, mine." She waved Pennance through before her and into the lobby. Beyond, through the plate glass windows, two cop cars idled, exhausts spewing. Both BMWs were designed for pursuit, not the clunkers uniform used. Fluorescent yellow livery, low slung, powerful engine, and handled by highly trained professionals only.

Outside, a drizzle had started. The driver, a bulky uniformed constable with a buzz cut and a once-broken nose, rolled his window down and glanced Pennance over. "You'll be more comfortable up front, sir." Windscreen wipers screeched across the window, scooping away the mizzle.

Pennance folded his long frame inside. Small vehicles were the bane of his life. The passenger seat had already been helpfully pushed back as far as it could, meaning his knees were below the fascia. He reached out for the door.

However, Meacham gripped the rim above the open window. "You're in good hands with PC Hamilton." She gave the door a good shove. "He'll have you there in no time." And she rapped her knuckles onto the roof before turning away.

"Don't forget your seat belt."

As Pennance pulled the strap across his chest, Hamilton accelerated away fast, enough g-force to press Pennance into the upholstery. Pennance glanced in the side mirror – Meacham trotting up the steps and inside the uninspiring architecture; an oblong lying on its side, four storeys of brown brick and square windows. Then she was gone.

"Any relation to the Formula One driver?"

"You wouldn't believe how many times I get asked that." Hamilton paused at the junction of Tinworth Street and Citadel Place, glanced fast in both directions before pulling out behind the lead pursuit car. "Cousins."

"Really?"

Hamilton reached up, flipped a switch and the blue lights came on. His eyes flickered to meet Pennance's. "No, sir."

"Oh."

The police pursuit vehicle on point took up a position a hundred yards or so ahead of Pennance and Hamilton, acting like a battering ram on four wheels, slicing through the traffic, headlights and blues flashing, sirens blaring, maintaining a line, forcing every other road user hurriedly out of their way.

Hamilton handled the car tightly and efficiently. Two hands on the wheel at all times, except to change gear, which he did with short, urgent movements before regaining his grip.

There was no pausing at any traffic lights, whatever the colour, or roundabouts and only the briefest pauses at junctions. Even the cyclists, who usually believed regulations were for everyone else, kept their distance. This was the way to navigate choked-up London.

Soon they were out of the city and on the M11 motorway. The lead cop car slowed and the driver, just a blur through the side window, pulled off at the first junction with their job done. Pennance leaned over, glanced at the speedo dial which hovered at 120mph yet the engine barely purred. He tugged his seatbelt tighter until it pressed across his chest like a committed lover's embrace.

Pennance pulled out his phone. The screen saver was a photo of him and Simone, heads side by side, an out of focus Christmas tree in the background. Simone was due to cook for them later as they had the rare situation of being in Simone's house by themselves – Simone's daughter was with her ex-in-laws, the grandparents. Pennance dialled and Simone picked up.

"Hi, you." Genuine pleasure in Simone's tone.

"I'm really sorry about this, Simone but I won't be able to make tonight. Meacham's sent me away on a case and I've no idea when I'll be back."

"I know. Vance called."

"Typical of Hoskins, sticking his nose in."

"He's our friend, Jonah. And the wine can stay on ice until you're back. Well, in the fridge. I haven't got any ice." Pennance laughed. "And, to be completely honest, I wouldn't have been such great company anyway. With Fulton away at the moment I'm run off my feet."

THE BLUE CODE

"When's he back?" Pennance wasn't a fan of Detective Chief Inspector Leigh Fulton, Simone's boss.

"He hasn't seen fit to share any information with me. Anyway, Vance said you'd need some clothes thrown into a bag to be sent up. I'm actually at your place now, going through your stuff. I haven't found anything juicy yet." Pennance stiffened and Simone's chuckle trailed off. "I'm joking."

"Sorry, it's weird having someone in my flat."

"I'm not just anyone, Jonah. You can trust me."

"I know."

"I hope so. Go and do your best." Simone disconnected.

Pennance wanted her to be right.

***

Hamilton slowed before swinging off the motorway at a junction. The signpost read, 'Huntingdon'. Hamilton switched the siren and lights back on, began weaving through traffic along a road which sliced an industrial area in half.

"Looks like this is it, sir."

Through the windscreen a uniform stood in the middle of the road, handheld out and palm forward, halting Hamilton's progress.

"I reckon you're right." Pennance reached for the handle. "I guess I'll be on foot from here."

Four

"DI Pennance with the NCA Major Crime Investigative Support Team." Pennance passed his warrant card to the PC who'd forced Hamilton to stop.

A roadblock consisting of a line of cones and a squad car at ninety degrees obstructed a roundabout turn-off to what was clearly an out-of-town retail area. Directly on Pennance's right lay a DIY chain store and ahead a drive-in coffee shop, about the only non-independent Pennance would entertain if there were no other alternatives. To his other side a large sign for a well-known supermarket – part of yet another corporation – was concreted into a grass verge. Traffic bypassing the scene crawled by as rubberneckers attempted to check out what the fuss was.

The PC was sufficiently rotund in shape that she'd probably bounce right back onto her feet if Pennance were to give her a good shove. She stole a glance at her male colleague, cap pulled down low his forehead, before accepting Pennance's ID. Her expressive eyebrows clambered upwards from the deep V they'd formed when Pennance first stepped out of the BMW.

Pennance didn't dress like typical police. No business attire for him. The suit and tie fashion were thankfully following the obligatory hat and umbrella of previous decades, burnt on the pyre of style history, leaving only politicians and the BBC as the outliers. A warm wind came from somewhere across the fields tugged at his clothes; a pair

THE BLUE CODE

of Converse Chucks on his feet, jeans, a shirt open at the neck, and sunglasses.

Hamilton performed a three-point turn to head back the way he'd come and nodded in response to Pennance's thumbs up.

Pennance said, "I'm here to see DCI Crosse."

The PC coughed into her crooked arm, the fabric of her uniform acting like a mask, while passing Pennance's card to her colleague who seemed not in the slightest bothered by the potential transmission of germs. He noted down Pennance's name on a list. A black Range Rover with heavily tinted windows rolled past, slowing right down to creep past Pennance.

"Sorry." She sounded like she was holding her nose, perhaps suffering the lingering effects of a cold. Or maybe hay fever. Once past, the Range Rover accelerated away, tyres squealing. "Take you about a minute to walk there." She pointed through a line of feeble trees to Pennance's left beyond the supermarket sign. "It's all pretty obvious."

Her colleague proffered Pennance's ID which he accepted gingerly, gripping one corner between two fingers.

"Give me bloody strength," she mumbled. Not at Pennance's behaviour but the driver of a car who'd rolled right up to the cones before loudly blowing their horn. The driver waved her arms, clearly irritated by the restricted access.

"I'll leave you to it," said Pennance.

"We can swap if you like?" Although the PC was already striding away to harangue the woman before Pennance could decline

A privet hedge, a couple of feet high, interspersed with the spindly trees, bordered the road. Beyond the struggling greenery, an array of cars of different models and colours in parking spaces, then a sprawling single storey building of orange brick with a tiled roof, pitched steeply enough for ski-jumping practice, and large glass entrance doors. Pennance took the short route, forcing his way between the shrubbery. It was only sticks and branches after all.

He weaved through the part-filled parking spots, heading for the inner cordon and the obvious knot of activity – people in painfully white evidence suits moving around the scene. Pennance volunteered his warrant card to another PC who approached at pace from the cordon, making to cut off his progress.

"I know who you are, sir. Warnock just radioed through." The PC, not much shorter than Pennance, tapped the Airwave fixed at his shoulder. Warnock would be at the roadblock then. "I'm PC Sumner."

"Where's Crosse?" Pennance's patience was beginning to wear thin with these obstructions being placed in his way.

"In the middle of it all, sir. You'll need to present yourself to Thriplow first. He's the CSM."

The acronym for Crime Scene Manager, the most senior of the crime scene investigators he'd be advising Crosse on forensic strategies – how to get the most out what was probably a chaotic state and gathering information in a legally compliant manner. Pennance had known prosecutions thrown out of court or culled by the Criminal Prosecution Service due to lax fact-finding practices which had subsequently compromised evidence and therefore the overall legal action.

"You can't miss Thriplow. He's the one with the nose. Well, it's kind of a beak."

Descriptions of anyone wearing an evidence suit devolved down to the most basic – short, tall, fat, thin – and any facial characteristics. The ensemble was effective at obscuring visual detail.

"And you'll need to stick this on." Sumner held out a suit, pre-folded into the shape of an over-sized envelope and encased in thin see-through plastic film that always set Pennance's teeth on edge when split, like now when Sumner helpfully tore off the wrapper before handing it to Pennance.

"I know the drill." Pennance allowed the legs to unfurl under gravity. As usual the suit would barely fit, like a jumper shrunk in a hot wash.

Sumner scrunched the plastic into a ball and glanced around. "There's never a bin when you want one these days." Sumner shoved the waste into a trouser pocket.

Pennance pulled the suit up past his hips, shrugged the material over his shoulders, raised the hood then worked the zipper as far as it would go. Sumner gave Pennance a pair of nitrile gloves next, which Pennance snapped on.

"Remember, the beak." Sumner tapped the side of his nose before turning away. Pennance got moving.

A road bisected the car park, ordinarily allowing access from the now-blocked carriageway, snaking through the space like a lazily bending river. The dozens of shoppers who'd ordinarily have been going in and out of the store were replaced by uniformed police and the suited investigators.

Pennance counted four squad cars, the same number of CSI vans with their logo prominent on the side, and a single ambulance. A pair of paramedics in green uniforms leant on the rear of their emergency vehicle, chatting and smoking. It never ceased to amaze Pennance how often health professionals tended towards the unwholesome.

The action was concentrated around a large, black Mercedes parked in a drop-off area delineated by white lines on the ground and large letters in the same paint which read 'Set Down Po-' the rest of the words obscured beneath the car. Tall, evenly spaced cylindrical metal bollards divided car park from pavement and pedestrians from apparent danger. Behind was a short terrace row of smaller concession shops, perhaps vaguely styled after an American strip mall – a shoe repairer and a dry cleaner's, separated by a narrow alleyway – then a couple of cash machines embedded into the wall.

The Merc's windows were almost as dark as the body paint, although a random pattern of marks peppered the rear passenger door. As Pennance neared he realised they were puncture holes – effectively exit wounds where the metal had been peeled back by high speed projectiles.

A man perched on the bonnet of the Merc, one leg swinging, the other a supporting prop on the ground. A second man loitered a couple of feet away, arms crossed. Both wore evidence suits, hoods down. The upright man eyeballed Pennance the whole way over.

Sumner was right: Thriplow's nose was unmistakable. Red and bulbous, implying the CSM perhaps appreciated a drink or several of an evening. Thriplow said something to make the seated man slide off the Merc, causing it to rock slightly, and place himself in Pennance's path, effectively blocking access to the more interesting end of the car.

"DCI Crosse?" Pennance held out a hand.

"This is the man of the hour, Frank." Crosse was of average build and height, elevated somewhat by boots, the heel a good, blocky chunk. He wore half-moon glasses and his hair was an impressive wave. The offer of a handshake was ignored.

"The NCA guy you mentioned," said Thriplow. "Or was it interfering bloody interloper?" Thriplow grinned.

However, Crosse's mouth tightened slightly. "I never said any such thing."

"I must have misheard." Thriplow chuckled.

"It's Jonah, right?" asked Crosse.

"To a select few people," said Pennance.

"Are you going to bring me bad luck?"

"My team and I are here to help."

"Not that I asked."

"Come all the way here from the capital," said Thriplow.

"London's not that far," said Pennance.

"Eighty miles. I checked."

"Whole different world," said Crosse and Thriplow nodded. They were right – London varied so much across the city. There was nowhere else like it in the country. A sink hole of power, influence, and money. Crosse continued, "Because the locals can't be trusted to do the job properly."

"And I thought it was your webbed feet," said Thriplow eliciting a snort from the DCI.

"You're here on my askance by the way, Inspector," said Crosse.

"And there's me believing the NCA's Director ordered your superintendent to allow access," said Pennance. Crosse rocked back and forth slightly on his heels. Pennance continued, "Are we done with all the posturing?"

Crosse briefly regarded his toe caps before shrugging. "Sure, why not?"

"I'd like to see the victim. I was assured he'd be kept for my arrival."

"Of course." Crosse gestured. "Take a gander at the mess back here. Everything's recorded, so if you put your size nines somewhere they shouldn't, it won't matter too much." He shifted out of Pennance's way.

"I'm a thirteen."

Thriplow whistled.

"Whatever anybody says we're efficient here, you know." Crosse trailed after Pennance.

"I'm sure."

"We get on with stuff. No messing around."

"Chief Inspector," said Pennance. "May I?" He wanted to focus and Crosse's verbal justifications were getting in the way.

"Yes, my Lord." Crosse wafted an arm and gave a half bow.

The driver's side passenger door stood wide open, the window gone. A few shards, the misshapen profiles of broken safety glass, lay on the ground. Between the door and the coachwork stood multiple small yellow markers, shaped in an inverted V and marked with synchronous numbers, scattered around an area a few feet across, including under the Mercedes itself. Sunlight reflected off round metal tubes the markers had been placed next to.

"How many bullet casings are there?" asked Pennance.

"We count twenty," said Crosse. "The cartridges and bullets will be analysed to determine the make and model of the weapon, although from witness reports the shooter used a machine gun."

"What about CCTV footage?"

"That's in process."

"I'd like to see it once you have it."

"Sir, yes, sir." Now Crosse threw a sloppy salute. Behind, Thriplow grimaced. Even he seemed to be tiring of Crosse.

Pennance shifted to where the driver and passenger doors met before bending over to give himself a decent view of the interior.

"Pleasant, isn't it?" asked Thriplow.

Pennance had never been to an actual slaughterhouse, but he imagined this may be how it would be decorated. The interior was white leather, or had been until the assault. Now, every inch of the material was stained with blood – seats, floor, ceiling. Even the rear window was splattered. The typical red had turned into a dark russet from the haemoglobin breaking down after exposure to the air. The colour depth could be used to approximate a time of death although he didn't bother to ask Thriplow for an estimate.

Elliott's corpse lay sprawled across the rear seat. One arm hung down into the footwell, hand pressed into glass debris beneath. Aviator sunglasses nearby. Branded, expensive ones.

His other hand rested on the door behind, the top of the skull pushed up against the fascia, lit by spots of light coming through the obvious bullet holes. More debris was sprinkled across the body.

"I guess he was shot through the window?" asked Pennance.

"According to witnesses," said Crosse, "a car pulled up next to the Merc, the shooter walked round, emptied the magazine in one go, before they drove off."

"Did one of you open the door?"

"No. It was like that when we arrived."

"You said you've already done the work needed in here?"

Thriplow nodded. "Be my guest."

Pennance shuffled right to the car body and squatted down so his knees hung over the footwell. He fancied the sulphurous fumes of a discharged weapon still hung in the air, though Pennance knew that was simply his imagination filling in the blanks. Any stray atoms would be long dispersed.

Now Pennance crawled inside, avoiding the speckles of glass spread round the interior. He paused directly above Elliott's corpse, the dead man's face just inches away. His skin was washed out, the colour of recycled paper. The moment the heart stopped pumping the blood settled to the lowest point in the body under gravity. Meaning the length of Elliott's rear – from heels to neck – would be a steadily developing maze of purple and red burst vessels, like a huge, aggressive bruise.

Elliott's eyes were wide, staring through Pennance to somewhere beyond. The pupils had narrowed into small black circles in the centre of a deep blue iris. Pennance felt he could dive in and search for Elliott's soul, wherever that now was. And Elliott's jaw was clenched; maybe he'd fought to survive right up to the end.

His face was largely clean of blood. However, the neck appeared like something from a butcher's block, thanks to a hole Pennance could put his finger inside and wiggle around, should he so wish. Though tempted, Pennance held back. People were watching, after all.

"The round severed his carotid artery." Thriplow was bent down, hands on knees. "He'd have quickly bled out. Even if there'd been a paramedic here immediately there was no saving him."

Pennance continued his assessment, moving down the torso, shifting back slightly as he did so. More puncture wounds, several in the bicep and forearm. More in the chest, stomach, thighs. Pennance reached out, clutched Elliott's dangling arm just above the wrist. The skin was cold. He bent the limb at the elbow, no rigor yet, revealing a handcuff, bright and shiny. A few links of steel chain hung below. "Why is he wearing this?"

"Something else we don't know right now," said Crosse.

Pennance wriggled backwards out of the car.

Thriplow held out a small plastic evidence bag. "We found a piece of metal in the footwell."

Half a link, the same type as the handcuff. "Looks like it's been cut." Pennance closely examined the metal.

"Agreed, and by a reasonably heavy duty tool," said Crosse. "Like loppers, rather than a saw."

"Quicker." Pennance handed the bag back. "The wounding isn't from what you'd call a tight firing pattern."

"Witnesses also stated the shooter laughed while pulling the trigger. Nice having fun on the job."

Pennance squatted by the open car door, closely examined the mechanism. He pointed to a small black catch. "That's the child lock and it's engaged. So Elliott wouldn't have been able to open up."

"I'll have the techs to investigate once the car is back at the lab," said Crosse. "I'm not getting inside that charnel house to check for myself." Pennance stood again, regarded the Merc for a long moment. Crosse continued, "This has Mercer's dirty little fingers all over it."

"Maybe." Thriplow rubbed his chin. "But murder? That's not normally his style."

"Criminals progress, Frank. That's how it works."

"Who's Mercer?" asked Pennance.

"He used to run a betting shop in town. These days he's a loan shark. Every pie – meat, veggie or vegan – Mercer has his fingers shoved right in them."

"The Chief Inspector has been after Mercer for some time," said Thriplow.

"What evidence ties him to this?" asked Pennance.

"Nothing at the moment." Crosse wagged a finger. "But mark my words, Mercer's involved somehow, and I'll prove it."

"Okay." Pennance glanced at Thriplow, who remained impassive. Pennance asked, "Where are the witnesses?"

"In the store café. Except Elliott's girlfriend, Olivia Bingham. She's down the station. Two of my best are looking after her. She's the reason Elliott was here." He pointed to several carrier bags on the concrete pavement twenty feet away. "Barbecue shopping." Then Crosse nodded towards the car. "Yet her meat is right here."

"Fuck's sake, Nick." Now Thriplow screwed his face up.

Crosse pushed his arms out, palms up, like he was feeling for rain, shoulders hunched. "What?"

"I'd like to speak to them," said Pennance.

Crosse tilted his head at Elliott. "Is that you done with him now, Inspector?"

"Yes."

Crosse removed his glasses and slid them into a jacket pocket before shifting his attention to Thriplow. "Then you can get the corpse cleared, doc. While Inspector Pennance and I go see the innocents." Crosse aimed a pistol shaped finger and thumb at the main entrance. "We're this-a-way." He moved off, unzipping his suit as he did so, taking them past the alleyway entrance. Pennance paused for a moment, peered into the gap. Just brick walls disappearing into darkness.

"Come on, Inspector." Crosse walked backwards now, then rotated on his boot heel in a move nothing like Michael Jackson. After a couple of strides Pennance, mimicking Crosse only in releasing himself from the suit's confines, fell into step beside him until they reached the two carriers Olivia had dropped.

Crosse abruptly paused, crouched down, pushed the bag open a little wider, searching inside. "Shame to waste all this food. My dog would appreciate the sausages. Mind you, he's already too chunky." Crosse stood, leaned against a large brick column, and removed his evidence suit entirely, revealing a shiny, black double-breasted jacket and collarless shirt, the top couple of buttons undone, which wouldn't have looked out of place in the early 90s. Scrunching up the suit, Crosse glanced around in both directions before he took a pace forward, got right in front of Pennance. "Bit weird you being in Huntingdon, Inspector."

"Not really." Pennance fought the urge to respond, to physically push back at Crosse. "As I'm part of MCIS I can be sent anywhere in the country to get involved in any applicable case."

"And why this particular 'applicable case'?" Crosse made air quotes before reaching out and plucking something from Pennance's shoulder like an attentive monkey. "A hair." He regarded the strand as if he were a child inspecting a worm. "And not one of yours. Girlfriend? Or superior, maybe?"

"What the hell's that got to do with you?"

"Unpleasant, right? Someone poking around in something that has no relation to them. It's like waving your dick at another man's wife." Crosse stared once more at Pennance. "So, why are you here?" He flicked the hair away.

"My boss didn't explain." Pennance spoke through clenched jaws. "And she's not the type to appreciate having her orders queried. She just told me to get my arse moving with only what I'm standing in."

"That's it, Inspector?"

"Cross my heart," lied Pennance.

"Is that a smart-arse play on words?" Crosse screwed his eyes up.

"I'm not the humorous type. I leave that to others."

Crosse stared at Pennance for a long moment before clapping Pennance on the same shoulder he'd plucked the

THE BLUE CODE

hair from. "Bloody management, eh? Always keeping the rest of us in the dark! Come on." Crosse spun in a half circle like an ungracious ballet dancer. "Let's get interrogating those witnesses."

Five

Crosse stopped dead outside the entrance to the superstore – a windowed oblong attached to the side of the building, large, plate glass doors at either end, creating a lobby area. Inside were some point-of-sale displays and a kids' coin-fed ride – a gurning elephant. Then a further pair of doors which divided entrance from main building.

The barrier remained firmly shut despite an audible click from the overhead sensor. Crosse focused on the piece of black plastic above him and waved his hands like he was trying to scare off birds. Still no response.

Crosse sighed, peered through the obstruction, nose almost touching the glass, and cupped hands either side of his skull – totally unnecessary as Pennance could see in perfectly well. Crosse's breathe fogged.

Beyond, two PCs stood shoulder to shoulder, facing inwards, deep in conspiratorial conversation accompanied by plenty of nodding and gesticulating, the pair setting the world to rights. Crosse mumbled something inaudible to Pennance before raising a fist and rapping knuckles on the door. Which didn't work either.

"Christ on a bike. Hang on a minute." As Crosse stalked over to the nearest squad car Pennance took the opportunity to remove his evidence suit. Crosse slid inside the car, lifted the receiver, said something into the mic.

In the store, one of the PCs uncrossed her arms, switched her attention to the radio at her shoulder and answered, still nodding to something her companion was saying. She turned, frowned at Pennance then visibly started when Crosse re-joined him and she recognised the senior man.

"That's it, get your arse in gear," said Crosse through a phoney grin, waving in mock cheer as the PC headed their way. She made for a panel beside the inner door, twisted a key before whacking an adjacent large red button, maybe trying to launch a missile for DEFCON 1. Finally, the door slid back, juddering as it did so. The moment the gap was wide enough Crosse slipped through. "Thank you *so* very much!"

"Sorry, sir." The PC winced at Pennance.

"Oh, don't worry yourself about keeping two officers waiting. It's only murder, after all."

The PC blinked, opened her mouth to reply, then clearly decided to maintain silence.

They'd entered the bottom corner of the store. The fruit and veg aisles directly ahead, the rest of the stock arranged in parallel rows. Immediately adjacent to Pennance stood a customer service section against the wall, where no-one was waiting for lottery tickets or cigarettes. Then banks of self-service tills without queues, although baskets of groceries had been left on the floor. Above, strip lights burned.

"Café is down here." Crosse pointed once more. As he led them past stacks of yellow bananas and red apples Crosse's phone rang. "What is it?" He listened for a moment. "Well, she'll have to sit tight. I'll be bringing the boy wonder back once we've spoken to the witnesses." Crosse disconnected. "That was Shapiro, my DI. The girlfriend is getting restless." He grabbed a couple of oranges from a display box and held one out for Pennance.

"No, thanks."

Crosse shrugged, began to peel, spraying juice into the air. For a moment it smelt like Christmas. "*You're* the boy wonder, by the way."

"I guessed." Part-filled trollies were ditched mid-aisle and Pennance weaved between them.

"Anyway, she can wait." Crosse bit into a segment. "The names of everyone still on the property when we arrived was taken down. Most people claimed to not have seen anything. If they were deep in the store, buying cornflakes, say, then that would be understandable. Ah, this is it," said Crosse needlessly as the café was obvious. There was even a sign, hanging over the entrance, which told Pennance so.

To one side lay a serving area, a stainless steel construct for displaying warm food. A pile of trays, and a rack on the front of a counter for people to slide a slab of fake wood along with their purchases atop. Behind squatted a serious coffee machine, a large lump of stainless steel, then a chiller for drinks and sandwiches and a till. The remaining space was taken up by identical Formica tables and plastic chairs, all fixed to substantial metal poles concreted into the floor in a strategy which had always puzzled Pennance. perhaps the store owner expected a furniture riot? Or that they'd be stolen and end up in a student's house?

Four people occupied the table furthest away. Two Pennance could immediately discount because they were uniform, hats off and at their elbows. Meaning the others would be the witnesses. The PCs hemmed the civilians in against the wall, neither could leave unless the cops budged. One of the uniform glanced over, nudged his colleague, tilted his chin in Pennance's direction.

"This is all of them?" asked Pennance. One of the PCs stood, short straw decided somehow, and made his way over.

"No." Crosse frowned. "It bloody well isn't."

"Sir," said the PC, a bulky guy, short sleeves revealing thick, hairy arms. His broad neck stretched the shirt collar to bursting point.

"Where's the rest, Jones?" Crosse waved an expansive limb.

Jones blinked, glanced around. "Sir?"

"The other witnesses." Crosse leaned in, hissed, "Have they all gone to the bloody bathroom or something?"

"They insisted they had to head home, sir."

"And you let that happen?"

"Their kids were making a load of noise. I didn't think we could detain them, sir. They weren't under arrest or anything."

"Last time I looked, decision making wasn't in the job description of a constable."

Jones sucked in air, expanding his chest even further and pushing the buttons closer to an eruption. "We've got their addresses. And the Yardleys are still here."

"Well, whoopee-fucking-dandy, Jones!" The PC curled his fists, yet Crosse wasn't backing down. "Gastrell is an ex-con, he could have been involved." Crosse ground his teeth. "I guess the Yardleys will have to do for now. Next time, contact a superior, of which you have many. Understood?"

"Got it." The cords in Jones's neck were stretched like cables.

"Right, now that unpleasantness is in the rear-view," Crosse scuffed his hands, as if brushing dirt off his palms, "get us all a coffee, would you?"

"I don't know how to use the machine."

"So, how did these get here?" Crosse pointed to four cups and saucers on the table. "Magic?"

"There's a kettle and instant, sir."

"So no wand, then."

"No, sir."

"Plenty of milk and sugar, son."

"Not for me," said Pennance.

"Take a bottle of water, if you want. No-one's here to object."

"I'm fine."

Crosse returned to Jones. "Actually, knock me up a bacon sandwich will you?"

"Excuse me, sir?"

"You know, bit of a pig? And no extra sauce, alright?"

"Not really, sir."

"I'll be getting an ulcer at this rate." Crosse rubbed his stomach. "This is me, giving you an order. Make me a buttie." Crosse peered at the PC. "What are you waiting for? Chop, bloody chop!"

The PC stalked away. "Arsehole," he murmured while passing by. Pennance clearly heard the insult, so Crosse must have, but the DCI didn't respond, instead heading over to the table.

THE BLUE CODE

"You can scoot, Squires," Crosse told the other uniform. "Help Jones with the food." Squires scooped up his hat, and Jones's too, retreating without a word. "DCI Crosse, we met earlier." Crosse gave a slack grin, as high a wattage as an energy saving lightbulb, and took Jones's space.

"Hello." A tanned brunette seated at forty five degrees to Crosse. "I'm Daisy Yardley." Her face was unlined, at odds with the wrinkles on her neck. Botox, probably. She smiled, perhaps with a little difficulty.

"Patrick, her husband." His full head of grey hair was slicked back. He wore chinos, a formal shirt, a cravat, cardigan and a chunky steel watch on his wrist. "Can we leave now?"

"Soon," said Crosse, eliciting a partially suppressed groan from Yardley. "This is DI Pennance," continued Crosse. "He's from out of town."

"May I?" Pennance indicated the chair beside Daisy.

Crosse briefly lifted his eyes to the roof.

"Of course," she said. As Pennance slid in next to her he got a whiff of musk from Yardley, reminding him of a barbershop.

"So are we," said Daisy. "Out of towners, I mean. We only relocated six days ago. From the Ribble Valley to be nearer our family, now Patrick has properly retired."

Yardley scowled, like he hadn't been quite ready to hang up his boots. "And look where that got us."

"You forget how much work moving house is." Daisy ignored her husband. "Particularly getting rid of the accumulated junk."

"There's nothing wrong with taxidermy."

"I'm not sure I'd agree." Crosse wrinkled his nose. "Fleas, and so on."

"That's what I told him!" said Daisy.

"I wanted to ask you about what you witnessed outside the supermarket earlier," said Pennance.

"We've discussed that already." Yardley folded his arms.

"Not with me so, if you wouldn't mind, I'd like to get your impression of events first hand. Maybe ask some additional questions?"

"We only popped in to buy stuff for our grandson William's birthday party. He turned one the other day. Our daughter is bringing him to see us," said Daisy.

"In fact, Suzi will be here soon." Yardley checked his timepiece. A Breitling, Pennance noted. Worth thousands. Unless it was a fake. They were hard to spot these days.

Squires returned then with the coffee.

"Sandwich coming, too?" asked Crosse.

"Of course, sir," said Squires.

"I'm sure the DCI will release you in time to meet her," said Pennance.

"Release?" said Yardley. "Sounds like we're being held captive."

"Not at all," said Crosse. "I'm sure it was just a poor turn of phrase from DI Pennance."

Pennance raised his hands, palms out. "My error."

"Let's help them." Daisy reached out, grasped Yardley's forearm. "I'm sure we'll be out of here faster then, right Inspector Dross?"

"It's Crosse, and I'm a chief inspector."

"I'm *so* sorry."

THE BLUE CODE

Pennance was certain a smile flickered across Daisy's lips.

Yardley massaged his temples briefly. "What do you want to know?"

"I didn't see as much as Patrick," said Daisy.

"Just tell me what you can both remember," said Pennance.

"What, since I got up?" asked Yardley. "Or after I stepped out of the shower? Some guidance might help."

"*Patrick*," said Daisy.

"It's just..."

"Just nothing, dear." Daisy gave her husband a grin bordering on the Arctic. Crosse slurped his coffee, watching the free show, eyes ticking back and forth, like one of those cat clocks.

"Alright, my apologies." Yardley sighed, slumped back. "We'd just gone into the car park. I'd loaded the bags into the boot and was in the process of returning the trolley."

"I got into the car while Patrick was away," said Daisy. "A people carrier parked in front and blocked my view."

"I just waited for someone to put their trolley in the bay and then shoved in mine when it all started."

"Be specific, dear." Husband and wife talked like a double act.

"Okay." Yardley wouldn't meet his wife's gaze. "Some kid launched his basket from about six feet out and walked off. I had a word with him, and then his father, about being better citizens."

"He was gone for five minutes, I was getting worried." Daisy looked daggers at Yardley. "If you'd just have ignored them we'd have been away before everything started."

"Shit happens, Daisy." Yardley shrugged.

"That it does." Crosse gave a sage nod.

PC Squires appeared at the table, wearing a grease spattered apron and bearing Crosse's sandwich on a plate. The bacon sizzled faintly in its bread wrapping. Crosse rubbed his hands together almost fast enough to produce smoke. He lifted the top slice, inspected the interior then reached out for a sauce bottle, pausing halfway. Crosse wafted his hands at Squires. "Dismissed, constable." Squires drifted away, trailing an odour of cooking fat.

"Did you know the man you argued with?" asked Pennance.

"No." Yardley watched Squires retreat. "As Daisy stated we only relocated here less than a week ago." He paused as Crosse loudly spattered sauce onto his sandwich.

Suppressing a grimace Pennance said, "Do you often remonstrate with strangers?"

"More than he should," muttered Daisy.

"Sometimes people need telling." Yardley paused again while Crosse splurted. "Maybe if more people did, then society wouldn't be in the state it is now."

"I couldn't agree more." Crosse tore a caveman chunk out of the sandwich and chewed, some crumbs spilling onto his jacket. "Go on."

"Anyway, I'd finally sorted out the trolley incident when the shooting started. I turned around. A masked man unloaded a clip into the back seat of a car. Whoever was inside had no chance. Once he was done, he calmly walked away and got into a waiting car and they drove off. The driver, he was more measured than the gunman, there was no burning rubber."

"What make was the vehicle?"

"Which one?" asked Yardley. "I used to be an actuary, Inspector. I've spent my career being precise."

"The getaway car, sir. We know what the other is." Crosse wafted his half-consumed sandwich at Yardley. "As it's still outside." He chuckled. No-one else joined in.

"A silver Audi saloon," said Yardley. "It had the four circles on the front grille. The engine was powerful, probably an A6 or A8. Beyond that..." Yardley turned his palms up.

"How many people inside?" asked Pennance.

"Three. Driver and shooter in the front. I couldn't describe either of them. They wore balaclavas. However, as the car went past someone popped their head up from the back seat and had a look at the Merc through the rear window."

"What did he look like?"

"Thin face, wild hair, like a scarecrow."

Pennance turned to Daisy. "And how about you, Mrs Yardley?"

"I just heard the gun, Inspector. I ducked down, as low as I could. God, it was horrible." Daisy squeezed her eyes shut. "I've never been so scared in my life. There was a long *brrrr* sound, a few moments of deathly silence, then the screaming started."

"That was a leggy brunette in a very short skirt," said Yardley. "She just kind of collapsed to the ground."

"That'll be Olivia." Sandwich finished, Crosse pushed his plate away and brushed crumbs off his jacket. "Bloody hell." The DCI noticed a spot of sauce on a lapel and reached out for a serviette. "Proper Italian suit, this."

"From which century?" asked Yardley to which Crosse cocked an eyebrow. Yardley continued, "There was also a mum with a young kid."

"Miss Dunne. One of the people Jones let walk out of here."

"I only raised my head when the door opened and Patrick was there," said Daisy. "He was just standing, looking at me." She said to her husband, "I was convinced it was you who'd been shot."

"How could anyone want to put a bullet in a charmer like me?" Yardley chuckled. Daisy dipped the sides of her mouth at him.

"I wonder," said Crosse.

"Then what?" asked Pennance as Yardley opened his mouth in reply to Crosse.

"I got out of our car," said Daisy. "I didn't see anyone driving off."

"The Audi was well away by then," said Yardley. "I approached the blonde, she sat there, knees drawn up against her chest, didn't say a word."

Pennance got a text notification on his watch. Hoskins. 'Will be at the station shortly'.

"I went over to the mum and her daughter, Dunne was it?" asked Daisy.

"Right," said Crosse.

"She was really shaken up. She wouldn't let her little girl go. Not long after, the police arrived and we were brought

THE BLUE CODE

here and gave a statement. One by one the other witnesses cleared off, now it's just us."

"And we appreciate your patience and commitment," said Crosse.

"The ice cream we bought for William will have melted," said Daisy.

"Better than being blown away," said Crosse. Daisy's jaw dropped open slightly.

"Did the shooter get into the Mercedes, Mr Yardley?" asked Pennance.

"Not the gunman, no." Yardley glared at the impassive Crosse. "Someone else. As the killer left, another person appeared from near the cash machines, opened up the rear door, and leant inside before they left again. It was over in less than half a minute."

"You didn't reveal this previously." Crosse tutted. "What happened to precision?"

"I remembered later. I guess as the initial shock wore off. I told one of your PCs." Yardley nodded towards the kitchen where Jones and Squires must still be.

"Can you describe them?" asked Pennance.

"Average height and build. They wore jeans, a jacket and a hat pulled low. Could have been a kid. Either way, they took a black case, a blocky thing, not the type you'd see a city gent carrying."

"You're certain?" asked Crosse.

Yardley pulled a face. "I've not got dementia, Chief Inspector. I'm crystal."

"This time, at least."

"Seriously?" Yardley leaned forward, jutting out his jaw.

"*Patrick*," warned Daisy.

"Tell him, too." Yardley jabbed a finger at Crosse.

"What about you, Mrs Yardley?" asked Pennance.

"I didn't notice anyone. I was too far away and there were lots of vehicles in between. But if Patrick says it happened, then it happened."

"Did you see where this person went?" asked Pennance.

"Across the car park directly away from me," said Yardley.

"There's an alley into the housing estate," said Crosse.

"And that really is everything," said Yardley. "We're leaving now."

"Thanks," said Pennance. "You've both been very helpful."

"There's the small matter of updating your statement with the new information you provided," said Crosse.

"Now? Seriously?" Colour seeped into Yardley's cheeks.

"Our grandson, Chief Inspector," said Daisy.

Crosse stood, leant on the table, fingers spread to support his weight. "I was going to say, before your husband interrupted, that I'll send someone round to your house in the next day or two."

"Oh." Yardley blinked. "Well, thank you."

"You're very welcome."

Pennance rose also, allowing Daisy out.

"If you want to pick up some ice cream as you leave, feel free," said Crosse. "I know the manager. I'm sure it'll be fine."

Daisy glanced at her husband. "I think we're okay, thank you."

Crosse shrugged. "Your shout."

THE BLUE CODE

Once husband and wife had departed the café Crosse said, "Released. What a word to use, Pennance. If you worked for me you'd be getting a bollocking right now."

"Well, I don't."

"Thank Lucifer for small mercies."

"I want to see that alleyway."

"Then let's continue the magical mystery tour." Crosse pointed his fingers like a pistol again.

At least this time he didn't make the sound of ejecting bullets.

Six

An arid wind ruffled Pennance once more as the superstore doors parted. Crosse pushed at his quiff as it lifted like a house roof in a hurricane.

The scene out front had already altered. A space where the ambulance had been, taking Elliott's corpse with it to await a post-mortem. A tow-truck, originally painted white and now smeared with brown mud, was parked in front of the Merc. The signage on the truck's door took some interpreting, what with the dirt and part-peeled off lettering. Pennance figured it read, 'Gaz's Breakdowns'.

A man with a startlingly bright mop of ginger hair, similar in hue to the hi-viz jacket he wore, squatted between truck and car, fixing a cable beneath the latter. By the time Pennance and Crosse reached the drop-off area hi-viz guy, presumably Gaz himself, stood beside his wagon, operating the winch which began to draw the Merc up the angled ramp.

Pennance trotted up to Gaz. "Hold on, please."

"Eh?" Gaz cupped a hand over his ear as the large chunk of wire continued to haul on the Merc, the motor chugging. Pennance reached out, slapped the stop button. Gaz spread his arms wide. "Oi, what are you doing?" His mouth worked, a cow chewing cud. Gaz had a cleft in his chin, deep enough that there were unshaven hairs in it.

"Gaz, right?" asked Pennance.

"What it says." Gaz hauled a thumb at his truck.

"I need you to put the car back."

THE BLUE CODE

"Why?" Gaz grabbed a rag from a nook above the controls and proceeded to wipe the cloth on his hands, moving oil from one part of his skin to another.

"Just for five minutes."

"Time's money, mate." Gaz leaned over to one side, glancing beyond Pennance to Crosse, who must have signalled acquiescence as Gaz sighed, and manipulated the level to lower the Merc.

"Thanks."

"Whatever."

Once the Merc was where it had started Pennance made his way over to the alley. The narrow entrance was only three or so feet wide. "Has CSI been in here?" asked Pennance.

"Of course." Crosse loitered nearby, watching Pennance while Gaz leant on his truck and shook a cigarette out of a packet.

Only a short distance along the alley Pennance immediately descended into gloom. His own shoes were barely a vague outline, yet the Merc was still clearly visible in the daylight. "Can you see me?"

Crosse squinted, craned his head forward. "Hardly at all. Which is a bonus." Pennance took another pace in reverse, bumping up against a brick wall. "Now you're completely gone."

Yet still Pennance had sight of the car – the passenger door behind which Elliott had sat. From here the person waiting would have seen and heard everything, emerging at exactly the right moment, while passers-by remained totally unsuspecting. Pennance re-entered the sunshine.

"What did you find?"

"Look for yourself."

"So, can I carry on now?" Gaz pinched out the tip of the half-smoked cigarette and returned it to the packet.

"Sure." Crosse, made a winding motion in the air with his fingers. Gaz raised his eyes to God before he ground out the cigarette. As Crosse disappeared into the alley the winch kicked in and began to drag the Merc once more. Moments later, Crosse emerged. "I get what you mean. Nice hiding place."

"Where's the estate you mentioned?" asked Pennance.

"Over there." Crosse pointed away from him at 45 degrees, into the corner of the car park.

"I'd like to take a look."

"Whatever you want, Mr N-C-A."

The DCI sauntered just ahead of Pennance, taking the lead, cutting right across the lot, heading for a high hedge bordering the estate. Crosse raised a mobile to his ear and made a quick call. Pennance couldn't hear what was said.

Now, Pennance spotted a petrol station and, much nearer, the square block building of a Click and Collect facility, where online pre-orders could be picked up – no need to even go inside the store anymore.

When Crosse had finished his conversation Pennance caught up. "What about Elliott's house? Has anyone been there?"

"Of course. I know my job." Crosse glanced over briefly. "I sent two uniform in to secure the location at the outset. The inside is apparently a right mess, like everything had been tossed up in the air. Maybe Elliott and Olivia had a fight."

THE BLUE CODE

Crosse brought them to where the hedge ended and a wooden fence took over. Just behind the barrier lurked a house, an upstairs window peeking over the route out of the supermarket car park, past the petrol station.

A concrete bollard pointlessly guarded a gap in the fence and an obvious footpath which, Pennance found, wound its way past new-ish houses, a row of narrow terraces and blocks of semi-detacheds, likely constructed around the same time as the store. Space had been treated as a premium, with the buildings crammed tightly together. The gardens were tiny patches behind the same wood panels as the border fence and cars parked everywhere, lining the pavements, two wheels up the kerb.

The sound of traffic was clear to Pennance. Like Dorothy, he followed the road for a few hundred yards as it continued until he reached a junction with the very route Hamilton had brought him along not even an hour earlier.

Pennance shoved his hands into his pockets. "Someone could have parked, hidden in the alley, waited until Elliott was shot and in the confusion lifted whatever they were after out of the Merc before returning and being back in traffic and away before the first cop car even set off in response."

Crosse merely grunted in reply.

"Which," said Pennance, "raises two questions. How did this person know to be here at a specific time? And what did they remove?"

"Maybe the girlfriend can shed some light," said Crosse. "But before that you and I will be having a little chat with Mercer."

Seven

The low-profile tyres squealed as Crosse took a corner in his Porsche 911, which had rolled off the production line before the introduction of modern technology like ABS and electric windows.

Where Hamilton had driven with focus, economy and control, Crosse was expansive, loose and showy. The Porsche constantly felt like it was going to slew off the road. Other vehicles swung out of Crosse's way. Not because of safety (though Pennance wouldn't have blamed them) but due to the blues Crosse had lit the moment they left the scene.

"Wayne Mercer, sixty two years old, single, originally an accountant by trade." Crosse was seemingly able to multi-task, driving and smoking an e-cig, though Pennance wished he'd just concentrate on the tarmac. "His earliest known legitimate employment was an analyst for an entrepreneur. Mercer's job was to assess distressed businesses – companies verging on bankruptcy – selecting the right ones which could be acquired for a few pence in the pound, then managed back to profit before being sold on at a much higher price. That's something about Mercer." Crosse glanced at Pennance. "Everything he does is calculated. What's his risk vs. the reward? What does he have to do to get something out of any given situation? Rumour has it that's why he never married – too costly should he divorce."

"Maybe he's right."

"For sure." Crosse grimaced. He swung the car off the main road and onto a street with shops either side. The

THE BLUE CODE

Porsche's tyres tripped over the cobbles, making a rattling sound, thankfully forcing Crosse to slow somewhat. "The bookies was one of these failing firms one his employers passed on. Or Mercer lied about the potential because he bought the lot for himself, including the building, sold his house and moved into a flat above."

"When was this?"

"Perhaps twenty years ago, before my time here anyway. Mercer became a collector after that."

"Of what, bagpipes?"

"Money and information, my friend. Mercer has eyes and ears everywhere. More snitches than MI6, that guy. A decade ago he left the betting business and entered into money lending, mainly to his old clients. He still uses his shop to trade from. As a rather nice side hustle, people who owe him cash also tell him stuff. Secrets learned, rumours whispered."

Crosse braked hard, throwing Pennance forward, before swinging through an archway, knocking Pennance into the door fascia, and entering a small stone-laid square surrounded by buildings. "This is it." Crosse parked up in the middle, slewed at an angle.

The bookies occupied one side of the quadrangle. The ground floor was curved glass windows bracing a doorway. The lower part frosted, the upper section clear, presumably to stop inquisitive passers-by peering in while allowing natural light to penetrate. A couple of posters had been taped up outside, but the words and pictures had faded and the edges were part peeled off. Dark blue paint flecked off the rotting wooden frames and he could just about read an old, hand-written sign above the window – 'Smith's Butchers'.

"We think he invests the rather sizeable profits into fixed assets like property, but we've never managed to get access to his finances. Tax returns to HMRC and accounts filed at Companies House are all clean." Crosse took a drag on the e-cig, filling the cabin with liquorice tinged smoke. "He's old school. As much of his dealings goes down on paper as possible which are often then disposed of, so finding any kind of trail, analogue or digital, has been impossible. We've raided him a couple of times but never found anything even mildly incriminating. Whatever we learn is just careless whispers by people who clam up once they realise what they've blurted. As for Mercer." Crosse tapped a fingertip on the window, pointing to the first floor. "He rarely descends into the shop and is never, ever seen outside."

"So who runs the place day to day?"

"Flic Ratliffe. She's his ever-present manager. Lives in a terraced house, her only asset, and walks to work. As watchful as Mercer is from behind the counter." Crosse tilted his head to one side. "Want to go inside? Just to have a look around."

"After you."

The slam of Crosse's car door echoed around the courtyard. Pennance gripped the brass handle and pushed on the shop door, itself frosted glass. Part-way, the door stuck, catching on a shred of decade's old torn linoleum.

"You've got to be definite. Crosse reached out. "Here."

Pennance gave up his space allowing Crosse room to pull the door back towards him, then swing it hard, catching on

THE BLUE CODE

the lino again, but the momentum stopped it from snagging. "*That's* how you do it." Crosse, in the entranceway, waved an arm like a concierge for Pennance to enter.

The interior was as grim and depressing as any Pennance had been unfortunate enough to witness. Bulky, dusty old TVs crouched on Formica shelves, the screens dead. Old because they were large – cathode ray tubes, the kind only seen on nostalgia shows these days.

Tall bar stools were set against the opposite wall, beneath another shelf made of the same composite chipped and scratched wood where scraps of paper, pens and newspapers were scattered. Pennance picked up a damp newspaper, a Racing Post, years out of date. The walls were peeling wallpaper, revealing crumbling plaster beneath. The lighting was a dim, a hue similar to cat vomit.

At the far end, a counter occupied the width of the room. Dark wood up to waist height then four adjacent inset metal grilles, each with a section of glass above and more wood up to the ceiling. Fabric blinds were pulled down over all but one section, the word CLOSED emblazoned across each. In the single open slice sat a woman with an angular face and towering beehive style hair.

"That's Ratliffe." Crosse confirmed Pennance's suspicion.

Next to the counter and set against the wall were the only seemingly modern items – a pair of slot machines, lit up and flashing in lurid colours. A white guy with long, greasy dreadlocks, baggy jeans half off his backside and a t-shirt emblazoned with 'FAC51' in yellow letters fed money into both; one after the other, coin after coin, back and forth, until he didn't. "What the fuck?" He began repeatedly kicking one of the bandits.

"Jerry." Ratliffe's tone was even. "Give it a rest."

"The bloody thing won't let me play anymore!"

"Because you've reached the limit." Ratliffe raised a comb to her hair. "We've discussed this. You know the score."

"Unplug it so it resets."

"I won't do that."

"Why not? You have before."

"I told you, no."

Jerry glanced at the cops, gave the casing another boot.

"Don't." Ratliffe kept her eyes on Pennance.

"Or what?" Jerry spat on the floor.

"Or one of our friendly police officers will have a word."

Jerry laughed. "Yeah, right. Like they scare me."

"After which you'll have to deal with Mr Mercer." Ratliffe lifted a phone receiver, a heavy old Bakelite design. "I can call him now, if you want?" She nodded at a camera lens above the slot machines.

"Okay, okay." Jerry raised his hands high in surrender revealing sweat patches under each armpit. "No need to get all unreasonable."

"Wise decision." Ratliffe gestured at the door.

"I'm going, I'm going." Jerry sidled past Pennance and Crosse, trailing pungent body odour, rewarding them both with a sneer.

As Jerry made his graceless exit, Ratliffe put the phone to her ear. Her lips moved, but Pennance couldn't hear what was said. Crosse reached the counter as Ratliffe replaced the receiver.

THE BLUE CODE

Behind the glass Ratliffe's legs were out of sight under a counter, the laminated wood worn away in places to white, doubtless from countless hands over the years. At her elbow rested a ledger which she'd closed so Pennance could only see the green cover. Ratliffe was hemmed in by a wall just a few feet behind her chair, more betting posters tacked up in a staggered pattern, then a door which would presumably allow Ratliffe into whatever area was out back.

"Morning, Flic." Crosse glanced around. "I like what you haven't done with the place."

"Chief Inspector." Ratliffe rubbed her neck with stubby fingers, the nails cracked and bitten down to the quick. "Come to take me out for that spin you promised me?" She winked.

"Unfortunately I'm here on official business." Crosse stole a sideways glance at Pennance. "To see Mercer."

"Your loss." Ratliffe smirked. "Got an appointment?"

"Just a friendly chat to introduce my colleague, Inspector Pennance."

Ratliffe gave Pennance the once over. "Only one of you can go up."

"Wayne will want to hear what I have to tell him and I'm not leaving the inspector down here. You'd tear him apart."

Ratliffe chuckled. "Chance would be a fine thing." Ratliffe held her hand out, palm up. "Alright, but first, mobile."

"No way," said Pennance.

Ratliffe shrugged, withdrew. "Then you're not meeting Mercer."

"How about I put them in the Porsche?" said Crosse.

"That'll do," said Ratliffe.

Pennance dug out his phone, turned it off, passed it to Crosse. Pennance's watch bleeped, informing him it was now disconnected and dumb.

"I'll be right back," said Crosse. "Don't kill him, Flic."

"You married?" asked Ratliffe.

"No."

"Divorced, then?"

"Also a no."

"Don't meet many of your sort."

"What's that?"

"Unsullied."

Thankfully, Crosse returned then and Ratliffe pointed towards a black painted wall between the slot machines and the counter. She must have pressed a button because a door-sized section popped, creating a gap six inches or so wide. "Close it behind you."

"Into the cheetah's den," said Crosse.

A bright and naked bulb revealed a steep set of stripped wood stairs which stretched upwards and bare brick wall, cold to the touch. Pennance glanced over his shoulder – Ratliffe already head down and paying them zero attention.

The lock proved to be an electronically controlled mechanism, one of several other latches and bolts which could be set from the inside. Pennance ran his fingers over a steel surround, there to protect against the door being kicked in. Mercer took his security seriously. Chirping sounds came down the stairs. "Is that birds?"

Crosse reached back, pulled the door shut. "You'll see."

THE BLUE CODE

As Pennance rose, the stairs creaked loudly beneath his feet, like some early warning system. His head popped up through a hole cut in the floor; he felt very exposed. A red rope with a large knot in the end hung close at hand, and Pennance hauled himself up. The hole proved to be a hatch, with a flap which Mercer could drop down, if he wanted.

The area was a spacious open plan rectangle, sofa and a big desk where a man, presumably Mercer, sat. Not behind in the chair, but on one corner, cradling a coffee mug. For now, Pennance ignored him, more interested in the layout. Where the shop below seemed like it was stuck in a time warp and hadn't been decorated for decades, Mercer's office was bright, clean, neat. And filled with what Pennance considered to be mini-prisons.

Brightly coloured finches, fluttering back and forth between perches but behind bars. Then green parakeets, Pennance recognised them – they were a growing menace in London. And a pair of lovebirds. Next to Pennance a white parrot rested on a chest high stand. Its plume lifted as Pennance regarded it.

A group of televisions (flat screens this time) mounted on an interior wall to the right of the desk displayed different CCTV feeds. The picture quality was excellent, better than most used by the police and councils. High definition cameras, for sure. On one a view of the stairs Pennance had just climbed. Another where Ratliffe dealt with a customer, her hands visible as she made a note in the ledger. Then a tight focus on the slot machines. Two more cameras within the shop itself.

Another of the entrance from inside and out, then a wide angle perspective of the whole shop, a fish-eye of the square out front and Crosse's Porsche. Finally, two images obviously outside on an alley, perhaps behind the building. The blocky bulk of a Range Rover slowly passed by as he watched. Seemingly, Mercer had every angle covered.

Three windows along the wall opposite the TVs were supposed to allow in light. However, the curtains were tightly drawn and bright LED lights recessed into the ceiling gave the required illumination instead. Pennance parted the nearest drape. The alley beneath was indeed the one on camera, another building with bricked-in windows opposite.

A fire escape, like the kind on American movies, a metal stairway reached by stepping out of the window before lowering a ladder to reach the ground. Finally, between each window, were fish tanks.

"Seen enough?" asked Mercer.

"Clearly it's not me who likes to watch," said Pennance.

Mercer chuckled. "Where are my manners, would either of you like one?" He raised his mug, revealing a large black O, maybe a logo for some business Pennance didn't recognise.

"I'll skip." Crosse grimaced. "Nothing of yours will be passing my lips."

"Where's your trust now?"

"In the same grave as your sincerity, Wayne."

"I never lie, Nick. So, Inspector Pennance, strong, black, no sugar, is your preference, right?"

"I sometimes take milk, depending on the quality of the coffee."

THE BLUE CODE

"Of course you do, and I only have the best here." Mercer slid off the desk and went to a pod coffee machine.

"Does that extend to your manager?" asked Pennance.

"Flic?" Mercer placed a small cup beneath a spout and pressed a button. "Certainly." The machine chugged loudly enough that conversation would mean raised voices, so Pennance waited. Shortly, Mercer sat the now-filled cup down on Pennance's side of the desk. "As a courtesy you can stay as long as it takes to finish your espresso."

"I'll drink it extremely slowly, then."

Mercer eyes twinkled. "Good man."

"There's been a shooting," said Crosse. "A man was murdered, and I think your fingers are all over it. So, we'll be here until I say."

"Private property, no warrant, Chief Inspector. So, no. The dead man is Logan Elliott, right?"

"You know that."

Mercer held out a hand, indicating a low-backed leather chair. "Please."

"You have it," said Crosse. "I'll stand."

Pennance sat and Mercer took his place opposite while Crosse perched on the corner of Mercer's desk, hemming the loan shark in.

"And, do you possess a shred of evidence tying me to the crime, Nick?"

"It's just a matter of patience."

Mercer switched his focus onto Pennance. "I've been looking into your background. You have a very interesting history."

"Does he now?" Crosse twisted to face Pennance.

Mercer said, "Born Jonah Revel Pennance in Lewisham, out of wedlock."

"Revel," said Crosse. "What kind of name is that?"

"Family tradition," said Pennance.

"Old French," said Mercer. "Translates as Rebel."

"Huh." Crosse grunted.

Mercer continued, "Your mother was an alcoholic. As a child you went by the name Joe, embarrassed by the association Jonah brought. You ended up in care for several years in Margate with your half-sister before your father withdrew you from the institution, but not her, which she loathed you for. You lived with your father before successfully applying to the Metropolitan Police at seventeen, eventually joining on your eighteenth birthday.

"Three years on the beat in Peckham before transferring to CID as a constable with a successful enough arrest record to reach sergeant, then a transfer to Sapphire, the specialist child protection agency based out of Southwark where you came under the auspices of boss and mentor Superintendent Devon Kelso and meeting Sergeant Simone Smithson. Eventually you gained promotion to detective inspector.

"Seven months ago you transferred to the National Crime Agency, MCIS team, reporting into Crime Team Manager Stephanie Meacham. This is your first case away from your patch, in a station potentially under special measures."

"That's supposed to be confidential." Crosse frowned.

"You're single, in an on-off relationship with the aforementioned Smithson; currently in the on phase after her recent tragedy. You're a high achiever and intelligent with an unorthodox investigative outlook, making the NCA the perfect place for you. How's that for a start?"

"None of that is particularly revelatory," lied Pennance. He tried to maintain a straight face under the glare of both Mercer and Crosse's examination.

"Challenge accepted. Let's get personal." Mercer steepled his fingers concentrating on Pennance. "You collect first editions, preferably signed. You don't have any personal social media accounts as you find the intrusion abhorrent and hearing from old school mates is something you intensely dislike, primarily because you moved institutions so often. This imparts a subconscious aversion to individual connections, which is principally what affects your partnership with Miss Smithson and results in a very limited friendship circle. Kelso is a father figure to you, replacing the man who died several years ago.

"You possess a difficulty in forming relationships with the living, yet you delight in the macabre of a crime scene. In fact, that's become somewhat of a speciality of yours and why you're here, in Huntingdon, albeit temporarily. No-one at the station wants you."

"He's right about the last part," shrugged Crosse.

Mercer rose, crossed to the fish tank and peeled the lid off a tin of food. "Why is that, Joe?"

"It's Inspector Pennance and I've no idea, nor is it relevant."

"Bad luck follows you around, I hear." Mercer sprinkled flakes on the water's surface.

"Your network is misinformed."

"Whatever anyone else says behind your back, Inspector, I rate your abilities."

Pennance drank the espresso in one shot. "Your machine needs cleaning out." Then he stood and made his way towards the hatch.

"Oh, are we finished, then?" asked Crosse. "I was rather enjoying that."

Pennance clambered down the stairs, Crosse close behind, aware of the camera lens observing him as he descended. As he reached out for the door the lock automatically unlatched. Ratliffe had the phone to her ear. She watched Pennance and Crosse all the way out.

When they were back in the Porsche, Crosse handed Pennance his phone. "Well?"

"He's a control freak."

"You got that right."

"Not sure I take him for a killer, though."

"Oh, Wayne Mercer never gets his own hands dirty. He's been poisoning this town for years. A certain section of society live in fear of him and it's high time that ended." Crosse narrowed his eyelids into slits. "He's going down for this, no matter what I have to do."

Pennance let that ride for a moment. "Mercer all but read out my personnel file."

"He did the same with me." Crosse started the Porsche's engine. "It's a rite of passage with Mercer."

"So he has someone on the inside."

"More than one I'd say."

"Who on your team has a money problem?"

THE BLUE CODE

"Could be any one of them. Have you seen how much we get paid?" Crosse put the car in gear and rolled across the courtyard. "But when I find out I'll hang them from a yardarm."

Eight

Huntingdon police station was awkwardly squeezed onto a narrow strip of land between a busy ring road and a housing estate, like it had muscled its unwelcome way into the space. Squad cars, their sides emblazoned with large blue and yellow chequers and the Cambridgeshire constabulary emblem, were parked wherever feasible – too many vehicles, not enough spots.

To Pennance the station itself appeared modelled unsympathetically with the neighbouring buildings – two separate narrow dark brown brick rectangles lying on their side, one two storey, the other three, both with a sharp roof and monotonously spaced windows.

The sections were conjoined by a narrow slice and it was into here, through a door marked 'No Entry To The Public' which Crosse led Pennance. Above, a large air conditioning unit whirred away, the noise cutting off when the door slammed shut behind Pennance, thanks to a badly adjusted spring.

Pennance followed the DCI through a warren of corridors and stairs confusing enough that he'd need string to find his way back.

"Elliott's girlfriend, Olivia Bingham, is being held for us," said Crosse. "I'll be handling the questioning."

"It's your patch."

Not that Crosse left room for argument. But he surprised Pennance by leaning on a door, holding it open for Pennance to enter. "This is your lot."

THE BLUE CODE

Three tables, each with a chair, butted up against each other in a tiny, windowless room. McAleney had her laptop open on one, a bulging backpack on the floor. Hoskins' feet on another, hat over his eyes, head almost touching the wall.

"Are we keeping you up?" Crosse pushed at Hoskins' legs, clearly aiming to shove them off the tabletop. He failed and Hoskins remained firmly in place.

"What's your problem, chief?" Hoskins raised his hat, swept back his hair, then focused on Pennance. "Oh, hey, Jonah." Now Hoskins straightened.

"It's DCI Crosse," he said. "I'm the boss round here."

"I think you'll find *she* is." Hoskins pointed at McAleney who rolled her eyes. "What are we working on, Ava?"

"*I'm* just getting set up, Vance."

"Almost ready?" asked Pennance.

"I would be, if people left me alone."

"See? I'm helping." Hoskins raised an eyebrow at Crosse. "Shut the door on your way out, would you, mate." Then he leaned back in his chair, cap over his eyes once more.

Crosse glanced between Hoskins and McAleney a couple of times before backing out into the corridor and pulling the door closed. "Is that normal behaviour?"

"Pretty much."

"It must be all fun and games at the NCA."

"You've no idea."

***

The interview room was empty. Of people at least.

"For f–." Crosse stopped himself before he finished the rest of the expletive. "Where the hell are they?"

"Not here," said Pennance.

"I can see why you're a detective." Crosse left Pennance alone, eyeballed by two CCTV lenses, mounted high in opposite corners overlooking a graffiti-scarred laminate wood table and the block of a digital recorder.

One wall was half-painted – part buttercup yellow, part magnolia. The tin and a brush, the bristles all dried out, on the floor nearby.

Moments later the door went again. A tall brunette in a short skirt, six-inch heels and a crop top revealing a toned stomach and pierced belly button entered. Olivia, Pennance guessed, closely followed by a man who'd be shorter than his charge, even if she were barefoot.

He wore a suit and blue shirt open at a thick, wrinkled neck. Bizarrely, rather than the standard cloth tie, he sported the kind of affectation TV cowboys wore – a piece of black braided cord and metal amulet with a blue stone in the centre. Pennance glanced down at the guy's shoes – standard loafers, no boots, no spurs. Pity.

"Who are you?"

Pennance would have liked the faux herdsman to possess an American accent. Instead, it was neutral Southern. "DI Pennance."

"Explains it."

"Explains what?"

Now a woman in a masculine grey trouser suit arrived. She was athletic looking with short, bleached hair, dark roots showing, a slight kink in her nose and a counterbalancing lopsided mouth. Both were definitely cops. Pennance could tell.

"I'm DS Keri Jansen," she said. "And this is my boss, DI Shapiro."

"She's a fortunate chick," said Shapiro.

Irritation briefly skittered across Jansen's face, but rather than reply she said to Pennance, "Would you like a coffee? It's machine unfortunately."

"I'll pass."

Then Jansen addressed Olivia. "Can I get you one?"

"Thanks, but no. I'm swimming in the stuff."

Shapiro patted a plastic chair designed never to be sat in for comfort. "Park your backside, love."

"I didn't realise we were still in the 1970s," said Pennance.

"You what?" Shapiro bared his teeth.

"Where did you get to?" Crosse filled the doorway, attention flitting between his two officers.

"We must have circled around each other," said Jansen.

Pennance's phone beeped. Text from McAlaney: 'Good to go.' Meaning she was hooked into the station's network, including CCTV.

"It's a bit over-stuffed in here now." Crosse blew air through his lips. "Ed, you can stay. Jansen you'll need to clear off."

Shapiro's face gurned into what Pennance assumed was a victory grin. "Better luck next time, Cupcake."

Jansen placed hands on hips. "It's me who's been with Olivia the whole time."

"Don't argue, Jansen. Shapiro got promoted, not you. Watch and learn if you like." Crosse hoiked a digit at a camera then grabbed hold of the door edge. "Or not. Either way, skedaddle."

"I'm sure we'll bump into each other later," said Jansen to Pennance.

Shapiro snickered. "Fast work, Inspector."

Crosse shut the door on Jansen before dragging a chair from under the table, metal legs juddering and setting Pennance's teeth on edge. Crosse settled down with a deep huff, like he'd removed the weight of Huntingdon from his soles, and shrugged off his jacket. Shapiro took the space opposite Olivia, leaving Pennance with the pleasure of facing Shapiro.

Pennance placed his full attention onto Olivia. Her expression was set at hard as concrete, lips a paper cut. Her eyes (brown pupils) were clear and her make-up perfect – no tear stains to ruin the careful, minimalistic application. Perhaps all that would come later. Or never.

"Just to reassure you, Miss Bingham," said Crosse, "You're here of your own free will as a witness to a murder."

"So, I can leave?"

"Sure." Crosse hefted one shoulder and Olivia began to stand. "However, that will lead me to believe you're unwilling to help find your boyfriend's killer and I'll be intrigued as to why that would be." Crosse regarded his fingernails.

"Boyfriend, that's quaint." It seemed she shared a similar outlook with Pennance. Olivia retook her place, crossed her arms. "Ask away."

THE BLUE CODE

"Do you mind if I record the session?" Crosse reached towards the machine, finger heading for the relevant button before she'd even answered.

"Yes."

"Thank you."

"Chief Inspector, you asked if I mind being recorded. I answered yes, which means I do mind and I don't want you to start your machine."

"Oh." Crosse blinked, dropped his arm. "Right." Crosse's accompanying beam possessed not a shred of good humour. "You were in the store buying food." He frowned when Olivia merely looked at him.

"That wasn't a question," said Pennance.

Olivia regarded Pennance now, a hint of amusement flickering across her features.

"Okay." Crosse nodded. "Clearly I need to be highly specific. When you exited the store what did you see?"

"At first, just tarmac. I was trying to balance in these bloody shoes." Olivia lifted a long leg and placed it on the table. She rotated her ankle, showing off the impressive heels. The sole was a bright red leather strip, hardly worn. Shapiro stared for a protracted moment along the length of Olivia's closely shaved calf, the oiled skin glistening under the light. "Logan liked me wearing them when we were meeting the boss." She lowered her leg back down and adjusted her dress. Shapiro licked his lips.

"The boss being Kai Naughton?" asked Crosse.

"The very same. I persuaded Logan to host a barbecue later so Naughton could watch me walk around the garden, eat a sausage, bend over, and so on."

Shapiro grinned, while Crosse looked like he'd kissed a slug. "Do you do that a lot?"

"Put on a show? Occasionally, when Logan needed it. But it was absolutely look, don't touch. Ordinarily, I prefer a nice, comfortable trainer and a tracksuit."

"Why?"

"Easier on the feet than these bloody skyscrapers."

Crosse ran a hand over his face. "No, I mean why did you get dressed up in clothes you wouldn't normally wear?"

"Because Logan was an excellent lover." Olivia arched an eyebrow. "And because he was a highly paid and ambitious man who I was happy to ride along with." She leaned forward. "I'm very good at getting what I want. Superb, even. But Logan, he was a challenge. I couldn't twist him around my finger, and I respected that. Naughton is a tough man to work for, he's intensely driven and expects his leaders around him to act the same. Naughton kept Logan very busy, so he valued his downtime highly, and if I could help by flashing a little skin then yes, I'd do it. Where's the crime in that?" Olivia rapped a painted fingernail on the tabletop. "Lots of other partners have done far, far worse." She sat back and regarded Crosse closely.

"So your visit to the supermarket was spur of the moment?"

"Right."

"What position did Elliott hold in Naughton's business?"

"Chief Something-or-other. Logan carefully separated work from social time as much as he could."

"What was in the case chained to his wrist?"

THE BLUE CODE

"Your guess is as good as mine."

"Was the driver always with him?"

"Ferrensby, yes. Logan didn't drive himself."

"Why not?"

Olivia shrugged. "He said he could afford to employ someone, so he did."

"Ferrensby was paid by Elliott?"

"Far as I know."

"What's his first name?"

"Matt, I think."

Crosse pointedly nodded at the camera. Jansen would be looking into Ferrensby. McAlaney too.

"Why all of these precautions?" asked Shapiro. "How many people have a lockable case?"

"I can't answer that for you." Olivia lifted a shoulder. "It's a statistic I've never had cause to verify."

"Go back to what happened when you left the supermarket," said Crosse.

Olivia thought for a second, eyes raised. "I walked out, tottered, really. Nice, sunny day. I stopped for a quick cigarette, but the lighter wouldn't spark. All normal until it wasn't." She stared off into the distance for a moment. "It was only when the machine gun began to fire I even paid attention. There was a guy wearing a balaclava, gun aimed into the Merc, at Logan. I dropped the bags and took cover behind a pillar until it was over."

"Did you recognise anybody inside the other car?"

"No, the driver wore a balaclava too."

"And did you see anyone entering the Mercedes afterwards?"

"I didn't even look." Olivia shook her head. "I stayed where I was until the police arrived."

"You failed to check on your boyfriend?" asked Shapiro.

"I'm not a fucking nurse," said Olivia. "There's no way he could have survived that."

"How would you know if you're not a nurse?"

"I guess you didn't want to see his body?" asked Pennance.

"Of course not." Olivia squeezed her eyes tight shut, shook her bowed head. "He was a good guy. Not marriage material, but decent to me."

Shapiro curled a lip. "Yeah, right."

Olivia snapped her head up, slapped an open palm on the table, almost a gunshot sound in itself. She glared at Shapiro. "Who the hell are you to judge?"

"Where do you want me to start?" Shapiro glanced Olivia up and down.

She turned to Crosse. "Are you going to let him speak to me like that?"

"I'll say whatever I want, love." Shapiro smirked.

"Okay." Olivia rose. "We're done. I'm not accepting blatant sexism."

"Hang on." Crosse reached out a hand towards Olivia but refrained from making contact at the last moment, like he realised that was going to be a mistake.

"I agree with the lady," said Pennance.

"Lady, *pffft*." Shapiro waved a dismissive hand.

"Don't forget the cameras," said Pennance.

"I could smack you in the mouth and get away with it."

Crosse said nothing, mouth slightly open.

THE BLUE CODE

"Oh, dear," said Olivia.

"Your call, Chief Inspector," said Pennance.

Crosse pointed to the door. "Leave, Ed."

"Nick?" Shapiro leaned forward, hands clasped between his legs. "You're really throwing me out?" said Shapiro.

"Go."

Finally, after one last shake of the head, Shapiro jerked to his feet, stalked out, slammed the door back on its hinges.

"Now can we continue?" asked Crosse. Olivia still towered over Crosse who couldn't bring himself to meet her gaze.

"Not quite," said Olivia.

"What else do you want?"

"For the nice Inspector Pennance to ask the questions." Olivia wriggled her eyebrows at Pennance.

"This is my investigation, not his."

"You can stay and listen, but we only carry on under my conditions." She tapped her foot like a ticking clock.

"Alright." Crosse sagged back into his chair. "Have it your way."

"Wise decision." Olivia took Shapiro's seat so she faced Pennance while Crosse closed the door. "See? Told you I was good at getting what I wanted."

"I believed you already," said Pennance.

"What's your first name? I can't call you *Inspector* all the time. So impersonal."

"It's Jonah."

"Interesting." Olivia chuckled before stretching out both her arms across the table, palms together like she was going to dive into a pool. "What else do you want to know, Jo-nah?" She split the name in half.

"Where did you come from before reaching the store?" asked Pennance.

"Logan picked me up outside my house."

"You didn't live together?"

Olivia wrinkled her nose. "God, no. I prefer my own space."

"Where's home?"

"Brampton. A mile or two outside town, if you know it?"

"Unfortunately not."

"I'll show you around, if you like."

"Perhaps another time. How long were you in a relationship with Mr Elliott?"

"On and off, for six months. We met at a club in Cambridge, the only club really. He was at some work event, I was with a few friends, both of us were bored. We've kind of drifted along from there."

"You were in the back seat of the Mercedes with Elliott?"

"No way I'd sit next to Ferrensby." Olivia grimaced.

"And Mr Elliott had the case with him?"

"That's right."

"Can you describe it?"

"Slightly smaller than a standard briefcase, I'd say. Hard plastic, combination lock. It seemed very sturdy, like you could run a truck over the top and it'd still be in one piece. Also, there was the chain and handcuff, of course."

"When you got out of the car, did you open the door yourself?"

THE BLUE CODE

"The handle wouldn't work. Ferrensby had to get it from the outside."

"Was that normal?"

Olivia rubbed her jaw with two fingers. "Now I come to think of it, no. Ferrensby said that the car's electrics had a problem and he'd have it checked tomorrow."

Crosse exhaled heavily.

"Is something the matter?" asked Pennance.

"I've been listening very closely to you two and something doesn't add up."

Olivia narrowed her eyes. "I expect I'll regret saying this, but go on."

"You claim going to the store was spur of the moment. Yet the killers knew exactly where to go and where Elliott was parked. Also, the rear doors were locked so Elliott couldn't escape. Finally, someone hid nearby, ready to remove the briefcase immediately after your boyfriend was murdered. The only way I see all of that being possible is someone told the killers where and when Elliott would be." Crosse leant forward, putting his weight onto his forearms, showing interest by how he peered at Olivia. "And I think that someone was you."

"That's untrue," said Olivia.

"Is it? You were conveniently out of the car when the attack happened."

"So was Ferrensby."

"I bet as soon as you got inside the store you made a call."

"Check my phone then." Olivia tossed her mobile onto the table.

"You wouldn't be so stupid as to use your own handset. I'd assume a burner. Dumped straight after you'd done the dirty on your boyfriend."

"Imagine all you want. I was walking back to the car when the shooting started."

"Right." Crosse shrugged. "Yet far enough away to be untouched."

Olivia stood again. "You know what? I've had enough of your crap. Arrest me if you want."

"Maybe I will."

The pair glared at each other for several moments.

When Crosse made no move Olivia said, "That's what I thought."

"You've been very helpful, Olivia," said Pennance. Crosse snorted. "I'd suggest you don't leave Huntingdon. In case we need to speak with you again."

"I've nowhere else to go," said Olivia.

"Oh, boo hoo," said Crosse. "I'll have someone show you out." He went to the door.

"I'd say thank you, but I wouldn't mean it," said Olivia.

"Now I reckon that's the first truthful statement you've made." Crosse tilted his head at Pennance. "With me." He went into the corridor.

"I hope I haven't got you in trouble," said Olivia.

"I'm good enough at that myself," said Pennance.

"See you soon."

"Maybe."

"Men always come back for more, Jonah. You'll be no different." This time there merely weary resignation in her expression.

Nine

Crosse leaned against the wall regarding his boots, waiting for Pennance as he swapped places with a PC who entered the interview room.

"Well, she's unique," said Crosse.

"I like her," said Pennance. "She bears a weight."

"You believe her?"

"Of course, don't you?"

Crosse's only reply was a snort. "They're often not to be trusted."

"They?"

"Females."

Olivia exited then, trailing the PC. She gave Pennance a long glance before allowing herself to be led in the opposite direction.

"And I'll remind you that I don't work for you, Chief Inspector," said Pennance. "I'm not yours to order around."

"This is my station. And my resources."

"Me and my team are here independently of you, remember?"

"Sure." Crosse scuffed the floor. "I don't have to like it, though."

Pennance sighed, leaned against the wall next to Crosse. "Look, I get why."

"You've had someone wander across your patch then?"

"More than once. You have my word that we'll be gone as soon as we can and you'll never hear from me again."

"That'll be a good day."

"I agree."

Crosse chuckled.

"You know this Ferrensby?" said Pennance.

"Part of a local family of career criminals. They seem to breed like rats. Not one of them has an actual, tax paying career. If Jansen's done her job properly she should have an APB out for him by now."

"Ferrensby lied about the door locks."

"You think?" Crosse curled a lip. "Clear as day, he set his boss up."

"Yet you went for Olivia in there."

"Just prodding around, seeing what falls out."

"And Naughton?"

"Now, that *was* interesting. He's a big name round here. A self-made man happy to share his wealth."

"A philanthropist?"

"Yeah, now there's a behaviour which has always made me suspicious. I mean, who in their right mind *gives* their cash away?" Crosse pushed off the wall. "I think we need to have a word with Naughton."

"Mind if I tag along?"

"Course, I'll give you a knock when I'm ready." Crosse pointed. "Your room's that way."

***

Hoskins was still reclining in his chair, feigning sleep, when Pennance entered.

"It's Jonah." McAlaney didn't look up from her keyboard.

THE BLUE CODE

"Oh." Hoskins straightened while Pennance settled into the remaining seat which immediately lurched backwards. "I forgot to say, mind that chair, it's broken."

"Brilliant." Pennance leant on the table. "I assume you saw everything?"

"Of course." McAlaney rolled her eyes. "I have access to each camera, their email account, and all their servers."

"Good work."

She pushed a plastic fob over to him. "Temporary ID, but this one will get you access to every part of the station." The lanyard was brightly coloured, some kid's cartoon characters.

"That's my gift to you," said Hoskins.

Pennance scooped the pass into a pocket. "What have you found on Matt Ferrensby?"

"He's a little minx." McAlaney turned her laptop around, Ferrensby's record on-screen, a photo of a rodent-faced man central. "Comes from a long line of ne'er-do-wells. Associated with multiple dodgy family members – cousins, uncles, nieces, mother, grandparents, even great grandparents. They've all got addresses in and around Warboys, wherever that is. All sorts of crimes from assault to theft. Fly tipping, racial hatred, even a case of public exposure."

"What about Matt himself?"

"The public exposure was Matt, urinating on a bus stop. Otherwise, it's car theft, speeding, handling stolen goods – they were car parts. He's been in and out of juvenile detention, then prison for half his life."

"How the hell did he end up working for Elliott?" asked Hoskins.

McAlaney's handset dinged. She lifted it and read the screen.

"Good question," said Pennance.

"Uh, Jonah," said McAlaney. "Did Crosse tell you he's having a briefing with his detectives?"

"No."

"Well he is. Right now."

"How do you know?"

"I accessed all their mobiles, too." McAlaney showed Pennance her phone. "Crosse just sent a group WhatsApp."

Ten

Pennance entered a large, open plan oblong-shaped space and immediately knew he was in the right place: CID detectives office. A group of smartly-dressed men and women, most seated, a few standing, turned almost as one towards Pennance.

Until Pennance's arrival their focus had been Crosse, positioned on a kind of low stage at one end of the room, behind a long bank of gunmetal grey painted filing cabinets next to a large TV on a wheeled stand. Behind Crosse three over-sized whiteboards fixed to the wall were already scrubbed clean.

Banks of desks, computers and screens, notice boards filled with data, documents and a large map of the area. Three windows along one side delivered natural light, although overhead strips burned, too. One flickered in an irregular, headache-inducing display.

"Don't mind me." Pennance leant against the wall, arms crossed. "Carry on with the briefing."

"To those of you who don't know, this is Inspector Pennance with the NCA. Up from London to show us country folk how it's done."

"I'm here to help, not get in the way."

"Damn right." Shapiro scowled at Pennance while Crosse propped himself with the cabinets, hands pressed down onto the metal.

"Starting over. Earlier today one Logan Elliott was shot to death by a man wielding a machine gun in a targeted attack. At this stage it appears to be a robbery – a briefcase with currently unknown contents was removed immediately after Elliott was killed. I've therefore classified the investigation as Category B, meaning a low risk to the public. This office will be our Major Incident Room with HOLMES being used to organise the investigation."

The Home Office Large Major Enquiry System, was effectively a piece of software, custom-built for the police, originally introduced in the mid-1980s. The huge swathes of case data developed by the otherwise independently operating police forces around the UK was loaded onto HOLMES, allowing an investigating officer to search and analyse existing data in one accessible location and potentially develop new lines of enquiry.

"I am SIO with Ed as my deputy. Speaking of whom, over to you." Crosse stepped backwards, allowing the junior man into his domain.

Jansen took the chance to tilt herself into Pennance. "Has Crosse sorted you out a temporary pass?"

"Got one already."

"And where are you staying?"

"No idea."

"Sergeant?" Shapiro dropped the folder from a few inches above the filing cabinets, generating an audible bang.

"Sorry, sir." Jansen righted herself again.

Shapiro flicked the cover of the folder open and held aloft a large, colour head and shoulders photo for the assembled to witness, like he had a decapitated traitor spiked on a pole. A line of magnetised coloured plastic circles ran along the bottom of a whiteboard and Shapiro used one to

THE BLUE CODE

fix Elliott's photo in place about a third of the way down, effectively starting a murder board where all the key case developments would be displayed as a visual central focus for the investigation to coalesce around.

"We have CCTV from the store." Shapiro pointed a remote at the TV, and a few seconds later a grainy coloured image came on screen. The perspective was from on high, and facing towards the drop-off point, revealing the Merc's bonnet. So the camera would be fixed above the shop entrance. Cars came and went, shoppers too.

"Bloody hell, the missus goes there," said someone in the office.

"Pity she didn't get struck by a stray bullet," said another, causing brief laughter. Jansen chuckled and Pennance hoped it was mock humour.

"Elliott was parked in the drop-off zone waiting for his girlfriend, Olivia Bingham." Olivia emerged, tottering slightly. Shapiro paused the footage. "Sir, if you wouldn't mind." A couple of appreciative whistles rang out as Crosse placed Olivia's photo on the board beneath Elliott.

"Really, guys?" asked Jansen, arms out.

"Jealous, Tinkerbell?" asked Shapiro.

"Children, shut it," said Crosse. "Carry on, Ed."

"Thank you, sir." Shapiro pressed play again and on screen Olivia moved forward a few paces before putting her bags on the ground. She was about halfway to the Merc.

"Another car, an Audi, arrives on the property now." Shapiro pointed as a car entered at the top of the image. "The Audi pulls up right beside Elliott's and his driver, Matthew Ferrensby exits, as does the shooter."

In almost perfect timing the doors of the two cars opened together. Olivia bent her head, hands up. This would be when she was struggling to light her cigarette. A large man cradling a machine gun slowly passed the rear of the Merc, seemingly in no rush, while Ferrensby moved in the opposite direction, round the bonnet. The gunman paused briefly outside the alleyway entrance as Ferrensby got into the Audi before aiming the weapon's muzzle at Elliott.

A couple of heartbeats later the gunman fired, a flame spitting from the barrel. Olivia and several bystanders froze. Magazine emptied, the killer moved fast this time while Olivia ran to a nearby pillar and cowered behind it, and bystanders scattered out of sight. Then the gunman was inside the Audi.

Shapiro paused the playback. "It's here things get interesting."

He started the footage again. As the Audi pulled away, a person darted out of the passage. Pennance was expecting the movement, but even he almost missed it. The person pulled open the Merc's door and entered before emerging again and disappearing off camera. Pennance had counted to twenty nine.

Shapiro turned off the TV. "Initial assessment from Thriplow is Elliott was struck from thigh to neck with thirteen out of twenty high velocity rounds."

"Unlucky for some." The same comedian who'd cracked a joke earlier. Nobody laughed this time.

"Casings have gone off to NABIS to determine if the gun has been used previously." Shapiro headed back onto the dais and to his folder.

THE BLUE CODE

NABIS was the National Ballistics Intelligence Service, primarily a forensics team who analysed weapons and ballistic material. Shell casings were like fingerprints and NABIS possessed a huge database to evaluate.

"We all know the driver, Matthew Ferrensby, and his family."

"Don't we bloody just," said one of the CID team.

Shapiro put up the file photo McAlaney had shown Pennance earlier. "On arrival at the scene we found the engine turned off and keys missing – probably Ferrensby took them. He hasn't been seen since." Shapiro closed the folder, drawing the curtain on his performance.

Jansen leaned in. "The Ferrensby's are local thieves. Combined, the Ferrensby's and Mercer are responsible for much of the crime around Huntingdon."

"I met Mercer earlier," said Pennance.

"Got something to add?" Shapiro stared directly at Pennance, like everyone else in the office.

"I was explaining who Ferrensby and Mercer are to DI Pennance," said Jansen.

"Bloody hell," said another detective. "Don't tell me Mercer's involved?"

"At this stage there's no indication of our favourite financier's sticky fingers on all of this," said Crosse. "However, my gut tells me that this is absolutely Mercer's work."

Jansen put a hand up. "Sir, we all know about the beatings and pressure tactics he's applied in the past, but that all stopped years ago. Murder, though? Is that really his way?"

"It's called progression, sergeant," said Shapiro. "Offenders start small, with the torture and maiming of animals, before moving onto people."

"Aren't you describing serial killers?" asked Jansen.

"And he had birds in his office," said Pennance. "They looked fine to me."

"I know Mercer better than anyone," said Shapiro. "I agree with the boss." Shapiro slapped a photo of the loan shark up on the board. "We just have to prove it."

Crosse picked up a dry wipe marker then circled Ferrensby's photo in red ink. "I want Ferrensby traced, soon as. Track his mobile phone, check into cash withdrawals from his bank account, social media, the lot. And talk to family and friends near and far."

"Do we have to? There's loads of them and every single one is a scally," said someone.

"Find Ferrensby, we may get a connection to Mercer." Crosse drew a dotted line between Mercer and Ferrensby. He then ringed Elliott's car, drew three lines down, angled away from each other, and finally a question mark beneath each. "Then, who's the shooter and the driver? And where's the getaway vehicle?" Crosse turned back to the room, tossed down the pen. "They're the broad lines of investigation we'll follow for now. Inspector Shapiro will give you each your tasks. Remember," Crosse tapped a finger onto his forehead. "Keep Mercer at the front of your minds." Then he clapped loudly a couple of times. "Chop, chop people, let's move!"

THE BLUE CODE

The assembled detectives began to break up and return to their desks as Crosse came down off the dais and stood next to Shapiro.

Pennance went to the two cops. "Why didn't you tell me about the briefing?"

"You found out anyway." Crosse narrowed his eyes. "How, by the way?"

"Overheard someone in the corridor."

"I call bullshit," said Shapiro.

"Pennance and I are going to see Naughton," said Crosse.

"Rather you than me," said Shapiro.

"Jansen, here." Crosse raised an arm, clicked his fingers a few times. She broke off the conversation she was in with another detective.

"Sir?"

"You're with us, Jansen," said Crosse. "Naughton appreciates a decent pair of legs."

"That's it?" asked Jansen. "My limbs are my only value?"

"Ah, suck it up, buttercup," said Shapiro.

"Can you stop calling me names, sir?" said Jansen. "I don't like you poking at me, calling me things."

"It's been a while since we did any poking, Keri. You know that."

Jansen's mouth fell open. "You bastard."

"Now who's name calling, sergeant?"

"Why don't we break this up?" Pennance stepped between Jansen and Shapiro.

"Ah, our hero," said Shapiro.

"Ed," said Crosse. "Apologise."

Shapiro shrugged theatrically, pushing his shoulders up as far as he could. "I don't mean anything by what I say, they're just jokes."

"Shall we see what HR think about this then?" said Jansen.

"That's a career-ending threat right there, sergeant," said Shapiro. "You need to remember who you're talking to."

"Enough!" Crosse held his arms out, palms up to Jansen and Shapiro. "Unless you've forgotten, we've a murder to investigate and Mercer to put away. So, park your differences until then. Alright, Ed?"

"Yes, sir," said Shapiro.

"Keri?" said Crosse.

"All fine, sir."

"Good, then let's go meet a millionaire."

Eleven

"Where are we heading for, sir?" Jansen bowed into the gap between the front seats. Crosse was driving his Porsche, blues on again yet tooting his horn when another road user did something Crosse didn't like – which was often.

Pennance, in the passenger seat, literally hung on, gripping the handle welded into the roof. He wished Jansen had picked a better moment to pose her question. Crosse didn't answer immediately as he negotiated a roundabout at speed on cantankerous tyres.

"To gate crash a party before they blow the candles out on the cake." Crosse leaned long and hard on the horn as he blasted past a tractor. Brightness bathed the rear window as the farmer flicked his lights to full beam in response. "Prick."

"Sir." Jansen, still squeezed into the space. "Unless you've got something else in mind I rang my aunt. She has a guest house and there's rooms spare for Inspector Pennance and his team."

"Good shout, Keri." Crosse pushed his foot down on the accelerator, pivoting the car round shallow bends, and the Porsche picked up speed, the shrubbery flashing so close by that if Pennance reached out through the window he'd be able to grab a fistful of leaves.

Without warning, Crosse slammed on the anchors and Pennance's restraint strained. Crosse whipped into a car park to the rear of a whitewashed building, spraying stones. Pennance braced, narrowly avoiding banging his head on the window.

"That was fun," said Crosse.

"Hardly," said Pennance.

By Jansen's silence, she didn't agree with Crosse either.

Leaving the engine running, Crosse grabbed a stalk next to the steering wheel and flicked the headlights on and off a couple of times. Another vehicle across the way responded in kind. Crosse rolled over at a relatively sedate pace and drew up beside the other vehicle. He killed the engine, lowered the window all the way.

"Evening, sir," said the driver. A second man sat beside him; both wore suit and tie. Cops on surveillance duty.

"He's still inside, then." Crosse unclipped.

"For now, sir. Gathering's wrapping up soon, so I'm told."

"What about the cake?"

"Being held for your arrival." The driver grinned. "Apparently Naughton's not happy."

"Let's not waste time adding to his distress then." Crosse popped his door, turned round. "With me, you two."

By the time Pennance was out, Crosse was striding across the car park, Jansen close behind, both aiming for the corner of the building. As they neared, a fire exit opened, spilling light from within, a man leaning out. He beckoned before disappearing again. Crosse and Jansen entered.

Pennance trotted to catch up and he too entered a space of sweltering heat and metallic clattering. Next to him, a cook in white uniform and cloying body odour lit the contents of a frying pan, generating a plume of purple and yellow flames, his forehead beaded with sweat. Pennance threaded his way along a narrow gap next to an oven

THE BLUE CODE

belching warmth to find Crosse remonstrating with a man in a suit and bowtie with greased back hair and a pencil thin moustache, who told Crosse, "You're late."

"Well, stop dithering, then, Barker," said Crosse. "Get the bloody candles lit."

Barker flashed a brief glare before shaking a match out of a box he held, striking, then holding the flicker to five candles arranged across a large chocolate cake in a train design seated on a trolley.

"I'll do the honours." Crosse grabbed the trolley's handle once all the flames were burning.

Barker manhandled his way through a swing door, closely followed by the cart and Crosse into the relative peace and calm of a restaurant of low ceilings and wooden beams. Several stacks of plates on the shelf beneath the confectionery rattled as the wheels rotated and wobbled. Heads turned their way and a little cheer rose. Crosse moved into the centre, before what seemed to be a top table with smaller circular tables dotted around the room, arranged like a wedding.

Jansen held Pennance back from following Crosse. She pointed. "That's Naughton."

She meant a dapper man with a carefully controlled, long silver mane dragged into a ponytail, who eyed Crosse from the top table.

"Now." Crosse had his arms wide, like a ringmaster. "Who's the birthday boy?"

"Me!" A kid next to Naughton with wild hair, wearing a shirt and skew-whiff tie, shot his arm up and energetically waved a hand, fingers splayed and wriggling like worms.

"Then come on here and blow the candles out, young man!"

The kid slid off his chair, ran over with a huge grin. He pored over the cake, sucked in a huge lungful and blew hard all over the icing. The guests cheered and clapped. If Pennance were an invitee he wouldn't be having a slice, now the glaze was misted with the kid's sputum.

Crosse wielded a long-bladed knife like an amateur butcher and hacked a chunk off the train, depositing the piece onto a plate before passing it to the boy. The kid took a bite a grizzly bear would be proud of, leaving chocolate smeared around his face like he'd fallen in mud. Crosse presented the knife to Barker for him to take over.

Naughton rose, only a few inches shorter than Pennance, then kissed the blonde woman next to him on the cheek before coming round to join Crosse. Naughton ruffled his nephew's hair before draping an arm across Crosse's shoulders, steering him along a corridor and away from the party.

"Now we move." Jansen and Pennance followed Crosse into a private dining room, just large enough for a table and four chairs. Naughton paused by the door. "I would prefer it if you went first. I like to be near to an exit."

Crosse snorted, hiked a thumb at Pennance and Jansen. "In you go."

Pennance drew out a chair and sat opposite Jansen, with Crosse next to her. Last of all, Naughton. He turned to Pennance, held out a hand. "Kai Naughton."

"Detective Inspector Jonah Pennance, National Crime Agency."

THE BLUE CODE

Naughton raised an eyebrow. "NCA? Interesting. I've never met one of you guys previously. Who would you be here for? The Chief Inspector, perhaps?" Naughton nudged Crosse in the ribs.

"I'm not Internal Affairs."

"I'd bet Crosse is as clean as a rusty whistle." Naughton laughed. Crosse did not. "I'm very pleased to meet you. And DS Jansen, of course. Your reputation precedes you."

"Thank you," said Jansen. "I think."

"I'm really sorry to be late, Kai," said Crosse.

"I should reckon so. Tommy was very upset when you didn't arrive. For some reason he wants to be like you when he's older."

Pennance and Jansen shared a glance. The two knew each other?

"I sent a text."

"Oh?" Naughton fished his mobile out of a pocket and powered it up. "I've had my phone turned off from when we arrived. One of Clarissa's stipulations. She's my wife." This to Pennance and Jansen. "A peril of running a successful business." Naughton flashed too-straight teeth at Jansen.

"The wife or owning a company?" asked Crosse.

"Excuse me?" said Naughton.

"I mean, what were the chances of choosing a haunted location for a gathering on the day one of your own is killed." Crosse glanced around.

"Hmm?" Naughton focused on the screen before he blinked and raised his eyes. "What was that?" He stared at Crosse.

"Logan Elliott, your COO, was shot to death in a car park earlier. He could be here, now, an ethereal being floating around. If you believe in that kind of thing."

"Good God." Naughton blinked. "Logan's dead?"

"Unfortunately. Somebody emptied a magazine into his car. And I don't mean the paper kind."

Naughton flopped back, then raised his hand at a passing waiter. "Get me a brandy, double." Naughton flipped pointed fingers between the cops. "Anyone else? I guess you'll be on duty."

"I wouldn't say no," said Crosse.

"Sir, you're driving," said Jansen.

"Then definitely not," said Naughton. "That's all, thank you." The waiter nodded, then was gone. "Why would *anyone* want to murder Logan?" Naughton ran fingers over his hair from front to back.

"That's what we're here to ask you," said Jansen.

"Kai, have you heard the news?" The woman Naughton had kissed leaned into the room; Clarissa then. She gripped the gnarly wooden post for support, revealing a large diamond ring and matching bracelet. "Logan's been shot."

"Nick and his colleagues were just telling me," said Naughton. "Sorry, I'm being rude. This is my wife."

Clarissa raised a hand to cover her mouth. "It's awful news."

"Were you friends with Mr Elliott?" asked Jansen.

"Not personally," said Clarissa. "He was always a bit too distant for me. His girlfriend was nice, though."

"Olivia Bingham?"

"That's her. We were seeing them both later, at a barbecue."

"I reckon that'll be called off now," said Crosse.

The waiter returned then. He placed a large, bowl shaped glass, with a large slug of brandy inside, before Naughton.

"What is it your company does, Mr Naughton?" asked Pennance.

"I'll leave you to it. I never understand what Kai is talking about," said Clarissa. "Don't be long, please."

"Sure." Naughton drank half the measure. "Where were we?"

"I asked about Obsidian," said Pennance.

"You did, sorry. I run a small but unique big data analysis company here in town."

"What does that mean?"

"It means he's very rich." Crosse chuckled.

"Jesus, Nick." Naughton shook his head. "My business uses artificial intelligence to analyse trends in huge blocks of information, the point of which is to help companies make faster, better, more efficient business decisions and improve their margins. Some of that extra profit comes to Obsidian. Our relative agility and ingenuity is Obsidian's USP, unique selling proposition. We might be modest, as Nick kindly observed, but we can run between the opposition's legs or rapidly change direction."

"Someone recently told me that data is more valuable than oil or narcotics," said Pennance.

"Whoever they are is right." Naughton had another drink, a smaller sip this time.

"How long did Mr Elliott work for you?" asked Jansen.

"Just over two years. I recruited him after an exhaustive executive search campaign. I used a head-hunter in London, cost me an arm and a leg but sometimes you do actually get what you pay for. Logan was on a short-list of three."

"Why select Mr Elliott in particular?" asked Pennance

Naughton shrugged. "Team fit. All three candidates had the right experience and attributes, otherwise they wouldn't have been a potential. Ultimately, it was down to who I felt I could work with the best. And that was Logan."

"Did all of the applicants have a forces background?"

"One was a retired chief inspector, another ex-MI6."

"If I'd known there was a job going, maybe I'd have thrown my hat in the ring," said Crosse.

"I don't think you'd have been suitable material," said Naughton.

"Wow, thanks, mate." Crosse even managed a pout.

"What was Mr Elliott like to work with?" asked Pennance.

"Same as everyone else in our company – committed, driven, resilient. If Logan hadn't displayed those characteristics he wouldn't have made it out of his probation period. Over the time we worked together I got to know him professionally. His private life was a very different matter, however. Logan was very closed off and difficult to truly know. Perhaps it's because of Olivia. She verges on over-sharing, always willing to display herself and recount the latest mishap she's got involved with."

"Did your company provide Mr Elliott's driver?" asked Crosse.

THE BLUE CODE

"Good God, no. We offer a very generous remuneration including well above average pay for our sector and significant pension contributions. Plus there are stock options for employees. But not personal staff. There comes a limit, Inspector. I drive my own car."

"You're listed on the stock market?" asked Pennance.

"Not yet, I'm sharing the limited ownership of Obsidian. My intention is to make as many of the team as much money as feasible. Disperse the wealth, so to speak."

"Olivia told us Mr Elliott was transporting something of high value in a security case," said Pennance.

"I've no idea what that would be." Naughton held his arms out wide.

Clarissa reappeared. "Kai, please. We need to go."

"I'm sorry everyone." Naughton finished the brandy. "A much higher power than you commands me." He stood then held out a business card pinched between two fingers. It was, of course, jet black. "Come in and see me, I'll show you around and we can continue our conversation."

"Mr Elliott wouldn't have told you if he was taking something of significance from your company?" asked Pennance.

"Not necessarily. He was fully empowered to make big decisions." Naughton nodded to Jansen and Pennance. "Nice to meet you both. Please feel free to take some cake on the way out."

Pennance turned the card over in his hands. A large 'O' emblazoned the front.

***

In the car park Crosse headed towards his Porsche, tapping something into his phone. Daylight was fading, the sun settling below the horizon. The other cops had left already. Pennance paused, one leg inside the vehicle, staring at a black Range Rover on the far side of the car park, reversed tight up against the hedge, no licence plate on the front bumper.

Crosse started the engine, revving it once before leaning over. "You coming?"

"Sorry." Pennance slid into the passenger seat, Jansen folded into the rear once more. Crosse backed out of the space. Pennance focused on the Range Rover as they passed, but saw no movement through the tinted windows.

Once on the country lane Pennance asked, "How long have you known Naughton?"

"Since I moved here. And I wouldn't say *know*. We bump into each other periodically at events."

"You're on first name terms, though."

"Small town and I'm an amiable kind of guy."

"You appeared to be friends. You were even invited to the party."

"That's just Naughton. He's a butterfly collector, Pennance. I'm potentially useful to him."

"And you never thought to raise this connection earlier?"

"If I recused myself from every case because I'd previously met someone, I'd work on barely anything. Right, Jansen?"

"If you say so, sir."

"This is a murder, though," said Pennance. He felt a touch on his shoulder; Jansen's fingertips fluttering.

"Sorry, sir. My aunt has just messaged. She's going to get the rooms ready, if you'd like to stay there?"

"Sure, if that's what you recommend."

"Where does she live?" asked Crosse.

"California Road," said Jansen.

"That's an okay location. Bit rundown. Walkable to the town centre and the station. I'll take you there. But first, Inspector, we're making a pit stop at Elliott's house because as the best and most experienced officer in CID here I'm the highest qualified to catch the killer. I'll pursue the investigation to my fullest abilities, regardless of how much or how little I know of Naughton." They drew up at a junction and Crosse turned to Pennance. "Feel free to tell your bosses that."

Twelve

Shapiro waited for them outside Elliott's property, about halfway along a small cul-de-sac with gated access called Waters Meet. Crosse drew up, blocking a drive and the egress of a squad car already parked in front of a double garage. The Porsche's headlights illuminated a stretch of grass and a couple of trees, one of which Shapiro leant against while he drew on a cigarillo.

To get here they'd driven through a short underpass, a double lane A road overhead. Despite being only a few hundred yards away, the traffic noise was surprisingly light.

Shapiro ditched the tab at his feet. "Nice place. I wouldn't mind living here."

"We couldn't afford it," said Crosse.

"Maybe I'll win the lottery."

"That's the River Ouse." Crosse nodded past the house, the kind of residence that communicated success – detached, large windows, plenty of garden. "Then beyond there's countryside."

"Front door's this way." Shapiro hiked a thumb. "Or maybe the back, I don't know. It's a weird set-up." Shapiro led them along a path, softly lit by LED bulbs inset either side. The entryway stood open, yet Shapiro paused before entering. "There's security everywhere." He indicated a video doorbell, then two CCTV cameras pointing at the door higher up the wall. Finally, uppermost, an alarm box. "Monitored 24 hours by a security company, sensors in every room, all controlled by an app."

"And nobody responded?" asked Crosse.

"Nope, not a peep out of the system. It was deactivated via Elliott's mobile."

"Which Elliott was carrying when he was attacked," said Pennance.

"Right."

"So, whoever went into the Merc, took Elliott's phone, too. Probably unlocked it with a thumb print or facial recognition."

"Possible," said Crosse.

"Either way," said Shapiro. "His house was wide open to access." Shapiro stepped in.

Pennance followed, into a spacious hallway with a door immediately to one side, stairs the other and a living room ahead. Shapiro continued forward, pausing a foot over the threshold.

Crosse whistled. Elliott's place appeared to have been liberally abused by a tornado as if twisting, violent air had sucked everything out of place, lifting furniture off the floor, ripping books from the shelves, tossing pictures and photos onto the floor. Yanking down curtains, peeling up carpets. Worse, even, than the aftermath of a drunken teenage house party.

Pennance picked his way through the living room, poked his head into an adjacent lounge and found similar destruction. Huge windows overlooked the back, illuminated like it was day by uplighters and down lighters. A strip of grass then tall, wavy reeds. Even the exterior furniture – chairs, a table, a large gas BBQ and an umbrella – were trashed.

The adjacent kitchen possessed a similar view. Yet the interest was in the cupboards which stood open, and seemingly had vomited their contents onto the floor. Smashed plates, glasses, bowls. Pans, cutlery, even the kettle and toaster had suffered. The oven doors sat wide, the shelves out, vents off the extractor fan.

Upstairs was little different. The clothes had been removed from all the cupboards, some even torn up – perhaps in anger as there was no way a shirt would hide anything incriminating. In the main bedroom, which delivered an extensive panorama over the river and fields that Crosse had indicated, the mattress was off the bed, eviscerated, and the light fittings yanked down.

The medicine cupboard in the en-suite bathroom was ripped apart, all the pills and lotions poured into the shower. The cistern lid to the toilet was off, broken in two. The other bathroom was the same, even the bath panel had been removed. The remaining three bedrooms were similarly destroyed, even the en-suites hadn't been spared.

Jansen was coming up the stairs as Pennance headed onto the landing. "This is as thorough a search as I've ever seen," she said.

"Agreed," said Pennance. "Somebody nearby must have heard something, seen someone."

"Uniform have already talked to the immediate neighbours. Nothing."

"Have CSI been over the house?" Pennance didn't think so, as there were none of the tell-tale signs, like fingerprint dust.

THE BLUE CODE

"Tomorrow, Crosse had the team focused on the supermarket."

"What were they looking for here?" asked Pennance.

"Your guess is as good as mine."

"Anything?" Crosse shouted up the stairs, Shapiro standing at his shoulder.

"No," said Jansen.

"Me either," said Pennance.

"We're wasting our time." Shapiro stifled a yawn.

"You're right," said Crosse. "Maybe CSI will be able to get a clue when they arrive."

"I'm bloody starving, though." Shapiro rubbed his stomach in a circular motion like a hungry child. "Anyone fancy a curry?"

"Now, that's a great idea."

"If you can take me to the station instead, I'd appreciate it," said Pennance.

"Not wanting to eat with us?" asked Shapiro.

"It's been a very long day."

"You don't know what you're missing."

"Not much. Just Shapiro sweating over a phall," said Jansen.

"It's good for the circulation," said Shapiro. "Gets the blood flowing to every extremity." He winked.

"Gross." Jansen looked like she might be ill.

"I'll drop you off, Pennance," said Crosse.

"And I'll see you at the restaurant," said Shapiro. "You coming with me or them, Marshmallow?"

"Tough choice, that," said Jansen.

Pennance didn't agree.

***

"Here's fine," said Pennance.

Crosse decelerated harder than necessary, but Pennance was properly ready this time.

A car horn blew from behind at Crosse's inconsiderate manoeuvere – he had stopped on the busy ring road near the police station.

Moments later the car slowly drove past. "Oi, grandad, sort yourself out," shouted the driver, a young man in a baseball cap, through an open window.

"I'll park where I want, son." Crosse held out his warrant card. "Have some respect." The other car accelerated off. "Yeah, you run away." Crosse turned to Pennance. "Right, see you in the morning."

"Enjoy your curry." Pennance unclipped his belt.

"As I'll be paying," Crosse raised his eyebrows briefly. "Not so much."

Crosse was already pulling away as Pennance shut the door. Perhaps in an effort to catch up with the kid in the other car. Or he was just hungry.

"Is it okay to swear at your boss?" asked Jansen.

In the distance the Porsche's exhaust popped.

"Under the circumstances, it'd be criminal not to."

Thirteen

"Your stuff's arrived," said Hoskins as Pennance entered the makeshift office. He nudged his chin towards a large black bag Pennance recognised, propped up against the wall. McAlaney seemed like she hadn't moved, still hunched over her laptop.

"This is DS Jansen," said Pennance.

"It's Keri, hi," said Jansen from the doorway. "Anyone want a coffee?"

"I wouldn't say no to a sandwich," said Hoskins. "I'm starving."

"You're always hungry," said Pennance.

"Shops are closed," said Jansen. "Shame I didn't know earlier as my boss is having a curry."

"Curry? Where? Nearby?" Hoskins got to his feet with surprising speed.

"The Bengal, it's on the High Street. Maybe a five-minute walk."

"I'll find it." Hoskins tapped his nose. "I have an intricately honed detection device."

"I don't think you need to spend time with Crosse and Shapiro," said Pennance.

"Why?" asked Hoskins. "It's always good, a couple of guys bonding over a spicy and a pint." He raised an eyebrow.

Pennance realised maybe it wasn't such a stupid idea. "Okay, but not yet. We could do with debriefing."

"But poppadums, rice –."

"Will still be there." Pennance turned to Jansen. "Can you give us a few minutes, please?"

"Sure. I'll be in the CID office." Jansen backed out, pulling the door closed behind her.

"I met with Naughton just now," said Pennance. "Interesting guy. Claimed he didn't know what Elliott was transporting in the case. He did invite me to visit his company for a walk around. Ava, I'd like you to come with me as I won't have a clue what he'll be talking about. We'll go tomorrow."

"Happy to," said McAlaney.

"What about you guys, find anything?" asked Pennance.

"I've been looking into the bystanders," said McAlaney. "They appear to be who they say. Nobody stands out, with the exception of one Clarke Gastrell." Another arrest record on her screen.

"Crosse mentioned him earlier."

"Gastrell's a safebreaker. Or maybe was. Seems to have steered clear of us for the last five years. Known associate of Matt Ferrensby." Pennance leaned over, skimmed Gastrell's RAP sheet. A name in Gastrell's associates list caught his attention. He tapped the screen. "Wayne Mercer. Crosse is convinced he's good for the shooting."

"Gastrell was believed to have done some B&E for Mercer a few years back. I've also kept an eye on CID's email and WhatsApp. Uniform has been to Ferrensby's property. They didn't find him and he's still officially missing."

"Crosse took me to Elliott's house," said Pennance. "It was upside down."

"I wonder what they were looking for?" said Hoskins.

THE BLUE CODE

"Crosse didn't have a clue," said Pennance. "And neither do I."

"Fairly normal state of affairs, then." Hoskins grinned while McAlaney snickered.

"Alright then, star detective, what have you turned up?"

"I've been delving into Naughton," said Hoskins. "He's a very interesting guy is our Kai. Ha, that rhymed."

"Do you want that Indian, Vance?"

"More than likely it'll be run by Bangladeshis." Pennance maintained a straight expression. Hoskins continued, "I take your point. So, Naughton is a local boy, state school educated, managed to get himself into Cambridge University. One of the decent colleges, too – Churchill. After graduating with a second, Naughton took himself off to California, did a postgrad course then worked for five years at a Silicon Valley start-up which was eventually bought by Palantir. They're a big data business based in Colorado."

"One of Palantir's founders' set-up PayPal," said McAlaney. "Billionaires, the lot of them."

"Naughton flew himself home about six months after the merger," said Hoskins. "A year on he began his own data-analysis firm in Huntingdon, which was unusual."

"Why?" asked Pennance.

"Like London, Cambridge is a sink hole, sucking in talent and retaining it there. Employing gifted staff even a few miles away is challenging."

"I'll take your word for it."

"Anyway, Naughton spent a couple of years developing algorithms before he somehow got found by the NCA. We funded him to the tune of £5M and were his first actual customer."

Pennance whistled.

"I know, right? That buys a lot of pies."

"Quant didn't mention this."

"What, the pies?"

"The contract, Vance."

"Oh."

"And Naughton told me he'd never met anyone from the NCA before me."

"So, that's a lie."

"Which came first, the contract or Elliott joining Obsidian?"

"The latter."

"So, Elliott introduced Obsidian to Quant?"

"Unless there were discussions already underway, it would seem so. Anyway, now Naughton runs one of the most innovative and nimble companies in Europe with a roster of impressive clients – mainly government departments in various countries. Rumour has it Obsidian is about to sign a deal with the British Passport Office to manage their data. And that's after inking another agreement with the Department of Justice in Ireland last month and HM Courts and Tribunals weeks before that."

"Naughton is doing well from the administration."

"He's got connections, that's for sure. And Naughton is a darling of his industry, journalists fall over themselves in their praise of him. Naughton brought some of the Californian practices he learnt. He pays well, everyone in his firm has a share of the company."

THE BLUE CODE

"He mentioned that earlier."

"Plus employees have flexible working hours and holidays – choosing for themselves their hours and breaks."

"How is that even possible?"

"You got me, buddy. And what's a day off? Anyway, Naughton is tipped to be a huge deal over the next decade, a tech entrepreneur with a household name. Our version of Shawn Fanning, so get his autograph while you can."

"Who's he?"

"Oh my God, Jonah!" McAlaney's jaw actually briefly dropped. "Fanning is the inventor of the first web browser, Netscape. He changed the face of the internet."

"Never heard of him."

McAlaney clapped a hand over her forehead.

"Us nerds worship at his digital feet," said Hoskins.

"It's geeks," said McAlaney. "Not nerds."

"I'll take your word for it," said Pennance. "Naughton can't be all good, surely?"

"Absolutely not. Big data has its detractors. There was the Cambridge Analytica scandal a few years ago when the now-defunct company scraped information from tens of millions of social media users without their knowledge, then used it to target political ads at willing recipients and, in the process, reputedly influenced the American presidential election and the Brexit campaign."

"All through adverts?" said Pennance.

"*Targeted* adverts, Jonah."

"There's a difference?"

"Absolutely, like you, me and Vance are different."

"Unique in my case," said Hoskins.

"Precisely," said McAlaney. "We have our own inclinations. Things like food or exercise preferences are relatively innocuous. However, if you drift into much more contentious areas such as politics or the environment, global warming, abortion or same-sex marriage, aspects people can really get worked up over, then you have trigger points that potentially make a person engage much more with a message."

"With Brexit you'd mean £350 million a day for the NHS or the number of immigrants apparently coming into the country and taking jobs."

"You got it." McAlaney aimed a finger. "The proper term is psychometric targeting, which is the science of measuring an individual's personality and their differences to others."

"Surely there can't be that many characteristics?" asked Pennance.

"I've seen claims that there are more than 250 variables."

"Wow."

"Data collection companies use various processes to capture these nuances, say through a quiz on social media – something seemingly simple such as whether you're a dog or a cat person – which the person completes and unwittingly gives access to *all* their information. Post comments, likes, dislikes and, in some cases, their most basic and personal data," said McAlaney. "This is fed back to the marketing company who design a message that they can be relatively certain the individual will respond to. In the case of Brexit and the US elections the tactic was highly effective in driving certain portions of the electorate out to vote, while ignoring or even dissuading others."

THE BLUE CODE

"This all makes me glad I'm not on any of these sites," said Pennance.

"Well," said Hoskins. "Everyone has someone who doesn't like them, right?"

"Even you, Vance?" asked McAlaney.

"It has been known," said Hoskins. McAlaney covered her mouth, eyes wide in mock horror. He continued, "A lone industry journalist, Erica Purnell, has voiced concerns about Obsidian. I spoke with her earlier."

"Was that who you were giggling with?"

"I wouldn't say *giggling*."

"Not Quant then?" asked Pennance.

"Hmm, could have been," said McAlaney. "I'll check his phone records."

"You will not." Hoskins glowered at a totally unaffected McAlaney. "During my *ultra-professional* conversation with Erica she revealed she'd been looking into Obsidian's government contracts and how fast they were spreading into other departments. Like a virus, she said. Erica's newspaper was about to publish an article on the risks of allowing one company unfettered access to so much personal data. Then it got spiked."

"Why?" asked Pennance.

"A law firm hit Erica and her publisher with a SLAPP, with two P's, which is some kind of lawsuit. The newspaper didn't want to fight, so they withdrew."

Pennance thought about a retired reporter he knew, Tommy Haas. "I'll reach out to a contact and ask some questions."

"Anyway, my stomach is becoming increasingly unhappy with me." Hoskins stood. "So I'm off."

"Jansen has somewhere for us to stay," said Pennance.

"Message me the details." Hoskins left the room.

McAlaney rolled her eyes at Pennance.

"Ready to go?" he asked.

"Sounds cool." McAlaney grabbed her laptop.

Fourteen

"This is it." Jansen drew up outside a detached property on California Road, marked out by voluminous hanging baskets crammed with brightly coloured plants fixed to the wall either side of the front door.

Mercifully, Jansen's aunt's house had only been a three minute drive from the station. Pennance was crammed into the passenger side of a two-door, roller skate sized Renault 5 – great for busy cities with limited parking, terrible for Pennance.

Even with the seat racked back as far as it would go his knees were up against the fascia. McAlaney was slightly better off on the rear seat, stretched out across the bench, hugging her laptop against her chest with their bags filling the footwell.

As Jansen switched off the engine, Pennance swung himself out of the car before dropping his seat to allow McAlaney to escape. Then McAlaney leant in and dragged out the luggage.

"Are you lot going to stand on the pavement all day?" A middle-aged woman silhouetted in the entranceway to the house pulled a cardigan tight about herself. Her expression was of someone who naturally frowned. "It's bloody freezing out here."

Pennance glanced at McAleney. The same warm wind pushed along the street.

"Don't exaggerate, auntie," said Jansen.

Pennance headed inside. The hallway, decorated in a striped wallpaper, felt balmy. Pennance held a hand out to a radiator. The metal gave off waves of heat.

"This is Auntie Melody." Jansen pulled the door shut behind Pennance. "DI Pennance and – ." Jansen paused briefly. "Sorry, Ava, I'm not sure of your rank."

"I'm privately employed. I'm not interested in all the yes sir, no sir, stuff."

"I like you," said Melody.

Pennance guessed Melody was early 50s. She wore a high-necked white shirt beneath the cardigan, pressed trousers. Tightly curled brown hair, Pennance unsure if either the style or colour were natural.

Melody pulled Jansen into a hug. Jansen kept her arms down by her side, grimace on her face. "Good to see you, love." Then Melody let go, ruffled Jansen's hair then frowned. "Are you okay?"

"I'm fine, I just over-exercised at the gym. My arms hurt."

"Sorry, love." Melody glanced at her guests. "I thought there were three of you?"

"There are," said Jansen. "Hoskins is out with my boss. He'll be along later."

"Crosse, ugh. Him I'm not keen on." Melody actually shuddered. "Nice to have some people staying born in this country for a change."

"Auntie!"

Melody waved away her niece's protest. "I'm not being racist, they pay my bills. It's simply that every fourth person round here is from Poland, or Hungary or the Czech Republic, and so on. Even some Russians." Melody glanced beyond Jansen to the pile of bags. "You've plenty with you then?"

"We're okay for a few days," said Pennance. "We might end up staying longer, depending on how things go."

"Well, if you get caught short, I think I can help. My ex-husband left some of his belongings behind. He was pretty tall, too. And there's a supermarket just up the road for pants and socks."

"I thought you took a pair of scissors to all his clothes?" asked Jansen.

"That was just for show," said Melody. She addressed Pennance. "I posted a video on Facebook of me chopping up my ex's stuff after he dumped me for another woman. Then I set fire to the remnants. It gained a bit of notoriety locally."

"I'll say." Jansen grimaced. "I was on the beat at the time. The number of people who came up to me, asking if she was alright in the head..."

"It would have been worse if I'd actually done what I wanted to," said Melody. "Which was cut his dick off."

Ava gasped.

"I don't think I could have let that one slide, auntie," said Jansen.

"Probably not. Right." Melody clapped her hands. "Let's show you to your rooms. Keri, you can piss off now."

"Charming."

"I try."

Jansen held out a business card for Pennance. "My number, in case you need anything."

"Thanks," said Pennance. "This is great."

"Tomorrow you can either walk to the station, or I can pick you up."

"I'll find it."

"I wouldn't mind a lift," said McAlaney.

"Just call," said Jansen.

"Stop fussing now, Keri, and be gone with you." Melody opened the door for her niece and tilted her head.

"See you," said Jansen.

"I thought she'd never go. I love my niece, but she can be intense to have around." Melody leaned against the door. "You've a visitor, Inspector."

"Excuse me?"

"I mean, someone to see you."

"Who?"

"I've no idea, he's not local. But I can guess his type." Melody raised a hand before Pennance could ask. "I don't want any involvement. He's in the lounge." She pointed. "In the meantime, let's get you settled in, love." Melody aimed McAlaney at the stairs before hefting two of the bags. "Good God, what's in here? A corpse?"

Pennance entered a room which had a style that could only be described as inconsistent, like the items had been collected from worldwide travel or an eclectic junkshop. An Oriental rug of red and orange weave, a wicker chair suspended from a chain on the ceiling, a wall full of pictures of various sizes, mainly racehorses, encircling a mounted bison's head.

Low wattage bulbs in lamps created from huge Chinese ceramic vases cast shadows across a man in an armchair. He placed down a folded newspaper and stood. He wore a three-piece suit. A gold chain stretched across the front of his waistcoat. He was totally bald and the light reflecting off the man's round glasses meant Pennance couldn't see his eyes.

"Good evening, Inspector Pennance." He reached underneath his jacket and withdrew a pocket watch. The lid flicked open at the press of a button. "My name is Connor O'Shea." His tone was smooth, well-spoken and precise. Irish roots without the inflection. The timepiece went back out of sight.

"How were you aware I'm staying here?"

"Excellent connections." O'Shea gave a thin smile. "I'm a lawyer and my client instructed me to make contact with you regarding the investigation into Logan Elliott's murder."

"I'm just attached to the investigation, Mr O'Shea. DCI Crosse is the lead. I suggest your client speaks with him."

"We are well aware of the pecking order and your position within it, Inspector. That's precisely why our preference is to negotiate with you, rather than DCI Crosse."

"Negotiate, Mr O'Shea? It's a murder enquiry, not a house sale."

"Perhaps not the best choice of words. And conveyancers handle property transactions." Another thin smile. "There is one condition to our discussion, Inspector. DCI Crosse must not be informed of this conversation."

"Why would I agree to anything when I don't have a clue who we're talking about, Mr O'Shea?"

"That's the process I'm following."

"I'm not playing this game." Pennance made for the door. "It's been a very long day."

As Pennance reached out O'Shea said, "I'm employed by Kai Naughton." Pennance paused. O'Shea continued, "He has certain ... issues ... he'd like to raise with you."

"Such as?"

"It's best Mr Naughton explain." O'Shea held out a piece of paper, hand-written words there. "This is where Mr Naughton will meet. You can easily walk from here which should take about fifteen minutes if you set off now." O'Shea glanced Pennance up and down. "Maybe less in your case."

"What if I don't?"

"That is, of course, your choice. However, I'm an excellent judge of character and you strike me as the naturally curious type, willing to take a risk." O'Shea checked his watch once more before he nodded at Pennance. "Good evening." Moments later the front door lock snicked as O'Shea departed. Melody entered carrying two mugs as Pennance picked up the newspaper O'Shea had been reading – the Racing Times, all about horses and betting form. A couple of names had been circled under tomorrow's date.

She offered a mug to Pennance. "I guessed you were a milk and two sugars man."

"Actually, it's black and none for me."

"Well, that was crap intuition on my part."

"Ava will take it, because I need to head out, sorry."

Melody fished around in a pocket. "Have these, in case you're back late." She pushed some keys into his hand. "Where are you going?"

Pennance showed her the address.

THE BLUE CODE

Melody wrinkled her nose. "That's a slightly macabre choice for this time of night. I hope you don't believe in phantoms."

Fifteen

When Pennance was a hundred yards or so away from Melody's house he dialled Tommy Haas, a retired reporter he'd met during a previous investigation.

"Inspector." Haas, a heavy smoker, inhaled deeply. He'd probably be outside a Fleet Street pub right now, lingering at old haunts. "How are you keeping?"

"All good, thanks. I could do with your expertise if I may."

"Shoot."

"Why would a newspaper shelve a perfectly good story because of a lawsuit?"

The scrape of a lighter reached Pennance before Haas asked, "What kind of lawsuit?"

"A SLAPP."

"Have you heard of reputation lawyers, Inspector?"

"Jonah, please."

"Okay."

"And no, that's a new one on me."

"The UK has some of the most stringent media laws in the world."

"I don't have an issue with that."

"Well, maybe you should, because with tough rules come intransigent lawyers. In this case ultra-high earning professionals who use regulations to protect their wealthy clients from *any* kind of investigation. Some of these clients are particularly dodgy. Russian oligarchs, gangsters, even so-called Royals. I assume you're familiar with the process of money laundering?"

"Unfortunately."

"Well, these guys are similar. Instead of cleaning cash they whitewash an individual's image. The so-called Magic Circle are the truly virulent. That's a journalistic term for the handful of the most profitable legal businesses in the UK. They weaponise the law to silence, intimidate, and threaten anybody who targets their clients. These firms employ not just lawyers but international investigators, journalists, cybersecurity experts and even ex-military intelligence."

"I'm surprised by that."

"Most people are once they start to look deeper. These aren't the guys in wigs we see on the news." Haas drew long and hard on his cigarette. "A SLAPP, which stands for Strategic Litigation Against Public Participation, is a blatant intimidation tactic to stifle or kill off an article by deliberately targeting the reporter. Most of the time the SLAPP isn't expected to be successful. The main strategy is to financially cripple the opposition, to tie them up in a lengthy and expensive legal battle most people simply can't afford."

"Has this happened to you?"

"Oh yeah. Any half-decent investigative reporter will have at least one SLAPP in their career. In my case the newspaper owner fought it to the end – he had significant resources too. Another colleague wasn't so lucky. She had to sell her house to pay legal fees to defend herself. Had young kids and was forced to move in with her parents. Recently I've seen others who've resorted to crowd-funding in order to survive. It's a bloody scandal, Jonah. It's suppression of free speech."

"Who are some of these Magic Circle companies?"

"Guardian Royal, Baskin Robertson or Cooper & Clarke are the cream of the crap. If any of those are involved, be concerned. Remember, whoever is behind the SLAPP has deep pockets. Look for a person or an organisation awash with money."

"Thanks, Tommy, I appreciate it," said Pennance. "For once I'm actually feeling a little sorry for journalists."

"You should. The death of democracy begins with eliminating a free press." Then Haas was gone.

***

The hinges of the metal gate squealed theatrically as Pennance pushed it open. He paused as a passing car's headlamps washed over him, briefly repelling the shadows.

Pennance's heart rate rose and his breathing quickened as he entered the full darkness of the cemetery. He passed between rows of grave markers, walking quickly, trying not to break into a trot.

He was fine with the recent dead, when they still had some form, and people – their friends and relatives – remembered them. But those in the ground, they were distant memories. Just names and the most basic of statistics – name, birth date, death date. Maybe they were mother, or father, or brother, or sister. Beyond that, they barely existed and that thought scared Pennance. Not mattering to anyone anymore.

THE BLUE CODE

Inside the church, where the temperature was several degrees lower, Kai Naughton awaited Pennance on the front row of pews in the lee of the pulpit. O'Shea was seated opposite Naughton, one leg crossed over the other. The lawyer checked his pocket watch. "Good timing, Inspector. You found it okay?"

"Obviously," said Naughton. "Detectives, detect, right?" The lawyer rested an arm over the back of the pew. "Why don't you sit down?"

Pennance selected a spot on the end of a bench, two rows back from Naughton and O'Shea so he could see them both. Naughton wagged a finger. "Forcing me to turn and face you, I like it."

"Why here?" asked Pennance. "Is religion your thing?"

Naughton's laugh echoed off the walls. Pennance didn't join in. His had been a genuine question, not an attempt at humour.

"Good God, no. I don't believe in the afterlife. Dead is dead. And religion has killed innumerable people over the centuries in its defence. However," Naughton shifted his posture, "there are two things I do appreciate about the secular. First and foremost is the resilience of its belief structure. Despite all the cultural changes and scientific developments over several millennia a higher power still rules over a large proportion of the population."

"I'd argue religion is hanging on, at best."

"In some parts of the world," conceded Naughton. "Although globally faith remains an incredibly influential constitution, and who can fail to appreciate significance?"

"Do you see yourself as that higher power?"

Naughton laughed again. "Not at all. I'm about empowerment, not control."

"And the second?"

"The architecture, Inspector. Even this little place is impressive, built off the backs of the poor. Did you see the brickwork outside?"

"Can't say I did." Pennance had been in too much of a hurry to escape the imaginary shades.

"It's very unusual; take a look when you leave. Although this place isn't the best example. I'd have preferred All Saint's on Market Square. The font where Oliver Cromwell was baptised in 1599 is inside, relocated from another long lost structure. Cromwell's father is buried there and Mary Queen of Scots' embalmed body apparently rested within the walls when it was being transferred from Peterborough to Westminster Abbey in 1612, twenty-five years after her beheading."

"Fascinating."

"History can inform the future, Jonah. May I call you Jonah?"

"I don't know yet."

"Interesting name you have."

"I'm often told so."

"I mean Pennance, actually. They're important, are names. Their etymology can often reveal the history of a person or a place. Take Huntingdon, a market town chartered by King John in 1205, although its foundation dates back at least three hundred years further and was probably a staging post for Danish invaders raiding the nearby countryside. It's a good position, defensible with the river bend. Dunne or don means hill so maybe the derivation is Hunta's Hill.

"I can trace my family back a long way, Inspector. Not quite to the Vikings, but to the Normans and 1066. A second invasion. And now we have a third assault, not marauding men with swords but the constant drip of immigration. Huntingdon is on the front line."

"What about Kai? What's the derivation of that?"

"Down to trespassers, Inspector. But the non-aggressive kind. There were camps formed here in the '70s, mainly by women, ban the bomb protests and the like against the US air force and their nuclear bombs housed on nearby bases. The time of make love not war means there are kids, like me, from then, many with more unusual names than mine."

Pennance sighed. "Fascinating. But why don't you tell me what we're doing here Mr Naughton?"

"I didn't reveal the whole truth to DCI Crosse earlier."

"You surprise me."

"Sarcasm is often a weak retort, Inspector."

"It amuses me, though."

Naughton briefly pursed his lips. "Elliott did in fact have a piece of proprietary technology in his possession. A drive loaded with the latest algorithm we've been developing. It's worth a lot of money, we're talking tens of millions, Inspector. I need it back."

"Why not talk to Crosse? He's leading the case."

"Crosse is decent. I wouldn't say we're friends. Certainly reasonable acquaintances. But for damn sure he isn't capable enough. Crosse is an example of nice guy, shame about the skills, promoted well beyond his abilities. I mean, have you seen what he wears? Right now he's out for a curry with that idiot Shapiro, rather than investigating."

"People do need to eat."

"Sure, although you and DS Jansen didn't join them. Why?"

"I was tired."

"Yet here you are."

"Your legal representative intrigued me."

"Well, that's good to hear."

"In your opinion is that why Elliott was killed? To get access to your knowhow?"

Naughton leaned over the pew. "Look, I'm a wealthy man, I've access to plenty of resources. I'm well connected. I can help with your investigation, find things out for you, have my people go where the police can't. I'm offering a quid pro quo – my assets are at your disposal and in return you keep me informed of progress and let me know when the drive turns up. Money can achieve amazing results when applied properly. And I'm sure Director Quant will be pleased when you succeed. What do you reckon?"

"I think it's a no from me."

"You'd turn down a concerned citizen's aid?" Naughton frowned.

"Every single time."

Naughton briefly slow clapped, loud and sharp, the sound reverberating back. "I commend your professionalism. However," he stood, O'Shea rising moments later. "If you run into brick walls and you think I can help, call Connor here." O'Shea held out a business card. Pennance was beginning to build up a collection. "Just remember, Inspector, I'm able to open doors, get you admittance to people Crosse simply can't."

Naughton left then, heels clicking on the stone underfoot, closely followed by his lawyer. The bang of the door closing sounded like a peal from Hell.

***

Outside, back on the pavement and the dead well behind him, Pennance called McAlaney.

She answered in two rings. "Yo, Jo."

"Jonah is fine, Ava."

"Yeah, but it takes longer to say."

"I'm assuming if I gave you a mobile number you could trace back the ownership?"

"Easy-peasy, long as it's not a burner. Though even then I could geolocate where it's been used."

"Good."

Pennance held O'Shea's card, just the name and the number printed there. No company details, no address. "Have you got a pen?"

"No."

"Seriously?"

"Nobody actually writes stuff down these days, Jo."

"I do."

"Okay, I'll rephrase that. Nobody *young* actually writes stuff down these days, Jo."

"Implying I'm old?"

"Kinda."

"Great, thanks."

"Welcome. Just take a picture on your phone and message it over to me. I'll do the rest."

"Will do."

Pennance paused under the wash of a lamppost, snapped a shot of the card and sent it by WhatsApp to McAlaney. Seconds later she acknowledged with a thumbs up emoji. Pennance pushed the phone into his pocket and got walking.

"Old," he said to himself. "Bloody cheek."

Sixteen

Using the key pass McAlaney had given him earlier, Pennance entered Huntingdon police station via the side entrance. Inside was quieter than earlier, maybe the evening lull before the pubs spilled out. Or the cops here worked part-time.

Pennance by-passed his temporary office and made for CID which he found near empty also. Considering a murder had occurred earlier the place should be buzzing with activity, yet there was simply the murmur of an officer taking a call and the irregular dance of fingers on a keyboard from another.

Murder board was a term originally coined in the US Pentagon – and used in project management circles – where a panel of senior executives interrogated staff to ensure a venture was properly thought through. Yet it seemed there was little interrogation underway, given the limited change in the display.

Another photo of Elliott had been placed next to his mug shot. The new one showed the dead man sprawled in the back of the Mercedes, bloodied and wide-eyed. And somebody had coloured in Mercer's eyes so they were now a solid black.

Beneath the photos an A4 piece of paper with the typed headline 'Witnesses' was stuck up with a coloured plastic tag. Pennance ran a finger down the list, recognised the Yardleys and Gastrell.

"Sir." Pennance straightened. Jansen. "I thought you'd be relaxing at my aunt's."

"Couldn't settle."

"Me either. I opened a bottle of wine but it didn't help."

"Nobody else seems too bothered." Pennance tilted his head at the vacant CID team.

"The focus is on Mercer. The tactics with him are always a long game, sir."

"Jonah is fine, Keri. Any sign of Ferrensby?"

"Zero contact since the shooting. Uniform has been to his home. Seemingly nothing is missing. And no large withdrawals from his bank account within the last twelve months."

"No preparation to do a runner, then."

"Right. So, either Ferrensby prepared to drop off the grid well in advance, or he's being hidden somewhere." Jansen tapped Ferrensby's mugshot. "His family own a lot of land – much of it remote and difficult to access because it's the Fens."

"What's that?"

"Low-lying ground partially reclaimed from water centuries ago." Jansen crooked her finger, led Pennance over to the map pinned to the wall. "Huntingdon." She pointed to their location before moving southeast. "Cambridge." Then back to Huntingdon and north. "Peterborough. Up to a hundred years or so ago most of the territory hereabouts was a waterlogged, bug-infested swamp. Small villages were scattered around on whatever higher terrain there was, maybe some houses on poles, and the people eking out a bare living from fishing. Over time, and thanks to drainage systems, most is now decent arable or grazing land although there are still parts which remain more wet than dry."

"Sounds divine," lied Pennance. He leaned against the wall, crossed his arms as a landline began to ring.

"Crosse has ordered a search of their property tomorrow. Maybe we'll find Ferrensby then."

"What do you think of Crosse's theory that Mercer had a hand in Elliott's death?"

"I'm not convinced." Jansen wrinkled her nose. "Crosse has been after Mercer pretty much since he arrived. Should Mercer be put away? Absolutely, but I just don't see him being involved in murder. I probably shouldn't say this." Jansen paused briefly. "No, I definitely shouldn't." She shook her head.

"You can trust me."

She lingered a little while longer before saying, "Alright, I heard Shapiro is one of Mercer's regular customers. Spends a lot of money with him."

"Where did you get that from?"

"Just rumours around the station. It's likely nothing."

"When I went to Mercer's earlier he pretty much read my personnel file back to me. Crosse is convinced Mercer has one or more cops in his pocket."

"That wouldn't surprise me. Over the last four years we've raided him as many times, but on each occasion come up empty. Crosse believes someone tipped him off."

"Could Shapiro have had a hand in it?"

Jansen blew air through pursed lips, eyes wide. "That's an accusation I wouldn't like to get into."

"There's no-one in earshot."

Jansen glanced past Pennance, like she was checking for herself. "It's possible, of course. But anyone in Mercer's network could have told him. And Crosse has a blind spot when it comes to Shapiro. He's the station golden balls. Anyway, forget all this." Jansen waved a dismissive hand. "Just do me a favour would you? Don't repeat what I said about Shapiro. I'd be in boiling hot water."

Nearby a phone began to ring. Jansen stood. "I'd better answer that." She strode over to the desk. "Jansen." She listened for a moment before beckoning Pennance over. "Say that again, sergeant." She pressed a button on the handset, the caller now on speaker. "Halloran, I've Inspector Pennance with me."

"Pennant?" said Halloran. "He's the NCA snoop, right?"

"It's Pennance. And I can hear you perfectly well."

"I'm pleased for you. There's a shout come in. A PCSO has requested back-up. Disturbance at a residential property."

"Who?"

"The flappy one who panics all the time; the blonde with the hair lip, what's-her-face." A clicking over the intercom, like Halloran was snapping his fingers.

"Donovan."

"Yeah, her."

"There's nobody else able to attend?"

"Would I be wasting my time talking to you if there were?" Pennance could hear the gritted teeth in Halloran's tone.

Jansen grabbed a biro. "What's the address?"

THE BLUE CODE

"River Lane in Brampton."

"House number?" asked Jansen.

"I don't have that."

"Great."

"Blame Donovan, not me. Best I can do." Then Halloran was gone.

"Olivia, Elliott's girlfriend, said she lived in Brampton," said Pennance.

"I'll get my keys," said Jansen.

Seventeen

Jansen swung her roller-skate Renault 5 into River Road, a narrow tree-lined street on the village's edge.

"This is a dead end." Jansen leant over the steering wheel, peering through the windscreen. "The River Ouse gets in the way."

"The same stretch that flows past Elliott's house?" Pennance was again squeezed uncomfortably into the limited space of the passenger seat, knees up against the dashboard.

"Eventually, yes." Jansen had the front windows open, allowing in a chill, damp breeze, yet the interior still smelt faintly of something meaty, like takeaway kebab.

Jansen rolled the car slowly along the dark thoroughfare, just sporadic streetlights emitting a sickly yellow hue, each cone only a handful of feet wide.

The well-spaced residences were difficult to see, set back behind high walls or thick greenery or both which, to Pennance, indicated wealth and a desire for privacy. "There." Pennance pointed to the car parked as far left as possible, though getting past would still be a squeeze. The siren on top and the flash down the side clearly marked it as police.

Jansen drew up to the bumper of the unoccupied squad car, flicked off the engine. She paused for a moment, hands still gripping the wheel. Pennance couldn't hear any movement, just the decaying hum of the fan in the bonnet.

"I don't see her," said Jansen.

"What's Donovan like?"

THE BLUE CODE

"She's lovely." Jansen reached over, between Pennance's legs, popped the dash compartment, the hard plastic knocking into his knee. "Far too nice to wear a uniform." She withdrew a box of nitrile gloves, handed a pair to Pennance. "Just in case."

"Why's she a PCSO then?"

She shrugged. "Wants to help."

Out on the pavement Pennance nudged the door shut with his hip. Inside the squad car a peaked cap lay on the passenger seat, no keys in the ignition.

Jansen touched a palm the bonnet. "Still warm."

"Sir, ma'am, I'm glad you're here." Pennance spun round. A shape moved towards them, stopped a few feet away when awash in the margarine light. "PCSO Donovan." She held a torch in one hand.

"DI Pennance. We haven't met before."

"Not officially, but everyone knows who you are."

"What have you got, Sophia?" asked Jansen.

"One of the homeowners, a Mrs Randall, called in to report shouting and screaming from her neighbour's house while she was outside looking for her dog. She was waiting for me when I arrived, in a bit of a state. Blood curdling, she said. And there was a loud bang. She thought a gunshot. Mrs Randall pointed me to here." Donovan hoiked a thumb over her shoulder. "I wanted someone else with me when I went in. Just in case. I wasn't expecting you." She gritted her teeth into an embarrassed smile. "Not that I'm disappointed, ma'am."

"I would be," said Jansen. Donovan chuckled, her shoulders relaxing a little.

"Where's Randall now?" asked Pennance.

"I sent her home for the moment," said Donovan.

"Good decision," said Jansen.

"What about Mrs Randall's dog?"

"It'll have to wait," said Pennance. "Let's go."

Donovan aimed her flashlight at the nearest entrance. She led Pennance and Jansen between two tall wooden gates pushed all the way back on their hinges against a thick, leafy hedge which Pennance guessed could be laurel. He was no horticulturist, in fact he didn't have a proper garden – just a few potted plants on his roof. The front door stood wide open, spilling out light and giving Pennance a view of an empty hallway.

As they neared the looming house a security light, fixed high on the front wall, flickered into life, illuminating a double fronted detached house with leaded windows on both floors and twenty feet of tarmacked driveway. "Who lives here?" No vehicle parked up. Unless there was one behind the metal garage door.

"Mrs Randall doesn't know. She's seen some movement, a man coming and going, but she couldn't describe him or tell me his name which seemed to be a source of frustration for her," said Donovan. Pennance glanced at the PCSO. "Just by the tone she took, is all."

The entrance was a deep porch of red brick set in a curve. Inside, a carpeted hall, stairs leading up to the right, doorways to the left and straight ahead. Every light bulb burned. There wasn't any furniture, no pictures on the wall, just a coatrack with a single jacket hanging there, a walking stick propped up in a corner and a pair of walking boots caked in dried mud dumped.

Pennance, Jansen at his shoulder, crossed the threshold, took a few paces, immediately picked up a tang he recognised – blood. A double doorway lay to one side, along the hallway the door stood open into an obvious kitchen and to the other a wide set of stairs stretched upwards. Under the stairs was another door, to a cupboard, perhaps.

"Police, anyone home?" Pennance cocked his head, listened, heard nothing.

"Sir." Donovan aimed a finger at randomly spaced dark spots on the hall carpet between the kitchen and the double doors.

"Call CSI and Crosse," he said.

"Yes, sir."

"We should check for proof of life," said Jansen.

"Agreed," said Pennance.

"I'll take the upper floor."

Pennance raised a thumb before proceeding along the hall as Jansen made for the stairs. He poked his head in through the entrance into what was a living room.

Feet.

Legs.

Pennance moved just inside the entrance, his shoes sinking into thick carpet, found a large man lying face down, arms spread like he was swimming the front crawl, face to one side. His neck was taut, eyes and mouth open, frozen as he drew in one last breath.

Impossibly pale skin indicated to Pennance the man was well beyond recovery. A pistol of a make Pennance didn't recognise lay a few feet away; long black metal barrel, and grip. Pennance glanced over his shoulder, Jansen was halfway up and staring through the doorway. She pointed to say she was continuing.

Pennance squatted by the corpse, lightly touched two fingers to the man's neck while being careful to stay out of the large pool of darkening blood radiating out from the body.

Noticeably cooler than normal.

No pulse.

He lifted an arm, gripping with two fingers at the man's wrist. The elbow and shoulder moved easily, no rigor mortis yet, revealing defensive wounds on the palms; sharp slices clearly from a blade. Tattoos radiated up from the back of the corpse's hand. The tip of one finger had been neatly sliced off some time in the past. Pennance laid the arm back down, rested on his haunches and slowly, methodically took in everything about the body.

Bald head, no eyebrows although a faint shadow on the skull – the man shaved. A small, bloodied nick just over a thick ear was perhaps a razor cut. The earlobe itself was pierced in several places, like there had been rings or studs. They hadn't skinned so the jewellery had been recently removed.

He wore a tracksuit top, no emblem or brand. More tattoos on his hairless neck of a crude, blue ink, likely performed by a non-professional. Then matching pants, a single strip of white fabric down the outside of the leg, and trainers without socks.

THE BLUE CODE

A gash in the tracksuit and sliced, bloody flesh beneath – a large and deep wound from a blade.

There was something else, a familiar odour emanating from the dead man. Pennance leaned forward again, got his nose close to the man's skin. Breathed in deeply, eyes closed, like he was assessing an expensive wine.

Body odour.

Urine.

Petrol.

Definitely fuel fumes. Pennance had no idea what it meant.

Next, he turned his attention to the surroundings; obviously a living room. A sofa nearby, covered in a thin clear plastic sheet which had protected the fabric from more than dust – more blood spatter. Empty of books. Curtains drawn at the windows. An armchair lying on its side. The dining table pushed at an angle. A computer monitor on the table, pitched over, and a keyboard. But no laptop, just cables with nothing to connect to. And a mannequin, leather jacket draped over its shoulders, neutral face watching over the corpse.

Pennance headed back into the corridor and opened the under stairs door – a toilet and sink – as Jansen descended.

"Nothing up here," she said. "One bed that's been slept in."

"I'm going to check out the kitchen," said Pennance.

"Who's the stiff?"

"No idea, maybe you'll recognise him."

All the kitchen overhead spotlights blazed, painfully bright pinpoints, though it was the blood which caught

Pennance's attention. He pointed to a large, red spray dashed up across the white fitted units which one wall. "Looks arterial."

"Jonah." Jansen indicated a handprint on the door jamb, just inches away from him.

Pennance stepped further inside, being careful where he put his feet. Two high chairs stood at a breakfast bar, then a range cooker beyond. A large drawer hung half open. Next to Pennance a small table with a pair of chairs. A half full mug of coffee sat towards the edge. Pennance touched the outside with a gloved knuckle; no heat.

He inspected the open drawer, within was cutlery, a bottle opener and other utensils. Pans hung from a ceiling rack, beneath which a wooden knife block lay on its side, the blades half out. Except for an empty space.

A cooling breeze wafted around the kitchen. At the far end the room morphed into a conservatory, a sloping roof and glass walls. The exit open, a few scrubby shrubs visible, and beyond, blackness.

At the door, Pennance dug out his mobile, flicked on the mobile torch app. The beam, wide and disperse, revealed trees, bushes and a broad strip of knee high grass that may have once been a close cropped lawn. No flowers, wood chip in the borders and weeds poking through. Pennance's kind of plot; low maintenance. He heard a nearby snuffling, a yap and a growl.

"What's that?" asked Jansen.

"Let's find out." Pennance swung the beam around as he proceeded, his shoes and the bottom few inches of his trousers getting wet as he waded through the green pasture.

THE BLUE CODE

Behind a hedge a dog dug in the dirt, paws scooting back and forth, scooping out chunks of earth. Pennance wasn't sure of the breed, one of the under-arm accessory sized things with chintzy collars he'd seen women lugging around in London. This one, though, had more the appearance of muddy rat, hair matted.

As Pennance moved closer the mutt eyeballed Pennance and growled, low in the back of its throat, teeth bared. Jansen placed a hand on Pennance's arm and he withdrew a step. The dog blew air out of its nose, lowered its head, grabbed hold of something out of sight, shook and tore.

"Stay here."

Jansen nodded.

Keeping a wide berth, Pennance skirted around the animal, no wish to have his ankle savaged. Once behind Pennance raised his phone, silhouetting what had the dog's attention.

"Jesus."

There, in the light, a hand reached out from the soil, flesh half chewed down to the bone.

Eighteen

While Jansen provided a distraction, Pennance managed to grab the dog by its collar and lift it away from the grisly feast. The hound thrashed, trying to claw and bite. He carried the animal at arm's length, while it continued to writhe like a mini dervish.

Under the lights inside the conservatory the dog appeared even more dishevelled. Mud smeared up its legs and blood round its mouth. Pennance opened the understairs door just wide enough and shoved the beast through the gap before releasing his grip and hurriedly shutting the door. The animal crashed itself against the wood, scrabbling and yapping.

"Sir." Donovan at the entrance. "Back-up has arrived."

Outside, River Road was experiencing a very different activity level to what would be usual. Donovan's call had stirred a wasp's nest and the cops buzzed.

Several uniform spilled out from a squad car. Under Jansen's direction, an inner and outer cordon was taped off – at the driveway entrance and twenty feet along the road in both directions, respectively.

Pennance noticed some dirt on his hand and peeled the glove off. Detritus from dealing with the hound.

Crime Scene Investigators, led by Thriplow the CSM, came close behind uniform, parking their vans beyond the cordon, and were currently in the process of getting themselves prepared – pulling on white evidence suits and blue overshoes and sorting out their gear – before entering

THE BLUE CODE

the house for an initial review. A couple of neighbours gathered in a small cluster at the entrance to a nearby house, talking and pointing.

Pennance leant against the wing of Donovan's squad car while Jansen propped herself on the bonnet, legs gently swinging.

"Okay," said Pennance. "Now CSI are here, the next step is to get door-to-door interviews underway, see if any neighbours heard or saw anything."

"I can get that organised." Jansen nudged her jaw. "Thriplow's heading over."

The CSM was dragging an evidence suit up over his shoulders. "Inspector, sergeant. What do we have?"

"Maybe two corpses, one in the living room who appears to have been stabbed and bled out and another in the garden."

"*Maybe* two?"

"I found a mutt digging a hole and gnawing on a hand. I couldn't see if there was more down there."

"Oh, joy." Thriplow rubbed his forehead. "I love exhumations."

"Will you want the cannibal dog?"

"What for?"

"Evidence. It likely ate some of the flesh."

Thriplow grimaced. "Not really. I don't fancy explaining to the owner why we had their perfectly healthy pet sliced into. And anything inside the animal will be decomposing in the stomach acid already."

"Just a suggestion."

"Where is the thing?"

"Locked in the under stairs bathroom."

"I'll have the door taped up." Thriplow turned to Jansen. "I assume you've been inside the house too, sergeant?"

"Upstairs only. Donovan didn't cross the threshold."

"I'll make a note of that. Is Crosse on the way?"

"I've no idea." Jansen shrugged. "Both Donovan and me have tried to reach him and Shapiro several times. Neither answered. I left voicemails."

"I tried Hoskins too," said Pennance. "He's one of my colleagues."

"Shame, they're missing all the fun."

"Crosse will be delighted when he realises."

"Well, we're not waiting for him, so that makes you SIO, Inspector."

"I'm not CID," said Pennance.

"But you are the most senior detective here, right?"

"I am."

"Decision made, then." Thriplow pulled up the hood of his suit.

Jansen glanced past Pennance. "You're wanted."

Donovan was at the cordon, signalling. Beside the PCSO stood a woman in paisley pyjamas and pristine white trainers, arms crossed over her chest.

"I'll crack on," said Thriplow.

"And I'll get door to door moving," said Jansen.

Pennance made his way over.

"Sir," said Donovan. "This is Mrs Randall, the neighbour who called in."

"It's Miss," said Randall. "Since my husband moved out."

"Sorry, ma'am."

THE BLUE CODE

"That's okay, how were you to know?"

"I'm DI Pennance." He ducked under the tape and Donovan moved away a few feet, giving the illusion of privacy.

"No-one has been to see me. I thought I would come to the mountain, so to speak." Under the streetlight Randall's face was the same colour and texture of over-stretched dough. Her hair held up in a rough bunch by a large plastic clip while a single curl hung down next to her face. She pushed it away with a finger, tucking the errant tress behind an ear, revealing a diamond stud at the top which Pennance knew (because Simone had one herself) was called the helix.

"We've been busy closing down the scene, Miss Randall. You were next on my list." Which was an exaggeration. "Thanks for making the effort."

"There's investigators everywhere. That means something dreadful happened, right?"

"We found a body inside."

"Oh my God." Randall covered her mouth with a hand.

"PCSO Donovan said you'd seen a man at the property. Could you describe him?" Randall pushed fingers through her hair. "Miss Randall?"

She blinked, like she was coming back into the present. "Big, broad."

"That's all?"

"I've never actually spoken to the occupier. Most of the time you wouldn't know he was even there. I'd see him from a distance, in his car, going in or out of the drive. While he was home the gates were always closed. Whenever Little

Willy escaped they'd ring my bell and I'd find him tied up on the doorstep."

"Sorry, Little Willy?"

"My dog. I named him after my ex-husband. Every time I shout, 'Little Willy' it makes me chuckle." She laughed, despite the circumstances. "Have you seen him?"

"The dog or your husband?"

"The dog, of course." Randall slapped Pennance with a flat stare. "He's been particularly troublesome the last couple of weeks. Seems to prefer my neighbour's garden to mine. I've no idea why."

Pennance did. "I found him earlier." He couldn't bring himself to use the dog's name.

"Is he alright?"

"He'll need a bath, I reckon." And maybe a colonic irrigation.

"Oh, thank God! Can I get him back?"

"Soon. Is there any more you can tell me about the occupier?"

"Well, Philby rented, rather than owned."

Pennance wasn't sure why that made a difference. Maybe it was a privilege thing. "Philby?"

"That's what we, me and Amanda, call our mystery neighbour after one of the Cambridge Five – the spy ring from the 1950s. I mean, everyone's got to have a name, right?"

"I guess. Who's Amanda?"

"A neighbour." Randall indicated somewhere further down the road. "Anyway, Amanda 'just happened,'" Randall made air quotes to emphasise her point, "to be on the road moving the bins when Philby turned up. And it wasn't even the day the rubbish gets emptied. It's best to be very careful with her around, unless you're going on holiday. Then having an Amanda is extremely beneficial. Anyway, Philby drove in, and the gates closed behind him. That was it."

"So?"

"No removal trucks delivering stuff? Really? I'll need two or three when it's mine turn to leave."

"Amanda might have missed them."

"Not a chance. Take my word for it."

"Alright."

"A few days later I rang his intercom bell, but nobody answered. I've tried several times. It's all been very strange. I mean who doesn't want to know their neighbours?"

"Most Londoners," said Pennance. "Let's come back to tonight. Tell me about the noise you heard."

"I was downstairs getting a drink of water in the kitchen. I went outside to stand on the patio and cool down. I have hot flushes most nights. Even sleeping with the window open isn't enough to deal with them. Hormones are like wrecking balls, Inspector. Be glad you're a man."

"I'll keep that in mind."

"I'd let Willy out for a run around, then I heard what I'm sure was a shout of pain. More like a screech. Made my blood turn to ice." Randall shuddered. "And then a very loud pop. By the time I got out to the front a car was heading up the road."

"Who was driving?"

"Have you seen the lighting round here? It's awful. I've complained to the council several times." Randall looked down at her feet. "I chased him."

"Excuse me?"

"I ran after the car." Randall met Pennance's gaze, said firmly, "I know it makes absolutely no sense." Her eyes flashed. "I blame the hormones. Anyway, I had my slippers on and I couldn't keep up. Then I realised what I was doing so I stopped, went back home, and rang the police."

"You said Philby rents, how do you know that?"

"Because Amanda keeps a close eye on property sales nearby. She knows the value of her house down to a penny."

"Which agent manages the house?"

"Everyone here uses the same one – Zinke & Co – I purchased through them. They've an office in Huntingdon."

"Well, thanks for your help. An officer will be around later for a formal interview."

"I've a spin class in the morning, is that a problem?"

"I'm sure someone will call you first."

"What about Little Willy?" asked Randall.

Pennance paused. He'd forgotten about the dog. "If you wait here a moment I'll bring him." He ducked back under the cordon tape, made his way to the front door, found Thriplow making his way out. "I need the animal," said Pennance. "The owner's here to take him away."

"Thank God for that." Thriplow pushed down his mask. "It's been making an almighty bloody racket. I've been on the verge of reversing my decision not to treat him as evidence." Back inside, Thriplow tore down several strips of plastic tape, pre-printed with DO NOT ENTER, secured across the door in a large X. Someone had even found a yellow 'radioactive' symbol from somewhere and stuck it up. Thriplow opened the door a crack before turning to Pennance. "The thing has crapped everywhere."

"It's a toilet. What's the problem?"

"The excrement is on the floor, not in the bowl."

"You must have come across worse in your job, surely. Do you want me to get the dog?"

"You're not suited up."

"I know." Pennance winked.

"Bloody hell." Thriplow opened the door wide enough to reach inside before withdrawing, holding Little Willy in an outstretched arm as the dog, which was even more of a mess than earlier, thrashed and snarled. "Aggressive little bugger, isn't he?"

"Just a second." Pennance found some string in the kitchen.

"We could just shove him into an evidence bag and seal it up?"

"I'm sure Miss Randall would be delighted with that." Pennance looped the twine through the collar and held the end tightly. "Okay, put him down."

Thriplow released his grip, dropping the dog three feet or so onto the tarmac. Little Willy landed cat-like on all four paws, legs bending to absorb the impact, then calmly sat. "Well, would you look at that."

"I'm sure he'd appreciate a pat or two," said Pennance.

Thriplow cringed. "Just get him out of here." He dismissed Pennance with a wave.

Little Willy walked up the drive with Pennance like a tiny horse in a dressage competition. When Randall caught sight of her pet she covered her face with both hands. "What have you done to him?"

"Nothing," said Pennance. "He was like this when I found him, digging in the garden."

As Randall opened her mouth, a vehicle turned into the road, headlights on full beam, illuminating Pennance and Randall like Christmas trees. Pennance raised a hand to shield his eyes.

The car stopped on the cordon's edge, engine and headlamps dying.

"Who's that idiot?" asked Randall.

Crosse got out of the driver's side, closely followed by Shapiro out of the passenger seat and Hoskins from the rear. Crosse paused, one hand on the door, the other on the roof, and glared at Pennance.

"Is he your boss?" asked Randall.

"Thankfully, no."

Without breaking his gaze, Crosse slammed the car door shut and stalked over, Shapiro and Hoskins in his wake, gunslingers in a one horse town.

"He doesn't like you very much," said Randall.

"Seems so."

"I'll go." Randall backed away.

"Why didn't I know about this?" Crosse nodded at the murder house. Hoskins tipped his hat at Pennance who could swear there was curry smeared around his colleague's mouth.

"DS Jansen attempted to call you several times."

THE BLUE CODE

"Blaming a subordinate? That's rather low. Perhaps you do that in your neck of the woods, but we don't around here."

"I don't have your number."

"Like I give a crap. You could have got it from Jansen."

"If you'd been paying attention to your phone, you might have been here sooner."

Crosse narrowed his eyes at Pennance while Shapiro widened his, not bothering to mask the grin. "I was having some down time after a rather long day."

"You don't need to defend yourself, Nick," said Shapiro.

Hoskins held his phone up. "Jonah's right. He did try and call. Sorry buddy, had it on silent."

"Feel free to do one, Pennance," said Shapiro. "The proper police are here now."

Crosse shuffled towards Pennance, moving inside his personal space. "I didn't want you here in the first place, neither did Malik. Now, it's my rules, my way of doing things. If you don't like that," Crosse shrugged, "not my problem. Is that clear?"

Shapiro smirked once more.

"Crystal," said Pennance.

Crosse got in even closer to Pennance, like he was after a hug, although there was no warmth emanating from the DCI. He whispered this time. "I want an excuse, Inspector. Any defensible reason to get rid of you."

"Come on now, Nick," said Hoskins. "We've enjoyed ourselves tonight. Why ruin a good evening?"

"That's his choice." Crosse tilted his head at Pennance.

"Jonah's a bit of a tight arse, but he's alright really."

"Thanks," said Pennance.

Crosse stepped back, giving Pennance some room.

"Excuse me, DCI Crosse?" Thriplow hovered nearby, blank expression on his face.

"What?"

"You and your team can access the house now."

"About bloody time. Let's get inside, Ed." Crosse finally broke eye contact and stalked away.

Shapiro, however, didn't move. "Back to London for you soon, I'll bet, *Jonah*." He winked at Pennance before squeezing Hoskins' shoulder, then turning and following Crosse.

"Let it go," said Hoskins.

Pennance made fists of his hands, digging his nails into his palms until they stung.

Nineteen

"Wriggle into these." Thriplow held out evidence suits for Pennance and Hoskins.

The trio stood just outside the entrance to the house, bathed by the powerful glare of floodlights on tripods CSI had set-up to illuminate the driveway, turning night into day. At least within this tiny bubble.

"That makes a change," said Pennance. "It fits."

Thriplow passed over masks and gloves. "See you both inside." Thriplow left.

"What do you think's going on over there?" Hoskins meant where Crosse stood in conversation with Jansen and Shapiro at the gate. Plenty of arm waving by Crosse. All three already wore evidence suits but only Shapiro's overshoes were pink.

"Probably nothing worth knowing," said Pennance. "How was your curry?"

"Decent enough that I'd go back."

"That wasn't what I meant."

"I know. We didn't discuss anything salacious, it was mainly bloke's talk. I'll learn more from them over time as they come to trust me. I think Crosse is alright. Shapiro, though. Not a fan."

As Pennance pulled on a glove Crosse continued to remonstrate with his team. A CSI paused beside Pennance. She said, "Looks like a bollocking is underway, knowing Crosse."

"I'll take your word for it."

"I'm Charlotte Abernathy, Charlie to my friends, the attendant Forensic Pathologist." Not CSI at all, then.

"DI Jonah Pennance."

"Vance Hoskins." Hoskins bowed slightly.

Abernathy nodded to herself. "Ah, the London snoops."

"Partly right," said Pennance.

"Not my words, by the way."

"Crosse or Shapiro?"

"Both, or neither. Could be somebody else, depending on whether you want to play politics, or not. Which I don't. Well, nice to meet you."

Shapiro caught Pennance looking at him, briefly raised a middle finger.

Abernathy grinned and waved in return. "Smile like you mean it, Inspector." Shapiro scowled then turned away. "I've found rude people hate a sunny disposition in response. And a woman has to stand up for herself, right?"

"No argument there."

"I've other ways of getting payback. You may be pleased to know Shapiro's pink overshoes aren't by accident. The standard ones weren't strong enough to fit over his stupid boots. He bitched about having another type, so I bought him those – hundreds of them. Crosse ordered Shapiro to wear them and now he has to wander around in pink for the next few years until the stock is used up."

"I like it."

Crosse wagged a finger right under Jansen's nose.

"I just wish Jansen would stand up for herself," said Abernathy. "There's steel inside somewhere, I know it."

THE BLUE CODE

After one last flourish to the group Crosse turned, heading for Pennance, Hoskins and Abernathy, followed by Shapiro and, a few seconds later, Jansen, her eyes downcast.

"What the hell are you waiting for?" Crosse jabbed a hand towards the house before pulling up his hood. "Let's get going!"

Abernathy fell in behind the DCI while Pennance raised an eyebrow at Jansen. She responded with a tiny shake of the head. Pennance slipped his mask on, then raised his own hood before stepping over the threshold once more.

Which was as much progress as Pennance and Hoskins could make because Thriplow was positioned at the bottom of the staircase, flanked by Crosse, Shapiro, Jansen and Abernathy.

"Now everyone's here I'll run through the timeline that Charlie and I think unfolded," said Thriplow." "First, note the open front door. There's no damage, i.e. entry was not forced. The locks are a Yale type, plus a seven-lever mortice and two bolts."

"A key was used to get in," said Pennance.

"Or a lock pick," said Shapiro.

"Not likely," said Thriplow. "There aren't any obvious scratches around the hole."

"So the Yale for day use," said Hoskins. "The rest for additional security at night. I have a similar arrangement at home."

"What about the corpse?" said Crosse.

"All yours, Charlie." Thriplow took a half step back.

"The assailant, let's identify him as 'A', moved along the corridor from the front door to the kitchen." The CID team trailed behind Abernathy as she proceeded, Pennance bringing up the rear.

When Pennance paused in the kitchen doorway Abernathy said, "Inspector, would you mind?" She beckoned Pennance over before positioning him like a dummy in a shop display, his back to the cabinets. "Let's call the inspector, 'B' and I'll take the part of 'A'. Note the knife block behind Inspector Pennance and the partially opened drawer." Eyes flicked towards each in turn.

Abernathy returned to the doorway and raised her arm, pointed her fingers like a gun. "I believe 'A' entered and fired a shot from roughly where I'm standing." Abernathy even mimicked the recoil. "Which struck 'B' although 'B' was likely only superficially wounded, a nick in the arm or shoulder."

"A neighbour said she heard a scream, then a gunshot," said Pennance.

"Okay."

"There's no blood," said Shapiro.

Pennance twisted. All he saw was white Formica. "It's been cleaned up to remove the evidence."

"Correct, Inspector." Abernathy pointed a small torch towards the cupboard which emitted a blue light, revealing a smear in a kind of electric purple colour. "But not so well. And we found a single shell casing against the wall." The pathologist raised a plastic evidence bag containing a small brass cylinder. "It'll go off for ballistics shortly."

"May I?" asked Crosse.

THE BLUE CODE

Abernathy passed Crosse the ordinance which he examined closely. "The wound would be painful, but not debilitating," said the pathologist.

"No need for hospital treatment then?" Pennance shook his head as Crosse offered him the casing.

"Medically it would be advisable," said Abernathy. "However, the injury could probably be managed with some butterfly stitches and a bandage."

"Let's get the hospitals checked anyway," said Crosse. Jansen made a note. "Carry on, Charlotte."

Not Charlie then.

"Probably 'B' pulled a knife from out of the block as 'A' was entering the house. Do the same, Inspector." Abernathy nodded at Pennance so he reached for an imaginary handle in the block.

Abernathy still had her arm up, index and middle fingers extended. "As 'A' raised his weapon, 'B' was swinging the blade." Pennance followed suit. Wounding 'A'. Note the arterial spray from the incision." Abernathy indicated a long line of blood stretching across the cupboards. "'A' then clasped a hand to their throat." Abernathy did the same. "And staggered out of the room, bleeding heavily." She indicated spots of blood on the floor, yellow markers beside each, larger and less frequent than the arterial spray. "'A' fell into the door jamb as they moved, leaving behind a bloody handprint. I haven't found any cast-off staining, that's when blood flies from the blade as it's being raised to strike again, although there is a defensive wound on 'A's hand."

Next, Abernathy moved into the corridor. "'A' staggers into the living room where he collapses onto the floor. And here we find an unidentified male, perhaps mid-30s."

Crosse positioned himself above the corpse, arms folded, braced by Jansen and Shapiro. Thriplow and Abernathy opposite. Pennance stood nearby with Hoskins next to him.

Abernathy squatted down, much like Pennance had. "The final wound was inflicted here, the knife driven into 'A'." Abernathy raised her hand in a fist and plunged it down towards the dead man. "And 'A' bled out. Note the large pool around the body."

"Would the final strike have killed him?" asked Pennance.

"It might have quickened his demise," said Abernathy. "'A' was probably motionless by this point, on the verge of death, if not gone already."

"The killer making sure he sealed the deal," said Hoskins.

"Right." Abernathy stretched out the vowel. "The knife has been removed, as you can of course see."

"Uniform are out looking for it," said Shapiro.

"Good work," said Crosse.

Pennance caught sight of Jansen squeezing her lips together. It was she who'd organised the search and at Pennance's request.

"I've taken fingerprints from the body and we'll carry out a formal identification once we've got him back at the mortuary," said Abernathy.

"What about the hand in the garden?" asked Pennance.

"It's best you see for yourself," said Thriplow.

THE BLUE CODE

The CSM led them outside. No need for Pennance to use his torch app this time; more floodlights on tripods, bathing the shrubs in a tungsten hue and banishing the shadows.

Two CSI were at the hole, slowly and carefully working away, removing dirt for a third to inspect. "Can you excuse us, please." Thriplow's team members shuffled back. The body had been further exposed, revealing flesh of a reddish colour and partially separated from the bone.

"I'll ask the inevitable," said Crosse. "How long has the corpse been interred?"

"And I'll give you the stock answer, Chief Inspector," said Abernathy. "It's impossible to be exact because of taphonomic factors – variables affecting the rate of decomposition. Heat and insect activity speed it up, cold and wrapping in plastic slow it down. The soil pH also has an impact. It's actually very difficult to actually get rid of a body. Cremation doesn't work – modern systems reach 1,000°C, but the skeleton still remains. The urn of ashes mourners receive are the result of a secondary process, a cremulator, which crushes the bones. So, usually killers hide bodies, like here."

"Has this one been burnt then?" asked Shapiro.

"No, I was just saying –."

"Take a stab in the dark." Crosse cut in.

"Not the best metaphor to choose." Thriplow raised an eyebrow while the DCI appeared unmoved.

"Three to five days after death the bodily fluids leak from orifices and turn the skin green," said Abernathy. "Then, as the blood decomposes, and gases accumulate the green turns to red after maybe eight to ten days."

"So, a week to a week and a half," said Crosse.

"Very roughly. But I'll make a closer assessment back at the mortuary."

"Will you be able to get an ID from the state of it?"

"Absolutely. I can carry out various analyses once the corpse is in my laboratory. DNA profiling can be done on a milligram of bone. Gender can be determined from peptides gathered from the tiniest scraping of a tooth."

Crosse raised a hand. "Great, that's fantastic, really glad to hear it, Charlotte. I always enjoy being a student of yours. But today, let's crack on, shall we?"

"As you wish."

"Anything else to add?"

"Yes," said Thriplow.

Crosse pushed his hands into his trouser pockets. "What?"

"This." Thriplow held out a clear plastic evidence bag. Inside was a cheap phone, a burner only capable of making and receiving calls and texts. The kind Pennance had found many times on drug dealers and pimps. "Discovered with the body."

"Get that to Cairns in Digital Forensics. Treat it as a priority." Crosse focused on Jansen. "Take our guests to your aunt's and then yourself home, Sergeant. There's nothing more here to see tonight." Then Crosse was inside the house and gone.

"Well that was rude," said Hoskins.

THE BLUE CODE

"I'm going to see upstairs first," said Pennance. "Whatever Crosse says."

"You're so tough," said Hoskins. He turned to Jansen. "You don't mess with our Jonah."

"Give it a rest, Vance," said Pennance.

"Yes, sir." Hoskins threw a slovenly salute.

***

Upstairs were five bedrooms, two en-suite, and a large bathroom. Pennance gave the latter a glance over – the shower was dry. Nothing inside the bathroom cabinet and just a scrawny bar of soap on the sink.

Jansen pointed across the hallway. "The master room."

Pennance flicked on the light. A peek through the drapes revealed the back garden.

An bed dominated the room which undulated briefly when Hoskins pressed down on one corner. "A waterbed," he said.

And clearly slept in, judging by the rucked-up duvet and squashed pillows – none of which had covers on. A large bag was kicked into one corner and clothes were strewn around the room. A funk hung in the air, the smell of sweaty sleep.

"It's like a student's room," said Hoskins.

"I wouldn't know," said Pennance.

The en-suite was a shower room. The toilet lid was up, the shower door open. A toothbrush (no paste) on the sink sat next to a packet of painkillers. Plastic had been shoved into the bin.

Pennance reached in and plucked them out. "These are for the bedding. And a sleeping bag."

Returning to the room Pennance turned back the duvet. No sleeping bag. He counted the pillows. "Only two," he said. "Yet there are three wrappers."

"Maybe it was a special offer," said Jansen.

Pennance checked out the remaining bedrooms. All were empty, the beds bare.

"Somebody else was staying here," said Pennance. "They took the sleeping bag and pillow with them."

"The dead guy had an accomplice," said Hoskins.

"Or a babysitter," said Jansen.

"So where are they?" asked Pennance.

Nobody answered.

Twenty

Jansen pulled up outside her Aunt Melody's B&B. Despite the hour, the downstairs lights blazed. Jansen yanked on the handbrake, turned the engine off. "I'd better show you two in. Just in case she's funny about you being back so late."

"I'll be fine," said Pennance. "I have keys."

"And no-one ever gets upset with me," said Hoskins.

However, by the time Pennance was through the gate, Jansen was tapping lightly on the door.

Melody opened up, backlit in the entrance. "You've been out a while."

"We had a shout to a crime scene," said Jansen.

Melody moved to one side, allowing room for Pennance. "I've a pot of tea on the go."

"I can't stay," said Jansen. She stepped up, pecked her aunt on the cheek. "Rain check?"

"That's what you said last time."

Jansen reached inside her jacket, read her phone screen. "The PM's scheduled for tomorrow morning. I'll pick you up first thing, okay?"

"When's that?" asked Pennance.

"7?"

"I can have some breakfast for you by then," said Melody.

"Sounds like a plan," said Pennance.

"I'll duck the PM," said Hoskins. "I can't stand all that cutting stuff up, not like Jonah here who always enjoys some gore."

"I wouldn't go that far," said Pennance.

"See you tomorrow, then." Jansen fluttered them a wave as Melody closed the door.

"Any chance of some food?" asked Hoskins.

"You've just had dinner," said Pennance.

"That was a couple of hours ago."

"If he wants to eat, let him, Jonah," said Melody. "Anything I should avoid? Like gluten, or meat or whatever? Seems like every day we're being told there's something else we have to dodge. It's tiring."

"Nope, I'm an omnivore," said Hoskins.

"Why don't you head up to your rooms and I'll bring a tray up in a few minutes."

"Thanks, Melody." Hoskins kissed her on the cheek.

Pennance trotted up the stairs, Hoskins following, Melody staring after him with one hand on her face. The door to number two was partially open. McAlaney appeared at the gap and beckoned them in. She returned to the desk, on which sat an open laptop. Pennance and Hoskins perched on opposite corners of the bed.

"How are you doing?" asked Pennance.

"Fine," she said. "Just working, as usual. Email never stops. Seems like you had a busy night. I've been monitoring the station's communications. A hand in a hole, yuck."

"Meanwhile, I had a decent curry," said Hoskins.

"I'm pleased for you." McAlaney rolled her eyes. "I looked into Mercer. He's an interesting fella. I found reports from several investigations by the NECC on the NCA servers."

"The New England Confectionary Company?" Hoskins loved his food references.

THE BLUE CODE

"No, you idiot, the National Economic Crime Centre."

"I know," said Hoskins. "They're a multi-agency team operating within the NCA. I was attached to them for a while. The NECC is made up of representatives from HM Revenue and Customs, the Financial Conduct Authority and the Serious Fraud Office."

"Heavyweight then," said Pennance.

"Not forgetting City of London police. As they cover the Square Mile – the Bank of England, and so on."

"And the records are on our database but not HOLMES?"

"See for yourself." McAlaney twisted her laptop around. Pennance began to read while McAlaney continued, "There's nothing been recorded by Cambridgeshire Constabulary. The most recent probe was just under a year ago."

"It seems the NECC were interested in several of Mercer's bank accounts."

"They were flagged up as potentially suspect in parallel investigations by JMLIT. That's the Joint Money Laundering Intelligence Task Force, part of the NECC."

"Too many acronyms." Hoskins groaned.

"Why hasn't Mercer been picked up?" asked Pennance.

"The CPS has never allowed a case to proceed due to lack of evidence or witnesses willing to testify. I spoke to one of the investigators at JMLIT, a DC Connors. Apparently Mercer is pretty good at persuading people not to go up against him."

"Violence?"

"It has been known, although not for some years. These days his main tool is apparently bribery."

"Did you find any connections to Elliott or Naughton?"

"None. At this stage it's hard to establish how Mercer could be involved in the shooting. He's probably a dead-end."

"That's not what Crosse thinks."

"I'm just saying what I see."

Pennance reached the bottom of the report. "Well I'll be damned." He pointed to the name of the investigating office. "DCI Leigh Fulton."

"Simone's boss," said Hoskins.

"Looks like he was seconded onto the case."

"Perhaps you could call him," said McAlaney.

"Maybe, though Fulton probably wouldn't go out of his way to be helpful," said Pennance. "What about O'Shea, Ava?"

"Who?" asked Hoskins.

"While you were stuffing your face I met Naughton and his lawyer, Connor O'Shea, in a church."

"Weird choice of location." Hoskins raised an eyebrow.

"Naughton told me Elliott was transporting a drive containing some data. That's what was in the case. Yet when we all met Naughton at the kid's party he said to Crosse he didn't know what Elliott had in his possession."

"Weirder and weirder," said Hoskins.

"Naughton offered me any help I wanted to get the drive back, under the condition nothing be discussed with Crosse." Hoskins opened his mouth to comment but Pennance cut him off. "Don't say weird again."

"So," said McAlaney, "I traced the mobile number on his business card. The service contract is owned by Baskin Robertson, on Bishopsgate. They're a legal firm."

"Let me guess," said Pennance. "O'Shea is a reputation lawyer."

"Yep, and one of Baskin Robertson's top lawyers, bills up to £500 an hour," said McAlaney.

"Big charges normally mean solving big problems," said Hoskins.

"Which leads to the question," said Pennance. "What's O'Shea covering for?"

"Or who," said McAlaney.

Pennance stood. "Get some sleep, guys. I suspect we have another busy day ahead of us."

"What are you?" asked McAlaney. "My dad?" She tutted.

"There's definitely a misconception about my age."

Hoskins laughed.

Pennance's room was next door. He pushed the door to with a foot, flopped on the bed, kicked his shoes off. Then grabbed a remote control off the bedside cabinet and flicked on the TV. Music blasted out, an advert theme tune, and Pennance hurriedly reduced the volume to zero before switching over to a national news station. The article seemed to be about the latest immigration issue in Kent – Pennance recognised the Dover docks. A group of ragged people, mainly women and kids, soaked to the skin, being taken off an almost impossibly small craft onto a coastguard cutter.

There was a knock before Melody pushed the door open a crack. "Are you decent?"

Pennance sat up, swung his legs off the bed as she entered, carrying a laden tray which she placed on the desk under the window. A plate displayed a proper doorstep sandwich – two thick slices of white bread, cut in half.

"I'm not hungry," said Pennance.

"The food is for Vance." She handed Pennance a mug emblazoned with a cartoon rendition of a ginger cat. "And my niece is annoyingly prompt. So if you come down at 6.30 I'll be ready for you." Melody picked up the tray. "Sleep well." She shut the door behind her.

Pennance sipped the tea, getting a belt of enough tannin to coat his teeth as brown as a lacquered fence. The news flipped to an external view of 10 Downing Street and a government minister scurrying towards a Jaguar, exhausts spilling smoke. Pennance had no time for most politicians.

Instead he focused on unpacking his things, pulling out any items that would crease, shirts and trousers, and hung them in the wardrobe. Smithson had used the classic traveller's technique – rolling, rather than folding. She'd thought to pack his running gear, too: trainers, shorts and a couple of t-shirts. The toiletries went into the bathroom, everything else stayed inside the case. Pennance didn't intend on settling in that much.

While Pennance brushed his teeth the news turned to Elliott's shooting – a long range view of the supermarket. The camera angle was from near the footpath Pennance had used to access the housing estate, perhaps beside the pick-up kiosk. It was early evening, the store itself dark while streetlights between the parking spaces were on, illuminating an empty expanse of tarmac. The Mercedes was gone, of course, and all that remained was the plastic cordon tape, flapping in the wind, and a uniformed cop.

Pennance grabbed the remote, raised the volume to a decent level. "... a shooting earlier today in a busy supermarket car park in Huntingdon," said a female reporter, off-screen as the camera panned around. "Police would not comment on the details of the investigation, nor the victim's identity. However, local sources named him as Logan Elliott." Elliott's photo flicked up on screen. "An employee at high-tech software firm, Obsidian, run by tech entrepreneur, Kai Naughton."

Naughton's photo appeared on screen next to Elliott's before the shot shifted to a vox-pop interview – a head and shoulders close-up with a man in a suit, tie pulled up high, and slicked back dark hair. A name flashed up at the bottom of the screen: Karl Greene, Manager.

"I was inside, near the Customer Services kiosk, so I didn't actually see the shooting, thankfully," said Greene. "But I heard it. A loud, buzzing noise, over in seconds."

"Did you go outside?" asked the reporter, still off-screen.

"Yes, it was chaos. People screaming and running. A woman was sitting on the floor, crying. I dashed back into the store and called the police."

Then, Crosse was on-screen, a street scene in the background. The reporter said, "We eventually tracked down the senior officer handling the case to central Huntingdon."

"It's too early to speculate." Crosse's name and rank were revealed in the same fashion as Greene's. "Why the victim was targeted is still under investigation. However, I would like to reassure the public that we see this as an isolated event and stress that everyone continue to go about their daily business without fear."

"Why do you say that, Chief Inspector?" asked the reporter.

"Our enquiry is at a very early stage, but the evidence right now points to a targeted, rather than general, attack. Now, I must be going, thank you." Crosse walked away, and headed inside a glass-fronted building. Then the camera panned out and revealed an Indian restaurant.

The camera shifted onto the reporter, a woman with long, curly hair and a mole above her top lip. "And there you have it," she said. "A brutal killing in a normally quiet market town, while the police enjoy a curry."

"A man's got to eat, you know!" The camera shot over to the restaurant entrance and took a moment to focus. Shapiro briefly glared at the reporter, before returning inside.

"Back to you in the studio," said the reporter.

Pennance turned the TV off, marvelled at Shapiro's reaction. Crosse's anger when he'd arrived at Wrigley's house hadn't entirely been because he was late, then.

Pennance's mobile rang. Simone.

"How are you doing?" she asked.

"Knackered. I was at a house earlier where there were two more bodies. And I've a PM early tomorrow."

"Sounds fun."

"That's one way of putting it."

"Will you be back by Saturday?"

"At this stage, I'm not sure."

"Because we've got Vance around for dinner, with his latest girlfriend, if you remember."

"Then we definitely won't be."

"*Jonah.*" Simone clicked her tongue. "He's our friend."

"I know, but he's always got some new woman on the go. Soon as you learn about them, they're out the door and replaced with the next one. I've no idea how he does it."

"Jealous?"

"Not in the slightest."

"Right answer," said Simone. "She's called Mindy, an American. Vance thinks Mindy might be the one."

"That's something else he says every time, too. At least it's not Quant."

"Director Quant, your boss?"

"My boss's boss, strictly speaking. Vance and Quant seem to know each other quite well."

"Wow."

"I know, the mind literally boggles." Pennance yawned. "Sorry, it's been a long day."

"I'll let you go. Love you," said Simone.

"Me too."

"You still can't say it, Jonah. We're not in the same city."

"Huntingdon is a town."

"Really? Now you drop into pedantic detail?"

"Small talk isn't easy for me. Even with you."

Simone sighed heavily. "No, it's me who needs to apologise, I shouldn't have said anything."

"I don't agree," said Pennance. "It's best to keep discussing how we feel. Let's talk more when I'm back. Over that bottle of wine in your fridge."

"Alright, now go and get your beauty sleep. You need lots of it."

"People keep thinking I'm older than I actually am."

"Well, there you go then. Night, Jonah." Simone cut the call before Pennance could answer. He rubbed his face with both hands. Relationships, they weren't easy. He got into bed.

Compared to London, with the constant background hum of traffic, of people, of life in general here was almost painfully quiet. He closed his eyes and tried to drift off.

***

What felt like hours later, Pennance was still tossing and turning. Despite being shattered he couldn't sleep for long before waking. It was the silence. He didn't trust it.

Pennance flicked on his phone and searched for an app. The second one from the top was perfect. He started the programme which ran on a loop. Within seconds he was unconscious, the sound of the city playing.

Twenty One

Pennance headed downstairs at 6.30am and found the door to the dining room open. Inside were four tables, all set for breakfast. One table was already occupied by a pair of builders in overalls, heads buried in red-top tabloid newspapers, plates marked with yellow and red smears pushed away from them.

Melody emerged from the adjacent kitchen, wiping her hands on a tea towel. "Morning, Jonah. What can I get you? I do a decent Full English."

Pennance didn't fancy a protein booster this early. "Porridge is fine, thanks. And some toast and coffee."

"Coming right up."

"Great tip yesterday," said one of the builders.

"Sorry?" Melody flickered a glance at Pennance.

"The 3.10 at Kempton came in by a nose at 10-1."

"Oh, good." Melody disappeared into the kitchen and the builders left.

Pennance picked up one of the newspapers they'd discarded. Elliott's murder was front page news – a long-range photo of the peppered Merc centre stage. The headline of large, bold letters read, 'In Cold Blood'. Pennance skimmed the story, which was light on actual information while heavy on speculation. At the bottom, in bold text, Pennance was directed to an accompanying article inside.

As Pennance flipped through the pages, Melody brought out his food. "Can I get you anything else?"

"I'm fine, thanks." Pennance began to eat.

Melody cleared the builders' plates as Pennance read. There was a photo of Crosse, seemingly lifted from the TV interview with him outside the restaurant, and the by-line, 'Curry Cop Out'.

'Detective Chief Inspector Nick Crosse of Cambridgeshire police preferred to be dining with colleagues last night, rather than trying to track down a vicious killer after the murder of a man in broad daylight outside a supermarket in the normally peaceful town of Huntingdon, a crime which has residents living in fear, too scared to leave their houses.

'This reporter understands DCI Crosse and two colleagues were dining on phaals, laughing and joking, while the very people they were supposed to be protecting quivered behind their doors. DCI Crosse briefly broke away from his feast to remonstrate with a BBC reporter about his conduct.

'Mary, a local resident I spoke to, told me, "The police round here are all rubbish. They let everyone get away with everything. There's kids making noise, drugs, even sniffing laughing gas and leaving their cannisters everywhere. They should all be got rid of." This reporter wasn't sure if Mary meant the kids or the cops...'

A car horn blew on the street outside, a single, long toot.

"That'll be my niece." Melody gritted her teeth. "I tell her every bloody time to knock on the door rather than make that racket. She does it on purpose." If it was Jansen then she was early, as Melody had predicted. Melody shook her head as Jansen tooted again. "Maybe you could mention it to her?"

"I doubt she'd listen to me." Pennance lifted his jacket from off the back of the seat. "Thanks for breakfast." He raised the newspaper. "Can I take this?"

"Of course, but before you go..." Melody briefly entered the kitchen before emerging with a thick square parcel of tin foil which she held out for Pennance. "A bacon sandwich for later."

"You don't have to."

"I've made it now." Melody wafted the package at him. "I'll bet you'll be too busy to stop somewhere, so take it. Just in case."

"Okay." Pennance slid the sandwich into a jacket pocket.

"There's one for Keri, too."

"I'll tell her."

"No, don't. It'll just put her off eating. She'll blame me for fussing." Melody waved a hand. "Now, get going before she makes anymore bloody racket and the neighbours start on me."

Outside, Jansen was leaning on her roller-skate car, the engine running, rapping her fingers on the roof to a jingle only she could hear. She needlessly waved before getting into the driver's seat, leaning over and popping Pennance's door for him, like he was some kind of invalid.

"You took your time." Jansen set off as Pennance reached for his seat belt. He strapped in then reached around to drop the sandwiches onto the back seat. "I assume one of those is mine?"

"I'm not supposed to say."

Jansen sighed. "My aunt is always trying to feed me up. Either that or get me married off." Jansen's eyes drifted briefly to the newspaper.

"Have you read this?"

"Oh, yes." She grimaced. "Crosse is going to be apoplectic."

"Where are we going?"

"Addenbrooke's Hospital, on the southern edge of Cambridge." Jansen negotiated a set of traffic lights. "We're usually shuttling between Cambridge and Peterborough for post-mortems." She blew the car horn and made a rude hand gesture at a van driver who cut in front of them. Funny how people changed once they were behind a wheel and a pane of tempered glass.

"Your aunt reckons you're noisy."

"I do it on purpose."

"She said that, too. How are your arms now?"

"Excuse me?"

"Last night you were in pain when Melody hugged you."

"Oh, right. Still hurts a bit, but better, thanks." Jansen navigated the dreaded ring road once more around Huntingdon's outskirts. "ID on the stabbing victim came in overnight. Alexis Draganov, Bulgarian by birth, specifically Varna."

"Never been."

"Me either, but as my aunt mentioned there will be people resident in and around Huntingdon who have, maybe including colleagues out of the station. Apparently, back in the day, Varna was the main hub in Bulgaria for organised crime. Various groups operated out of the city.

People smuggling, prostitution, illicit gambling, drug trafficking, extortion, and so on."

"Draganov had a record, then?"

Jansen's face knotted. "Extensive, is probably the best description. From assault to rape and a suspect in the murder of at least four people. Apparently, he particularly enjoyed beating people to death." She drew up as traffic lights turned red and twisted in her seat. "According to his file, Draganov was a freelance operative. Whoever paid, got his services. His only actual convictions were from relatively minor teenage crime. After that he stayed out of police stations."

"Nice guy."

"His lack of loyalty meant eventually he pissed off the wrong people and he went from being ally to enemy."

"So, he escaped to the UK?"

"How did you guess?" Jansen tapped the steering wheel with a finger, eye-balling the signals. "Officially resident here since 2007 when his country joined the EU. He came over in one of the first waves of immigration and the Bulgarian authorities must have been delighted to have got rid of him."

"He should have been denied entry at the border and put straight back onto a plane."

"You'd think, right?" Jansen accelerated away hard the moment the amber bulb lit. "However, communication between Bulgaria and the Home Office wasn't efficient. He managed to slip through and disappear."

"Great, then what?"

Jansen swung onto a dual carriageway, largely empty of traffic. "This used to be the main A14. Before the new road was built this would be bumper to bumper. But now..." She put her foot down.

"Are we running late?"

"Nah, ages yet. Speed cameras aren't working, so why not?" She shrugged. "Draganov's file from then on is pretty patchy. Seemingly he got up to his old tricks, just in a different country, for different employers. It's believed he worked for several London firms, next Manchester, Birmingham, Glasgow, possibly Belfast, too."

"He moved around, then."

"It's his M.O. and there's no shortage of prospective employers across the UK."

"So, how did he end up in Huntingdon?"

"That's something I'd like to know too, Jonah."

Pennance shut up, leaving Jansen to concentrate on the road. Soon she moderated her speed, moving in tandem with the vehicles around them.

"Now the cameras are on?" asked Pennance.

"Sadly." Jansen huffed. "Just a couple of junctions down before we pull off." Which was exactly what they shortly did, entering a more built-up area, Trumpington. "I've no idea where the name comes from," she said before Pennance could ask. They waited to turn at a junction, indicator ticking. "When I was a kid I used to live right there." She pointed at the middle of the road. "The council decided here was the best place to put a highway through to the hospital so the house and four or five others either side got taken out. All this was once fields. We even had an orchard. Yet now look."

THE BLUE CODE

"That's progress," said Pennance, to which Jansen snorted.

Jansen took them through the edge of a new-build housing estate and soon she was skirting a sprawling series of large modern buildings constructed of a pale yellow brick. A single decker green bus rolled by, heading in the opposite direction. "We're here."

To Pennance the hospital seemed more like an industrial complex than any medical centre he was used to in London, where existing institutions expanded rather than building from new. Jansen swung into a car park, taking the first space she saw.

"Come on." She turned off the engine. "I need a coffee before we watch someone get chopped up."

Twenty Two

Pennance couldn't fail to miss the distinct drop in temperature as he entered the examination room. Nobody with a pulse could.

He'd just scrubbed up, standing next to Jansen at a large sink, washing with plenty of hot water and soap before donning one of the surgical scrub suits which hung nearby on a hook. Cap, plastic glasses, nitrile gloves, knee length wellington boots followed.

Heavy double doors slipped shut behind him, creating a seal; autopsy suites operated under negative pressure relative to the room outside. In the background came a steady whisper of the atmosphere being constantly filtered and the sharp chemical tang of disinfectant that scraped the back of his throat hung in an airborne blanket.

The suite seemed at odds with the hospital estate he'd seen so far: worn, well-used and certainly well-scoured. Pale tiles of a yellowing white, dulled stainless steel and a floor which sloped down towards a drain, standard procedure as the most straightforward route to removing the blood and gore resulting from the evisceration process. Overhead, strip lights hummed; no natural illumination in here.

Two examination tables were occupied; long and narrow humps, clearly corpses, beneath large white paper sheets which completely covered the bodies and hung down either side; a recyclable shroud.

And the dead had company. Under the surgical gowns Pennance recognised Shapiro's bulk and Crosse's disdain.

THE BLUE CODE

"Inspector, sergeant," muttered Crosse.

"Sir," replied Jansen.

"Muffin," said Shapiro. "And dickhead."

Pennance said, "How is it being infamous?"

The door went again before Crosse or Shapiro could respond. Abernathy entered, mask down off her face, followed by another person, obviously the photographer given the large camera with wide lens and extensive flash attached. "Good morning all," said Abernathy. "I'm glad you're on time. DI Pennance, nice to see you again."

"Don't get used to the sight of him," said Crosse. "He won't be here long enough."

"What a shame." Abernathy turned to the photographer. "This is Miss Clemson and that's everyone introduced so let's get started."

The lack of stenographer meant Abernathy would transcribe her own findings later. No assistant, either. Several pathologists Pennance had met worked this way.

"For expediency I measured the particulars of both victims prior to your arrival," said Abernathy. "Mr Elliott's height is 1.75 metres and his weight a shade below 75 kilos. Under the imperial system, that's 5 feet 9 inches and 11 stone 11 pounds. Given Mr Elliott's age of 47, the victim immediately prior to death was a reasonable weight, towards the upper end of acceptable at least, and with a BMI of 24.4, if you believe in that kind of thing. Mr Draganov's height is 2.03 metres and his weight at 98 kilos or 6 feet 8 inches and 15 stone 6 pounds.

"In addition, I took blood and urine samples, clippings of fingernails and scrapings from underneath along with hair samples. Finally, I swabbed Mr Draganov's hands for potential gunshot residue. All these have been sent away to the labs for evaluation. I expect a 24- 48 hour turnaround."

"What about the burial?" asked Pennance.

"As that corpse was well on the way to putrefaction, Inspector, it is elsewhere. The PM will have to be carried out under very different conditions."

"No point filling the room with the stink of decay," said Crosse.

"I think you'll find deterioration all around us, Chief Inspector. Your skin renews itself entirely every 27 days. I note your hair is greying as it dies at the roots." Crosse half-raised a hand before stopping himself. Abernathy continued, "The body is permanently on a knife-edge, with nature poised to return us to our constituent atoms. Ours is just a temporary and borrowed form."

"Well, I feel much better now, thank you, doctor."

"You're welcome. So, who would you prefer I start on first?" Abernathy motioned, palm up, towards the bodies like a magician's assistant prefacing a great illusion. "The shooting, or the stabbing? Take your pick."

"I'm more interested in Draganov," said Crosse. "I'm well aware what killed Elliott."

"This is he." Abernathy wheeled a tray of instruments over beside the veiled hitman.

Abernathy adjusted a microphone which extended from the ceiling on an umbilical, bringing the receiver closer to her while Pennance placed himself opposite the pathologist, flanked by Jansen and Shapiro, Crosse taking up a position by Draganov's feet.

THE BLUE CODE

The pathologist raised a hand encased in a surgical glove and fixed her mask in place. Beneath the nitrile would be another layer; cut proof mesh gloves to guard against any slippages with razor-sharp instruments – each blade was honed by a technician after every procedure, and no pathologist wanted to expose themselves to the deceased's bioliquids. Then she placed a visor on.

"Prior to the Anatomy Act of 1832, dissection after death was viewed as a post-mortem punishment for executed murderers." Abernathy drew back the paper shroud without flourish, revealing Draganov's naked corpse lying on a burnished steel table. Holes had been drilled in the metal to allow the excess bodily fluids to conveniently drain away. "In other words, they suffered in the after-life."

"Sounds good to me," said Crosse.

Abernathy neatly folded the cover, handling it like a large tablecloth, before dropping the resultant square into a tall, flip top medical bin which would be emptied later and the contents sent for incineration.

"Disembowelling dead bodies in the name of science was an ancient trade," said Abernathy. "The word anatomy was Grecian – *ana*, meaning 'up' and *temnein* 'to cut' – and first attributed to Aristotle. However, Herophilos, born more than three hundred years BC, was recognised as undertaking the world's first human dissections and the earliest medical and anatomical references occurred 1,300 years before even that. Burke and Hare had nothing on the Greeks."

Somehow, Draganov seemed more imposing than in Philby's house. Perhaps it was the breadth of his chest, or the bulge of his muscles. Maybe the over-sized hands, palm down on the shimmering steel. Or because the full scale of Draganov's tattoos were finally revealed. Symbols and letters in a muddy blue ink marked almost all of his body – skulls, anchors, naked women, words in a language Pennance didn't recognise – sprawling from Draganov's ankles, to his ears, to his fingertips. It was like someone had used Draganov as a doodling board.

Shapiro whistled, shrill and brief. "I wouldn't like to meet him in a dark alley."

"According to his file, sometimes people did," said Jansen. "And only came out again in a body bag."

"Never seen anything like it," said Crosse.

There was something odd about Draganov's face. Then Pennance realised; he didn't possess eyebrows.

"There's also the total lack of body hair," said Abernathy. "Mr Draganov regularly shaved his whole body. Or someone did."

"Sack, back and crack, too?" asked Shapiro.

"The lot, I reckon," said Crosse.

"According to his file, Draganov developed a bizarre ritual," said Jansen. "Before and after every hit he washed himself down with petrol. He'd stand butt naked while one of his comrades poured fuel onto him and he'd scrub away. And he kept his entire body closely shaved."

Pennance remembered the smell of hydrocarbons from last night when he was close to Draganov. "Presumably his way of eliminating any DNA?"

"It would be pretty effective," said Abernathy. "You'll note several clear signs of an incised, sharp force trauma on Mr Draganov. I count five in total. And Inspector?"

THE BLUE CODE

Abernathy beckoned Shapiro over. "Would you mind? I'd like you to be the victim and me the attacker." The pathologist evidently liked her play-acting.

"Sure." Shapiro moved beside Abernathy.

"Let's start with Mr Draganov's gullet. As a data point, one third of all homicides are the result of a cervical wound, whereas 46% result from an injury in the upper half of the body."

A long, thin line ran the width of Draganov's throat, peeled open slightly to reveal raw flesh.

"Here we see the single slash wound I referred to yesterday at the scene which ruptured the external carotid artery, creating the spray pattern noted at the time."

"Cause of death?" asked Crosse.

"Possible, but too early to be sure. The wound resulted from a tangential movement by the attacker." Abernathy manoeuvred Shapiro so they faced each other, standing ninety degrees to the examination table before she mimicked swinging a weapon across Shapiro's neck. "This movement produces an incision longer than it is deep." Abernathy took a ruler from the tray and measured the injury. "Wound One is 5.6 cm in length and runs at an approximate angle of fifteen degrees from right to left, three millimetres in depth on the right and less than two on the left. In addition, the margins are slightly abraded, meaning it was caused by a somewhat blunt edge."

Clemson leaned in and took a photo, flash off, with the gauge still lying on Draganov's neck to give a sense of scale in the image.

"So, the attacker was right handed," said Crosse.

"It's an assumption that the end of a wound with the greatest penetration means the initiation point. However, it's next to impossible to determine who was standing in what posture from a single cut. The attacker may have swung forehand or backhand, so to speak. What's more indicative is the wounding to the victim's left hand side, caused due to how attacker and victim were standing." Abernathy turned back to Shapiro and plunged the side of her fist into his stomach, below the rib cage. She then indicated the location on Draganov. "From these two data points it's possible to propose that the attacker was at least *holding* the knife on their right."

"That'll do me."

Abernathy returned her attention to Draganov. "Moving onto the torso there are a further four lesions, referred to as Wounds Two to Five, all the results of stabbing, which is characterised by the width of the injury on the surface being less than the depth of the penetration into the body."

"The opposite of a slash wound," said Pennance.

"Correct, Jonah." Abernathy made a fist again and this pushed her hand towards Shapiro, over and over.

"Okay, I get it." Shapiro rubbed at the imaginary injury. "Anyone would think you had something against me."

"Three of the stab wounds I measure at 2.6 to 2.9cm across," said Abernathy. "I can only ascertain the depth once I go inside Mr Draganov to make an analysis." Clemson snapped photographs with and without the ruler. Abernathy moved the scale from Draganov's neck to his torso. "Wound Two we've already discussed." More photos. "Wound Three is 0.9cm wide and we'll come back to that momentarily.

THE BLUE CODE

"Wound Four is located in the victim's back, 3.5 centimetres to the right of the midline." Abernathy went around the rear of Shapiro, pushed her fist near his spine. "The lesion passes between the fourth and fifth ribs of the right hemithorax, possibly nicking one of the bones on the way through and, I expect, transfixing the right lung. The blade penetrated entirely through the torso, resulting in Wound Three." Now Abernathy reached around and placed two fingers on Shapiro's chest, showing the route the blade would have taken.

"Doctor, I didn't know you cared," said Shapiro.

"We're done now." Abernathy gave Shapiro a light shove before she made to roll Draganov over.

"Do you need a hand?" asked Pennance.

"Need?" said Abernathy. "No, thank you. I'm well versed in how to lever an inanimate object."

Shapiro tutted at Pennance. "Sexist."

"Better to offer and be rebuffed than make no attempt at all, surely Inspector Shapiro?" asked Abernathy.

"I wouldn't know," said Shapiro. "Rejection isn't something I'm familiar with."

"Oh, please." Jansen raised a hand to her face.

By now Abernathy had Draganov on his side. "Here you can note the injury I referred to." After the detectives had had a good look Abernathy lowered Draganov back down.

"And finally, the victim's hand." Abernathy lifted Draganov's arm, held out the palm, displaying a ragged vertical gap. "There's extensive yellowing of Mr Draganov's index and middle finger, the result of nicotine. And then Wound Five. Here the blade passed entirely through the soft tissue. This is a classic defensive wound. Draganov was holding one or both of his hands out, trying to ward off his attacker."

"Didn't work," said Shapiro.

"I note that the lesions all display the same abraded appearance as the slash at Mr Draganov's neck. A neat, thin slice would indicate a sharp blade. This favours something duller. Whenever the knife is found I would expect it to be approximately 15cm in length with a rounded tip and serrated cutting edge."

"A bread knife," said Pennance.

"Murder by baguette." Shapiro grinned.

"He wasn't killed by a bakery product," said Abernathy.

"I know, it's just..." Shapiro tailed off at Abernathy's under-the-eyebrows stare.

"What about time of death?"

"We know when," said Jansen, "because of the gunshot."

"The shooting and the stabbing could have occurred at different times," said Pennance.

"But there's the cleaned-off blood spatter on the cupboard," said Jansen.

"Again, they don't necessarily need to be connected," said Pennance.

"No jumping forward," said Abernathy. "There's a procedure to follow."

"She's right," said Crosse.

"For the benefit of my audience, several changes occur within the body, triggered by the cessation of a heartbeat, and proceed in a straight line progression, each with their own characteristics.

THE BLUE CODE

"As the blood stops flowing, cells become deprived of oxygen and acidity increases. Internally, at around four minutes following death, *autolysis*, which means self-digestion, initiates. Externally *pallor mortis* becomes visible after maybe fifteen minutes, i.e. the person no longer possesses their natural looking colour and vibrancy. The body cools, steadily losing heat until it reaches whatever the ambient temperature is, like the central heating has been turned off.

"Enzymes digest the cell membranes which then leak as the cells break down, accelerating the process, initially in the liver and brain, but soon all other tissues and organs begin to degrade. The damaged cells spill out, aided by gravity, eventually settling in the capillaries and veins at the lowest point in the body, presenting as a bright pink colouration with a bluish tinge, similar to a well-developed bruise. This is known as *livor mortis*, or *hypostasis*. Typically at least thirty minutes or up to four hours are required for *livor mortis* to be observed. Maximum lividity occurs at between eight to twelve hours. When I arrived at the scene I noted *hypostasis* had not begun to occur. The ambient temperature within the room was only fourteen degrees, the central heating was turned off, low enough to slow the process.

"In parallel, muscle cells are contracting and relaxing due to the counter-movement of two proteins. The loss of energy from the body means these proteins can no longer bypass one another and become fixed in place which causes the body to stiffen up. This is what we call *rigor mortis*, beginning with the eyelids, jaw and neck and spread downwards, somewhere between two and four hours after death. *Rigor* was also not present when I first examined the body."

"So he'd been dead less than half an hour," said Pennance.

"A reasonable judgement at this stage," said Abernathy. "That completes my external assessment. Now we go inside."

"My favourite part," said Shapiro. "I'm lying by the way."

Abernathy reached out towards the instruments tray, the rush of cold air through the vents the only sound in the examination room. She selected a substantial knife possessing a broad blade, as yet unsullied with blood, and a wide handle which fit snugly in Abernathy's grip.

The pathologist hauled down a hose vent – a wide, umbilical tube and large inlet – for a more localised extraction to capture any stray particles from Draganov. Abernathy placed the blade on the skin at the base of the dead man's neck.

"I'll start at the sternal notch," said Abernathy. "That's the finger-wide dip at the top of the rib cage, and cut straight down to the base of his stomach, followed immediately by another across the chest, in a crucifix shape." The blade cut as easily as Abernathy drawing a line with a pencil.

Abernathy continued her slicing, saying nothing throughout, concentrating, until she revealed the rib cage. She placed the tool back on the tray. Abernathy gripped the section at the top. "Skin is truly amazing. It's a part of the integumentary system – *integumentum* means a covering."

Pennance concentrated on Abernathy's words in an attempt to block out the vomit-inducing sound as she rolled up Draganov's skin like a rug, producing a slurping noise as it parted.

"Depending on the definition, the body possesses 78 or 79 organs, including the skin. There are three layers to the latter – epidermis, which is the part we now see. This is affixed to the dermis and is where the ink from Mr Draganov's tattoos ended up, and finally the hypodermis, mostly made up of fat of which Mr Draganov possesses a minimal layer – that's the buttercup yellow line you can see, by the way." Mercifully, Abernathy placed the gory cylinder onto a nearby table. "And, we're done."

"Thank you for that," said Crosse.

Abernathy bumped a shoulder. "All part of the job." The pathologist went back inside Draganov with the knife, making more incisions, before she lifted out the bloody ribcage itself, which ended up on another table separate to the skin, leaving Draganov's internal organs on display.

"See here." Abernathy placed the tip of her knife on a section of one lung.

Pennance bent in, saw a small slit said, "The result of Wound Four?"

"Correct." Now Abernathy wheeled the table away over to a large sink against the wall. Using a tap sprinkler she washed off the ribs before placing them carefully back on the table. She bent at the waist, examining the bones closely.

After a few minutes Abernathy crooked a finger. "If you'd care to join me." Once Pennance and the others assembled by the table in a ragged semi-circle, Abernathy said, "I'll need to spend more time reviewing the bones but, as I expected, there is a clear mark on the fifth rib where the blade struck."

She indicated to a V-shaped notch. "And there's a further indentation here." Abernathy pointed to the other side of the ribcage, higher up to the third rib, where a rough hole was about visible. "Now, returning to the body."

Next, Abernathy made several cuts around Draganov's gullet, severing each connection between the organs, removing and weighing one tissue after another, examining and listing the data for the benefit of the digital recorder while Draganov's blood dripped out and down through the holes in the examination table. Eventually, Abernathy blew out a lungful of air and placed down her blood-covered blade.

"Such a waste." Abernathy rubbed Draganov's plasma between her fingers. "Blood is humanity in a literal microcosm but multiplied massively. The circulatory system of veins and arteries is about sixty thousand miles. The heart pumps a litre of blood every ten seconds. Our bone marrow manufactures two million red blood cells every second. There are thirty trillion red cells in a person and they can travel some twelve thousand miles through the body's network. Carrying oxygen, nutrients, heat and hormones; regulating energy, sleep, bodily functions and mood. Removing carbon dioxide, fighting infection and repelling interlopers."

"Wonderful," said Crosse. "But I'm more interested in your findings."

"In life Mr Draganov was not a healthy man. And I'm talking body, rather than spirit. Despite Mr Draganov's reasonable mass to height ratio his internal organs were displaying stress from a rather harmful personal regimen.

THE BLUE CODE

Both kidney and liver were overweight; I'd suggest due to a high consumption of both alcohol and fatty, highly processed foods. Mr Draganov's left anterior descending coronary artery exhibits signs of calcification. That he was a heavy smoker will have added to his problems. All in all, Mr Draganov was probably a couple of years away from a serious and potentially debilitating stroke."

"Thankfully he's gone sooner," said Crosse. "And what about cause of death?"

"Yeah, cut to the chase, doc." Shapiro nudged an unmoved Crosse.

"Wound One sliced the carotid artery while wound Four caused internal haemorrhaging," said Abernathy. "Either on their own could have proved fatal without extremely prompt medical attention. Together, Mr Draganov had virtually no chance of survival. Everything will be detailed in my report."

"Great, we're done then." Crosse clapped his hands together.

"I was going to move onto Mr Elliott."

"I said already, we know what killed him – lots of bullets. I'll just read your notes when you send them over." Crosse removed a glove. "Besides, I've some land to search for Ferrensby. My interest is in finding the living; the dead aren't going anywhere."

"What about the unidentified male from the garden?" asked Pennance.

"I'm in the process of organising some body scans to determine cause of death," said Abernathy.

"Can I see the corpse?"

"Are you sure?" Abernathy peered at Pennance. "It's pretty grim."

"I seem to remember Dr Abernathy saying she'd need to assess the remains all by herself, due to the decay," said Crosse.

"Not quite –," replied the pathologist.

"Nevertheless," said Pennance. "I'd like to take a look."

"You're on your own then," said Crosse.

"I will too," said Shapiro.

"No, you won't," said Crosse. "I've better things to be doing with your time. We're off, Ed." Crosse left the examination room trailed, a few moments later, by Shapiro.

"As I drove Jonah here I guess I'll have to stay," said Jansen. "I'll be in the café, just don't take too long."

"The body's in the cold store," said Abernathy.

"Can't wait," said Pennance.

Twenty Three

Abernathy led Pennance past the scrubbing up station where Shapiro was washing, soap as far as his elbows, while Crosse removed his medical garments.

The pathologist's destination proved to be a room a hundred yards or so further on, entirely devoid of both furniture and warmth. The space was markedly lower in temperature than the post-mortem suite; this was a proper chiller and Pennance wouldn't like to spend too much time inside.

One wall was a series of stainless steel doors in rows and columns, each with a large pull handle, the metal polished so bright the reflected glare from the overhead bulbs assaulted Pennance's eyes when Abernathy threw the light switch. One drawer was already open, the metal gurney extended out and a half-eaten sandwich in a wrapper lying there.

"It's this one." Abernathy paid no attention to the part-consumed food, heading for a drawer at her thigh height. She tugged on the handle and the table slid out on entirely silent wheels. Ice-cold air spilled, a distinct funnel of frostiness which slid across Pennance like the caress of Death himself. A cadaver pouch lay on the metal, the form underneath indistinct, though obvious enough.

Abernathy paused, one hand gripping the body bag, the other pinching the zip between two fingers. "Ready for this?"

"No."

"Do you want some vapour rub to put under your nose?" The strong menthol odour from what was usually used on an infant's chest to help keep the airways clear was a common trick used by CSI technicians to keep strong smells at bay.

"Only if you will."

"I'm fine."

"Then so am I."

"Okay." As Abernathy worked the zipper a stench of rotting flesh and earth filled the examination room, like a wall of bad meat. Pennance stood his ground, forced himself to stare at the wreck of what was barely a person.

"I measured the John Doe's height at 1.6 metres and his weight at maybe 53 kilos so 5 feet 3 inches and roughly eight and a half stone," said Abernathy. "Male."

Pennance wasn't getting accustomed to the rotting odour, an olfactory battering raid. "How long has he been in the ground?"

"There are three methods of decomposition: putrefaction, which is the commonest, mummification, which is self-explanatory, and adiopocere, which occurs under cold and damp conditions and is the saponification of body fat."

"We turn into soap, then."

"Pretty much. The skin takes on a waxy or crumbly appearance."

The body just looked like a tangle of flesh. "I guess we're talking about putrefaction."

"Correct. Most people see death as the end. In fact the human body teems with life once the heart stops beating. Dying is just part of the natural process and we return to the swamp of chemicals that makes up the planet to be recycled once more. Something we will all confront at some point, ready or not."

"I'm not concerned about my own demise, doctor."

"You're in a minority," said Abernathy. "A putrefying body is where the tissues turn from solid to liquid and the speed depends upon temperature. Hotter means faster and vice versa. In our climate this starts at around three to four days.

"Animals and bugs move in, laying eggs. Most internal organs are free of bacteria when alive as the immune system keeps them that way. After death the microorganisms roam free and unopposed, beginning in the gut and radiating outwards. By the time there's any external evidence, visible as a great splodge on the stomach, the bacteria will be causing devastation inside, using blood vessels like highways to speed around the body, digesting the intestines, then the liver, spleen, heart and then the brain.

"The skin blisters as fluid collects in pockets, which subsequently burst. Gas is generated as a by-product and the body swells up; genitals first, then face and abdomen. Eyes and tongue protrude as liquid moves up from the lungs, leaking from the orifices – mouth and eyes in particular – which pop. After seven days or so, depending on the environment, body cavities burst, tissues liquefy and the skin sheds from the body. Certain body parts are more resistant to putrefaction – prostate, tendons and ligaments take months to break down before the skeleton is fully naked and exposed."

Pennance felt slightly ill. "Based on all of that, do you still apply the seven to ten days you told Crosse?"

"I'm thinking now he's been dead for maybe two weeks. I could bring in a forensic entomologist to determine insect types and growth, or a forensic anthropologist to examine the taphonomy of the body and be more accurate but for now, that's the best I can do."

"Crosse will need to know the timelines have altered." Pennance pointed to an arm where there seemed to be some colouration. "Is that a tattoo?"

Abernathy bent and looked closer at where Pennance had indicated. "Could be." She straightened. "I'm going to have the body examined by magnetic resonance imaging. Hopefully the scans will throw up some clues on cause of death. And I'll also take photos of the corpse with an infrared digital camera, which should capture any markings." Abernathy reached out for the zip again. "Shall I?"

"I guess there's not much more to reveal."

"Not until the results come back, no." She sealed the bag once more, slipped the body away and shut the door. Out in the corridor Pennance slid back his hood and took off the mask.

"Sinks are this way." Abernathy pointed.

Once they'd removed and disposed of the suits the pair began to scrub up, using a torrent of hot water and plenty of soap. As Abernathy nudged off a tap with her elbow she said, "Look, if you're stuck for something to do one evening, just let me know." She tugged a wedge of paper towels from the dispenser and rubbed her hands with several before holding the remainder out for Pennance. "I can show you the sights, whatever they are."

"That's very kind of you," said Pennance. "Although I'm pretty certain I'm going to be working all hours to get the case finished and then go home."

"Well, keep me in mind." Abernathy dropped the paper towels into a bin before producing a business card from a pocket and offering it. "My mobile is on there."

***

Jansen was speeding up the A14 back north towards Huntingdon before she asked, "How did it go with Doctor Abernathy? Are you two heading out on a date?"

"Nothing like that. She offered to show me around Huntingdon."

"Oh, yeah?" Jansen crooked an eyebrow.

"I'm sure that's not what she intended."

"Did she give you her number?"

"Maybe."

"She did then." Jansen shook her head. "She's enough self-confidence for the three of us."

"That's one way of looking at it."

"You're aware she lives in Saffron Walden?"

"Which means?"

"It's a market town about half an hour south of Cambridge, so she'd have more than an hour's drive to just, 'show you around' Huntingdon."

"Oh."

"Yes, *oh* indeed."

"I've already got a partner."

"So what?"

"I won't be ringing Abernathy anyway."

"Good, that leaves you all to me." Jansen gave Pennance an arch look before she burst out laughing. "You should see your face, Jonah! Such a prude." She slapped the steering wheel a couple of times with an open palm. "Ah, that's going to keep me amused all the way to Huntingdon."

"I'm pleased."

"Anyway, while you were canoodling with Abernathy, I was making some calls. We're on our way to see Zinke and Co. They're the bunch who rented the River Road house. But a brief stop first to meet an ex-gambler who can tell you more about Mercer."

"We weren't 'canoodling'. There was a decomposing corpse and a rather powerful stench between us."

"Sounds like the perfect date for a pathologist."

"Yuck."

"And the more you defend yourself, Jonah, the less I believe you."

Pennance decided silence was the best option, which left Jansen chuckling away for the rest of journey while he stared out of the window, watching the vegetation flash by.

Twenty Four

Jansen parked next to an over-sized chopper motorbike outside the Fenstanton Church Centre, a single-storey block of 1970s architecture adjacent to the much more traditionally built village church.

The inside was rectangular, painted cream walls, a vaulted ceiling and blond varnished floorboards. A low stage at the far end and a kitchen area to one side, obvious through a large hatch cut into the wall.

A man in jeans and a black leather jacket paused stacking metal chairs when Pennance entered. "Mr Ingle?"

"Sorry, mate. You'll have to come back next week, we finished fifteen minutes ago."

Jansen followed. "Hi, Mr Ingle."

"Sergeant, good to see you." Ingle hefted another couple of chairs into the pile. "You could have got here sooner and helped me with this lot." Ingle hiked a thumb at the pile of seats. "The urn is still warm if you want a coffee?" He nodded towards the kitchen.

"Depends how it comes," said Pennance. "I'm a coffee snob."

"That's the best kind of pretentious to be." He led Pennance and Jansen into the windowless galley, a pronounced limp to his gait. The space felt tight, packed with units and cupboards, sink and drainer along with the fridge which hummed noisily, like it needed to be read its last rites, threatening to vibrate off several fridge magnets of tourist traps from around the world – Eiffel Tower, Statue of Liberty, Pyramids of Giza, among others.

Ingle withdrew a French press and three mugs from a cupboard, poured in some grounds – from the branding on the bag the source was supermarket, the one where Elliott had been shot – and added hot water from a large, stainless steel urn. Then Ingle flicked a switch on the wall, turning the urn element off.

"Mr Ingle runs an outreach charity from here," said Jansen.

"Sean is fine," said Ingle. "And we're called 'Don't Bet On It'. Sounded good at the time. We help gambling addicts. I don't do much, just set out the seating three times a week, see who turns up and wants to speak, then put everything away again."

"You're just being modest, Sean. No more trouble with the kids?"

"Not since last time." Ingle faced Pennance. "We had a series of break-ins, Sergeant Jansen helped put a stop to it."

"How do people find you?" asked Pennance.

"When they're not trying to rob me, it's either word of mouth or social media. I've a Facebook page because it's free. I don't have a marketing budget."

"Do many people come along?"

"Varies." Ingle tilted his head. "At least fifteen, sometimes over twenty five." He ladled in a couple of sugar scoops then pushed down on the plunger, poured the coffee into the mugs. "Milk's in the fridge."

"I'll pass," said Pennance.

THE BLUE CODE

Jansen popped the fridge door, leaned in as her phone rang. "Hello, sir. Yes, we're in Fenstanton." Pennance heard no more as Jansen moved away into the hall.

"Do any cops come here?" asked Pennance.

"Some, why?"

"Just interested." Pennance glanced into the hall. Jansen was still talking. "Is Nick Crosse one of them?"

"No, definitely not."

"What about Ed Shapiro?"

"I don't like him."

"Me either."

"He's never passed the threshold and I doubt he ever will."

"But he's a gambler, though?"

"Oh yes. Heavy duty."

"With Mercer?"

"Like almost everybody."

Jansen returned, slipping her phone into a pocket. She nodded at Pennance.

"What about Matt Ferrensby?" asked Pennance.

"Ferrensby was here for the first few weeks," said Ingle. "Probably because my girlfriend at the time is his best friend and to check out what I was doing. He's the kind of guy who was always on the make – the sly, watchful type. I counted the mugs after he left a session. I was glad when he stopped coming. These days I see him occasionally in passing. When we do, we give each other a wide berth."

"When was this?" Pennance drank some of his coffee.

"Just over two years ago. As local healthcare support has been withdrawn, more people have come to us for help."

"It must be frustrating."

"We're all creatures of habit and temptation is constantly placed in our way."

"Sounds rather biblical."

"Sometimes it does feel like holding back a tide and I know that from personal experience."

"Has internet gambling had an effect?" asked Pennance.

"Absolutely. You can throw away money you don't have from the comfort of your armchair these days." Ingle leant back against one of the units, grimacing as he took the weight off a leg.

"What about your own addiction?"

"I manage better than most, probably. Cards were my thing, poker mainly. I was good. Really good. I made decent money. I was in a stable relationship then, nice house I'd bought outright, my girlfriend had plenty of trinkets. It all seemed perfect. Until it wasn't." He drank half his coffee. "You'll have noticed I walk with a limp."

"Yes," said Pennance.

"A few years ago I lost a game, an important game, lots of money riding on it. I'd borrowed from Mercer and was massively in debt to him. This," Ingle hit his hip with the side of his fist, "was my reward for screwing up. I took a bloody good kicking and then some. I ended up in hospital for weeks, barely able to move. I couldn't even get to the toilet. Mercer's men came round my house, demanded payment from my girlfriend. And the bailiffs were on the doorstep, wanting access so they could take my stuff. That's why Lesia dumped me, and I could hardly blame her."

"Sounds like a difficult period," said Jansen.

"That's an understatement. All I could do when laid up in bed was think and reflect. I decided I was done with it all." Ingle drank some of his coffee. "As soon as I was mobile I went to the bank and took out a mortgage on my house. I withdrew the lot as cash, went to Mercer and dumped it on his desk – all the money he'd loaned me, plus a 12% compound interest. I told him I was never coming back, that we were done. Mercer took the bag off his desk, so I limped out of there and never went back."

"That doesn't seem like Mercer," said Jansen. "Once he has you, getting free is impossible."

"That's just the image Mercer cultivates. He assesses the probabilities of everything he does. Are they in his favour, or not? Like giving me that shoeing. I took a measured risk by paying him, but I kept it discrete, said I'd disappear and be no bother. Mercer had all his cash back, and more. What did he have to gain by refusing?"

"The house wins." Pennance's watch vibrated, a message from McAlaney, 'Phone from the hole working. Waiting for you'.

"Always," said Ingle. "The odds are permanently stacked in their favour, that's what I tell my friends who come here every week. No matter how close a big win feels, a much more significant loss is trailing behind. I guarantee it. So yes, I know how Mercer works. He draws people in slowly, until they're in his pocket. He's dangerous, extremely dangerous. And untouchable. I was very fortunate. I tell myself that every time I have the slightest temptation to go back. And my limp is a constant reminder."

"What about Mercer's manager, Ratliffe?"

"Tough woman, totally loyal to her boss, almost as dangerous as he is. Best I can say with her is, watch your back."

Twenty Five

The Digital Forensics team was based a couple of doors along from the Detectives Office in a space with enough room for two desks, both occupied, and two tables, loaded with technical equipment that Pennance had the barest knowledge of, near which McAlaney idly span around in a chair.

Crosse stood beside a man seated at one of the desks, put a hand on his shoulder. "DI Pennance, this is Kim Cairns."

Cairns possessed a mullet and wore a black polo shirt, arms exposed. He nodded at Pennance in greeting. Crosse didn't bother to introduce his female colleague. She briefly glanced their way before returning to her work.

"Cairns has been looking at the mobile found with the burial," said Crosse.

"So have I," said McAlaney.

"Over here." Cairns scooted next to McAlaney at the table of technology where the phone was hooked up. "The device was out of power so I had to get some electrons flowing."

"Show them the call log," said McAlaney, who'd returned to spinning in her chair, a sure sign of boredom.

Cairns scroll down through a short list. "There's quite a few on here. Mainly incoming, and several outgoing."

"Who was he talking to?" asked Crosse.

"They're other burners," said McAlaney. "So at this stage, we don't know."

"The last call was made fifteen days ago," said Cairns.

"Which fits with Abernathy's assessment of approximate time of death," said Pennance.

Cairns wiggled a mouse and a computer monitor came to life.

"Once we got the RIPA authorised," said McAlaney, "we accessed the GPS and triangulated the phone's movements."

Mobile operators were required to keep a record of every call and text for a year. The police had a direct link to the database via a single piece of software supplied by Charter Systems and didn't require a warrant to do so under RIPA – the Regulation of Investigatory Powers Act.

Now Cairns opened a map on-screen. A series of pins of various colours dropped into place, obscuring Huntingdon.

Crosse pulled his half-moon glasses out of a pocket and perched them on the end of his nose. "What the hell is this?"

"All the activity of the numbers to and from the burner. However, when we look at where the actual phone was used and eliminate all other communication, we get instead..." Cairns clicked his mouse, leaving two groupings of red pins. "Activity broadly grouped around two locations. The town centre. And here."

Crosse tiled forward. "Mercer's."

"Right." Cairns nodded then hit the mouse button again. "This is the last movement of the phone." Yellow pins appeared, though tracing a route across Huntingdon. "They run from Mercer's to River Road. Then the phone is powered down, presumably as it ran out of juice."

"Not electrons?" asked McAlaney.

Cairns ignored McAlaney.

"So, we've a connection between Mercer and the murder site," said Crosse.

"Not necessarily," said Pennance. "All we know is the victim travelled between those two points, not with who, or why."

"Mercer is involved." Crosse bunched a fist. "I can feel it in my water."

"We need proof."

"More's the pity."

"There's nothing else visible in the memory," said Cairns. "But we can run a deeper scan, see if anything's been deleted."

"There won't be," said McAlaney. "The handset was used for trading, drugs probably."

"Keep going anyway, maybe there's something we can use," said Crosse. "Good work." Crosse removed his glasses and then patted Cairns on the shoulder.

"What about me?" asked McAlaney.

"Sure," said Crosse.

"Anything from the search of Ferrensby's property, sir?" asked Jansen.

"Just muddy boots. Wherever Ferrensby is, he's well hidden." Crosse pushed his hands into his pockets. "Uniform spoke with Ferrensby's mother earlier but didn't get anything out of her. Ferrensby doted on her and vice versa. If anybody in that family knows anything, she does. Someone could do with having another go." Crosse stood. "Someone who's good at getting stuff out of people, sergeant."

"You flattering me now, sir?" asked Jansen.

Crosse smirked. "Am I that obvious?"

"First we've an appointment with Zinke, the estate agents," said Pennance.

"Get going then," said Crosse. "Find me what I need."

Twenty Six

"We can walk from here," said Jansen as they exited the station. "It'll only take five minutes."

"Fine by me." Pennance felt shorn of exercise. All he'd done for the last 36 hours was sit or stand. Normally he'd be out every day for a run but there'd been little chance of that. "Have you got your car keys?"

"Yes." Jansen pulled them out of a pocket. "Why?"

"Open up, would you, please?"

Jansen did so and Pennance leaned into the back, grabbed the foil-wrapped sandwiches Melody had prepared. Jansen's expression cleared. "Good thinking."

"I try."

"And occasionally succeed."

As Pennance unwrapped the food, Jansen led them across the adjacent road, threading her way between a short row of cars at the end of a cul de sac. Pennance held out the double-decker monsters.

Jansen took half. "You only need one of my aunt's sandwiches. They're always bloody massive."

"Try telling Hoskins that." Pennance lifted his and scrunched up the foil before taking a bite. The bacon was crispy enough to snap between his teeth.

They continued along a narrow street of mainly old buildings, including a small, converted church. After a few hundred yards Jansen headed right onto an equally narrow block paved road, parked cars and shops both sides and meandering pedestrians. "This is the High Street." She still chewed. "All the estate agents are along here. I counted, there are nine."

"Wow." Pennance dropped the wrapper into a nearby bin. "Prime location, I guess?"

"Kinda. As you've seen already, leave the town and you're in fields. Not much for miles around in every direction, remember."

They skirted takeaways, salons, hairdressers, bars – then an estate agent one side of the street, and another almost opposite, neither of which were Zinke and Co. Two women, one pushing a buggy, walked in the opposite direction, chatting in a language Pennance didn't understand.

"Not far now." Jansen led them past the George Hotel, which had once been a coaching inn by the large portico. The High Street swung right but Jansen carried on straight, beyond another church with a large sign declaring it to be St. Mary's. Clearly, Huntingdon had once been a God-fearing town.

The entrance to the office of Zinke and Co. Estate Agents, stood right on the pavement, the old building angled like it was preparing to offer a greeting. Pennance paused outside and scanned the array of houses for sale in the window as he finished the last hunk of the sandwich – some were in the town, others in locations Pennance didn't recognise like Little Catworth, Great Stukeley and Offord Cluny. Several properties had red 'sold' flashes across them – an unsubtle reference to the agents' ability to trade such a prized asset.

A young couple holding hands next to Pennance tapped the glass over a place they were plainly interested in. A cookie cutter starter home on a new-build estate, two bedrooms, small back garden with grass, a fence and some shrubs. Somewhere to move into as a married pair, sizeable enough for a first child before scaling up as the family expanded and the career developed. No thoughts of divorce that afflicted more than 50% of the population. Humans were conditioned to forget failures of the past and ignore potential pitfalls in the future. Until old age crowded in and the road behind far outstretched that ahead.

Pennance shook himself, chasing away his thoughts. "The prices are quite low."

"Compared to what?" asked Jansen.

"London."

"Isn't everywhere?"

"Probably. I've never really had reason to check."

"City boy?"

"Born and bred."

"Live and die?"

"If I'm lucky." A farmhouse with 65 acres of land caught Pennance's attention. He could buy it with the proceeds from his first floor, two bedroom flat and have cash to spare as a pension. Could he imagine sharing all that space with just one person? Keeping all the world's troubles at the fence and leaving someone else to solve them?

Pennance had never considered himself capable of living with anyone but himself, never mind sharing a child. Recently he'd got himself a pet; Lars, the iguana. Even that commitment to keeping another being alive sometimes felt like a stretch. He hadn't thought any person could fit into the jigsaw that was his life. Until Simone.

"Anything take your fancy?" Jansen watched the couple walk away, arm in arm.

"Not really."

"Inside then?"

"Crumbs." Pennance pointed, and Jansen glanced down at her chest before brushing off the offending particles. Jansen's personal grooming complete, Pennance pushed on the door, causing a brass bell fixed on the jamb to jangle. He held it open for Jansen. "After you."

"Thank you, kind sir." Jansen performed a diminutive bow.

They entered a low-ceilinged sales office, smaller in floor space than Pennance's bedroom at Melody's. More house-for-sale notices affixed to bare brick walls, front-lit by slightly too powerful LEDs, the glare reflecting back off the protective plastic sheeting. The bell was total overkill because no-one here could fail to be aware of incoming customers, and it rang again when Pennance allowed the door to drop shut of its own accord.

Two desks sat at ninety degrees to the entrance, the nearest positioned just feet away. It would receive a blast of frigid, bitter air in the winter, sultry, vaporous air in the summer and everything else in between. This was the junior's position, the one who had to prove themselves.

The more senior staff member, presumably the supervisor, would have the desk positioned further away from the vagaries of the weather, while beyond at the rear and up a couple of steps lay a separate section with one, much larger desk facing a window, where the manager, or perhaps even the great Zinke himself, would reside.

THE BLUE CODE

This was a structure repeated in offices and businesses all over the world for generations past; power positioned above the lower ranks. The police were no different – Pennance was forced to go up several floors at NCA HQ if he wanted to see Meacham face-to-face and it was the same for Meacham with Quant.

"Morning, sir, madam." The lad occupying the lowest echelon put down his phone and half rose out of his seat. By the acne-ravaged cheeks, spiky hair and peach fuzz on his top lip Pennance guessed he was barely out of school and would probably prefer to be scudding around the market square with the skateboarders.

A woman at the adjacent desk, a thirty-something brunette in a smart trouser suit, nodded and smiled at Pennance. Rather than return to her PC she leaned back in her chair, observing goings-on, though making no move to become involved herself.

"I'm DS Jansen." She flashed her warrant card. "And this is DI Pennance." He held out his ID, too. "I called earlier, we're here to see Mr Zinke."

"Oh, that's me," said the lad. "I'm Zack."

Pennance blinked. "Zack Zinke?"

"Correctamundo."

Pennance glanced over at the woman. She remained focused on Zack, expression bland, like Pennance and Jansen weren't present.

"We're enquiring about one of your properties," said Jansen. "On River Road in Brampton where an incident occurred yesterday."

"Incident?" Zack's lips widened into an O as he considered what that might mean. Meanwhile, the woman turned to her PC and was tapping away at the keys.

"It's probably best I take over this conversation." A dapper gent poised on the steps leading to the upper office section, steaming cup of coffee in hand. He wore suit trousers, shirt with cufflinks, open at the neck without a tie, and red braces. "Zack's my son, he's a trainee. His mother thought it was a good idea." Zinke Senior raised an eyebrow to infer he didn't agree, and Zack may be dangling on the short rope of unemployment soon enough, legs kicking. Zack waved like he was on holiday before returning his focus to his mobile. "I'm Adam Zinke. Come on up." Zinke shifted sideways, held out an arm, Pennance and Jansen important enough to be allowed into the sanctum.

Zinke patted the back of a chair, one of a pair angled towards each other and fronting his large, oak bureau. "Take a pew." Pennance sat while Zinke lowered himself into a leather executive seat. The woman efficiently trotted up the steps, heels clacking, before placing a file on Zinke's desk.

"Thanks, Elaine. Do you want a drink, by the way?" Zinke indicating Pennance and Jansen in turn. "We've a proper bean to cup machine."

"It's Columbian at the moment," said Elaine.

Zinke raised his mug. "Rather good, too. Roasted locally."

"Great, thanks," said Pennance. His typical coffee intake was at least five cups in the morning and he was well below a happy medium and feeling it. "Just black, if that's okay?"

"Of course," said Elaine. "And for you, Sergeant?"

THE BLUE CODE

"Have you got a peppermint tea?" asked Jansen.

"We've everything these days." Elaine delivered Jansen a thin smile. "I'll be back momentarily." She retreated.

Zinke opened a drawer, pulled out a pack of gum, withdrew a strip. "Nicotine based, better than reaching for a cigarette."

"Anti-stress?" asked Pennance.

"Tension, strain, and several other synonyms I can think of. Divorce, running your own business, bills to pay, employees to support and so on." Zinke glanced down at his son then back to the detectives before he tossed a piece into his mouth and got rampantly chewing. "I founded the company more than three decades ago, before I met his mother." Zinke tipped his head at Zack. "Ran it out of a bedroom. Before then I worked for another agent, got to know how everything ticked, figured I could do it better and I was right. After a couple of years, I was managing well enough, gradually opened more offices, right up to the credit crunch in 2008. That hit me hard."

"Drop off in sales?"

"Stroke. Mainly brought on by pressure. On doctor's orders I slowed right down. I'd already made more money than I could spend, so I took us back to two offices. One for residential," Zinke opened his arms wide. "The other for commercial; offices, shops, agricultural and the like, based in St. Ives. Zack's been working over there recently. It's better that way."

"What, dad?" shouted Zack up the steps, not taking his attention off his phone.

"It's Mr Zinke when we're at work, remember."

"Oh, yeah. Sorry, dad."

"He isn't the brightest." Zinke spoke in a lowered his voice. "Takes after his mother."

"Decent hearing, though."

"Gets that from her, too. I learnt the habit of speaking quietly, or not at all." Zinke bared his teeth. "For house sales we tend to focus on the middle to top end of the market in terms of quality. Superior properties sell themselves."

"What about rentals?"

Zinke rested on his elbows. "Now, that's a different prospect. There I'm intensely choosy; I only take on top-notch stock with high rates on long-term contracts. I earn a percentage, so I want that to be as strong as possible. Others can wade around in the 'crappy end' of the market, with DSS claimants and the like that you never know are going to pay from one month to the next. My first boss, that's what he still does." Zinke hiked a thumb back in the direction of the police station. "He's down the road from here." They'd probably walked right past.

Elaine returned then with three cups on a tray. She reached to put an espresso in front of Zinke but he raised his hand. "Guests first." So instead Pennance got his coffee, followed by Jansen's peppermint, and finally Zinke's. "Thanks." Elaine leaned against the wall, all the chairs taken. "You mentioned a property on River Road?" Zinke opened the file and glanced over the contents, raising his nose like he was a short sighted bird hunting for seeds.

"Two bodies were discovered at the house. One inside, one buried on the garden."

THE BLUE CODE

Zinke's eyes flicked up from the folder. "Good gravy." He reached for the gum packet and shook out another piece before adding a second and tossing both into his mouth. "I wasn't aware."

"Nobody from the station called?"

"Not until you did, no."

Zinke closed the folder, sat back and steepled his fingers, chewing vigorously, his jaw muscles flexing. "River Road is currently not on the market."

"Yet someone was staying there," said Jansen. "We found at least one bed had been slept in."

"Then they must have broken in."

"There's an alarm on the property and plenty of locks. It's not exactly what I'd call low security. And we didn't find any evidence of forced entry."

"That's very odd."

"Do you recognise this man?" Jansen held out her phone, a mug shot of Draganov on-screen.

Zinke wrinkled his nose as he focused. "No, definitely not."

Jansen showed Elaine next who shook her head.

"Who is he?" asked Zinke.

"One of the people found dead at River Road."

"How long has the property been off the market?" asked Pennance. Zinke didn't answer. He seemed to have zoned out. "Mr Zinke?"

"Sorry, coming up for three months."

"Is that unusual?"

"Not particularly with the higher-end properties. And we receive a management fee from the owner regardless of whether the house is occupied or not. We win regardless."

"Someone was interested in taking the place." Elaine chipping in. "But the owner declined to rent."

"That's right. I remember now." Zinke snapped his fingers. "The old brain box isn't what it was. A married couple, professionals, were keen."

"Simon and Sandra Carnforth," said Elaine. "They knew exactly what house they wanted, gave me the address and offered to pay up-front for the full year long term. Including three months' rent as a deposit, we'd have picked up £18,000."

"Very nice," said Jansen.

"Absolutely, except we couldn't take it."

"No, no, no, quite right," said Zinke.

"How so?" asked Pennance.

"The client must physically see the property and only then sign the contract to declare acceptance in case of future disagreements. Avoiding buyer's remorse, so to speak, or just side-stepping a con – they complain about something, like poor decoration, and then refuse to pay anything until we go to court. Months of lost income."

"So, I drove the Carnforths over and showed them around," said Elaine. "They spent half an hour inside, giving each room a good going over, and the garden. They even went back for a second look while I waited outside."

"And the payment?" asked Pennance.

"£18,000 in cash raises all sorts of questions these days, Inspector," said Zinke. "Anti-money laundering, et cetera.

THE BLUE CODE

I was perfectly happy to have all the fees, just transferred electronically. Every agent would take the same view. Even my old boss."

"Then, despite all that, the owner decided to take a pass and said no to the Carnforths," said Elaine.

"It happens sometimes," said Zinke.

"All the information on previous occupiers is in the file," said Elaine. "Along with the ownership."

Zinke pushed the file over to Pennance. "I've been doing this for nearing four decades. Not much I haven't seen. Lots I've been burnt over. I'm sure it's the case for you, too."

Pennance almost said then that he wasn't quite that old.

***

Once they were on the pavement and fifty yards away Jansen looked up from her phone and said, "Text from Crosse. He's holding a case review soon as we return."

"And who are we to argue?" Pennance fell into step beside her. "What did you think of Zinke?"

"Seemed like a straight shooter to me," said Jansen. Pennance pulled a face so Jansen asked, "What did I say?"

"Americanisms."

"Not a fan?"

Pennance thought of Simone's ex-husband. "No."

"Alright, he came over as honest. A self-made man not willing to take risks for a bit of cash he doesn't need."

"I agree. What about the son?"

"Seems more like a chip off someone else's block. I'm not sure he'll be what his father may want."

"Somewhat like Shapiro with Crosse, then?"

"My lips are sealed," said Jansen as she lengthened her stride.

Twenty Seven

As they entered the station Pennance said, "I'm going to drop in and see my team first."

"Crosse said to come straight back," said Jansen.

Pennance shrugged. "He can wait."

"But –."

"Sometimes you need do things your own way, Keri." He shouldered through into the temporary office.

"Vance, can you handle this for me." Pennance tossed the folder Zinke had given him onto the desk. Hoskins snagged the file and started looking through the documents. "It's the rental details and ownership of the property on River Road. Have a chat with Alasdair Tremayne."

"The forensic accountant? Sure."

"What about Crosse?" asked Jansen. "He'll need to see it, too."

"I trust Vance to get to the bottom of the data faster than anyone," said Pennance.

"Even me?" said McAlaney.

"If the cap fits, Ava," said Hoskins. "I'll take a copy, then give pass it onto Shapiro or Crosse."

"Thanks." Pennance turned to McAlaney. "After the case review with Crosse we're going to see Naughton at Obsidian. I'll need you with me. I suspect I won't have a clue what he's saying."

"I'll be here, idly awaiting you," said McAlaney.

Back in the corridor Jansen said, "I'm not sure you should be keeping things from the SIO."

"I'm not," said Pennance. "There will just be a short delay." He paused outside the Detectives Office. "Do you trust me?"

"We barely know each other." Jansen glanced at her shoes. "But, yes, I do."

When a significant case was underway a Major Incident Room always reminded Pennance of a beehive, a hub of seemingly random activity with everyone centred on the queen – the senior investigating officer. The movement of people in the room would seem random and chaotic to the inexperienced, but the reality was a pattern of focused activity. Drones would leave the hive, collect information like pollen and bring it back to the nest to be turned into analytical honey.

The Elliott investigation continued to be very different. The whiteboard over on the office wall had a couple of additional hand-written squiggles in marker pen, definitely a new photo of Draganov and the corpse in the hole. Other than a single ringing phone, the office was remarkably peaceful.

Beehive, this was not and bees, they were becalmed.

"Where the bloody hell have you been?" Crosse held onto the open door with one hand, beckoning Pennance and Jansen across the library-like office with the other. "Come on, chop, bloody chop!" As Pennance approached, Crosse let go, forcing Pennance to lurch forward and grab the door. He let Jansen in first before entering the meeting room himself.

Shapiro was already settled, TV remote in one sagging hand, elbow resting on the table above a laptop and nearby notepad, his arm and shoulder forming an approximation of the square root mathematical symbol. Beyond Shapiro sat Thriplow.

The screen fixed to the wall displayed Abernathy and a bespectacled man with a buzzcut and wideset eyes who Pennance didn't recognise. Both were joining via video conference from different locations by the look of it. The pathologist waved, but said nothing, her background a shelf of academic books. Buzzcut guy, squinting at the screen and typing right now, wore a large pair of headphones like an air traffic controller.

Crosse took his chair at the far end, leaving Pennance and Jansen the places nearest the frosted glass dividing meeting room from the Detectives Office. Pennance shuffled around until he faced the television.

"Ready, Inspector?" asked Crosse.

"I am now," replied Pennance.

"Right." Crosse cracked his fingers, the sound like snapping dry twigs. "An initial analysis on the bullets and cartridges found at the scene has been carried out, and Dr Hewson is here to outline his findings." On-screen buzzcut guy raised a hand in greeting. Crosse continued, "And Dr Abernathy is present to update us following the PM on Elliott and the unidentified burial. First, over to you, Dr Hewson. Perhaps you can introduce yourself, then take us through your findings."

Hewson began talking, but no sound came out of the speakers.

"You're on mute," said Shapiro.

Hewson reached an arm out, pressed a button off-screen, asked, "Is that better?"

"Fine," said Crosse.

"I should know better by now, been long enough making calls like this." He chuckled. "Anyway, as DCI Crosse mentioned, I'm Dr Huw Hewson of the National Ballistics Intelligence Service. We're headquartered in Birmingham with forty staff in the team which includes four regional forensic hubs. Here at NABIS, we gather intelligence on the criminal use of firearms, which we share with police forces across the country. As for me, I'm an expert in ballistics with a specialisation in military weapons. I'll just take control, if I may."

"Be my guest," said Crosse.

Hewson squinted, focusing on his own computer screen. Moments later photos of a shiny brass cartridge and a squashed bullet filled the television.

"What you see here is a sample of the munitions recovered from the scene. NABIS maintains a directory, called the Integrated Ballistic Identification System, which records photographs and data on every recovered weapon, cartridge or bullet fired in every case since 2008. Weapons manufacture is a high-volume production process, yet every gun which comes off the line is slightly different at a microscopic level. These flaws provide all bullets fired with a distinct imprint, meaning we can track a specific gun's use and link cases together. This data is what we store on IBIS. The catalogue has an automatic search tool which narrows down the options and then I or a technician spend our time visually inspecting each cartridge."

THE BLUE CODE

"Like our fingerprint database," said Pennance.

"Quite."

"Easy then." Shapiro shrugged. "Run the evaluation, find your weapon."

"Almost, but alas, no. Each bullet basically tells an experienced analyst what it's been up to. Where it's been, what it's done – in today's terms it's like a blog."

"Nobody writes blogs anymore," said Shapiro.

"It's an analogy," said Pennance.

"Carry on, doctor," said Crosse.

"Take the base of the cartridge." Hewson flipped the image on screen to an end-on shot, a shiny metal yellow circle with letters stamped around the circumference. "This reveals the shape of the firing pin and the pressure applied. From the bullet itself." The screen was now filled by a dark grey with spiral lines of a lighter colour cutting through. "The sides outline the barrel rifling – also known as spiral lines or striae. Rifling design dates from 1498 – they're rotating grooves cut into the barrel interior and cause the bullet to spin, improving the directionality and therefore accuracy. As the slug passes down the barrel under extreme heat and pressure, what we define as 'setback deformation' occurs, resulting from minor imperfections in the rifling or tool marks. And we can potentially extract material from the nose which can tell us what it passed through – clothes, flesh, wood, and so on."

"Very interesting, Dr Hewson. But what about our weapon used on Elliott?" asked Crosse.

"It's an assault rifle, specifically a Russian-made Kalashnikov AK-74M, an updated version of the more well-known AK-47." Hewson put photos of two similar looking guns up. Long barrels with a wooden handguard for the shooter to grip, a butt, curved in a wide inverted C shape to fit into the shoulder, and a magazine in front of the trigger. "The AK-74 is above, the AK-47 below. The original AK-74 design halted in production in 1991, although the M- variant is still manufactured today in high volume. It weighs approximately 3kg, is 94.3cm in length and takes either a 20 or 30 cartridge magazine. In the US they're classified as pistols for legal reasons because of their similar caliber.

"Assault weapons are selective fire rifles first produced in quantity during the Second World War, starting with the German StG 44. They're effectively a lightweight variant of the heavier and less accurate sub-machine gun. They may be set to fire automatically or semi-automatically, which means the design uses the recoil generated by the previously discharged cartridge to eject the empty case, load the next live round, and cock the hammer without the intervention of the handler. As a result, cartridge cases are expelled with considerable force, so they're usually always left behind at a scene. Also of note, armaments like these are more expensive and not so commonly used."

"The average scally on the street can't get their hands on one?" said Crosse.

"Highly unlikely, so, typically, they're handled by the larger Organised Crime Groups," said Hewson. "The gun operation forces some design comprises in terms of size, shape and material. First, the cartridge." Hewson returned to the photo of the shell on its own – a long cylinder with a point at the top, like a rocket. "Which comprises a case, primer, propellant, and bullet." Hewson circled the point at the very top for the latter. "The case is made of brass. During discharge the metal expands with the heat, so occluding the barrel and stopping gases escaping, which would reduce the effectiveness of the gun or cause dangerous blowback. The most effective construct is a bottleneck, making the cartridge shorter and fatter, allowing for higher quantities of powder to be packed in."

Hewson flipped to the end-on shot once more. "The lettering is termed a head stamp which details the manufacturer's origin. In order to cause the explosion, a firing pin in the rifle strikes the primer which is described as rim or centrefire depending on the location. In this case we have a centrefire." Hewson indicated a dark circle in the middle.

"As for the bullet itself, lead is technically the best material due to its high density and low cost, but it easily softens and smears the barrel interior which affects performance, so typically lead is alloyed with other materials or jacketed with a harder metal, such as copper. Most bullet names have little to do with physical measurements. The .30-06 results from it being developed in 1906. .357, .38 special and 9mm all essentially have the same diameter. The AK-74 itself uses a 5.45 x 39mm cartridge which is steel cased." Another image on screen – this time the shell was a darker, dull colour.

"Where's this going?" asked Shapiro. "It's like being in a lecture."

"There is a point to all of my information," said Hewson.

"Let him talk," said Crosse. "I'm finding it interesting."

Shapiro started spinning a pen around his thumb.

Hewson said, "Lead actually contains up to 26 common elements. Different material types are used by the various bullet manufacturers. We can assess the composition – the type and quantity of the constituents – by a rubeanic acid test which detects copper and nickel. Therefore, I can tell you that the ordinance used to murder Mr Elliott was manufactured in Belarus."

"Does that matter?" asked Pennance.

"To this case, perhaps not," said Hewson. "But when tracing the routes of illegal weapon imports and arresting the perpetrators, it certainly does."

"So," said Crosse, "we know it's a Russian-made weapon, with Eastern European bullets, and handled by an Eastern European hitman, right?"

"In this particular event, that's correct," said Hewson. "Your CSI team recovered two bullets from the scene and Dr Abernathy couriered me the rest subsequently extracted from the corpse. This is they." Hewson put photos of several lumps of misshapen metal on-screen. "Deformation in shape doesn't occur until the impact velocity is over 800 feet per second. At 800 – 100 fps a slight flattening of the nose results. Over 1,000 is when you get the kind of appearance you see on-screen. Also, at these speeds, the copper jacket tends to separate and is found elsewhere in the body. A velocity of 163 fps is needed to break skin, 213 fps and above to break bone. I'd prefer a test firing of the weapon itself, however from the data I've generated I can be confident in stating that this particular AK-74M has been used in the murder of five other people, from London to Liverpool to Dundee."

"And now Huntingdon," said Crosse.

"Meaning Draganov is a serial killer," said Jansen.

"The assault rifle certainly is," said Hewson. "Though not necessarily Draganov himself. The gun could be rented out for a particular hit, returned, and then handled by someone else in the next crime. Equally, it could belong to Draganov and he's simply used it on multiple jobs. Either way, we want this weapon off the streets."

"For damn sure," said Crosse. "When we find it. Good work, doctor. Is there anything else?"

"Dr Abernathy and I have already conferred on her findings from the Elliott autopsy," said Hewson. "So, I'll comment when necessary as she proceeds and relinquish control to her now." The images of the battered bullet disappeared, briefly replaced with the Cambridgeshire police logo until it in turn was substituted by a photo of a bloodied Elliott, lying prostrate on the back seat of the Mercedes.

"This is the position of Mr Elliott's corpse when I arrived on the scene," said Abernathy. "Following your departure yesterday I carried out a post-mortem on his body in order to determine cause of death."

"It's totally obvious, isn't it?" said Shapiro. "He was shot."

Abernathy ignored the interruption. "First, an external review revealed thirteen entrance wounds between the neck and the thigh. I also counted eleven exit wounds and during the procedure I was able to find the two projectiles within Mr Elliott and these are what I sent to Dr Hewson."

"If you remember the bullet blog reference I made earlier," said Hewson. "I discovered a microscopic piece of cotton from Elliott's shirt in the tip where the projectile punched a wad of the clothing into the body. However, there's also the weapon design itself. Ballistics refers to the science of a projectile in flight, from the moment it's fired until it impacts the target. Controlled expansion of gases from burning gunpowder generates pressure – energy transmitted to the bullet – mass multiplied by force multiplied by time. The time is determined by the length of barrel up to a certain point when the forces begin to oppose each other and speed decreases. Bluntly, the longer the barrel the more the energy imparted as the expanding gases have further to push the bullet and speed it up. The shorter barrel and cartridge design of compromises mean the wounds from an assault rifle are less severe than those from say, hunting rifles."

"They'll still kill you, though," said Jansen.

"Under the wrong circumstances, absolutely."

"The exit wounds on Mr Elliott," said Abernathy, "were in his back, forearms and shoulder."

"He held his arms up as a reflex to protect himself?" asked Pennance.

"It would fit with the evidence," said Abernathy. "Now, wounds resulting from very close or actual contact of the weapon typically display marks from the discharge such as a muzzle imprint if the gun was right up against the person when it was fired and a soot mark on the skin, like a dark ring. The force of the exhaust gases also causes laceration. However, none of these elements were visible on Mr Elliott."

"Witness reports put the shooter several feet away," said Crosse.

"Which concurs with my observation and I've consequently classified the firing range as intermediate," said Abernathy.

"Noted," said Crosse.

"Prior to the post-mortem I had Mr Elliott's body analysed via Standard and Multiple Detector Computed Topographic scanners. By taking images in planar slices that are then combined we're able to build up a 3D internal image of the bullet's path and its impact on internal organs."

Abernathy put on screen what seemed a cartoon-rendered photo of a body.

"We'll ignore the limb damage for now, as these are largely superficial and not life threatening, and concentrate on the torso instead. The channel created through a body by a passing projectile is a permanent void, lined by crushed cells and tissue, next to which is an area called a temporary cavity, where the pressure wave from the bullet's passage stretches and shears the tissue. Think of a canal being dug – a straight line of destruction and the waste piled up either side.

"Next, the type of tissue and its properties, specific gravity and elasticity in particular, affects wounding potential and depth of penetration. The more elastic the person's skin, the less visible damage the entry wound creates. A higher specific gravity means greater injury. So, measuring the dimension of an entry wound is not a reliable guide to the bullet calibre."

"Why are things never simple?" asked Crosse.

Abernathy zoomed in on Elliott's CT scan, the perspective dropping through the dead man's digital shell, before pausing.

"This is what I term Entry Wound Seven in my PM report. The bullet proceeded downwards at a shallow angle, clipping the fourth rib, which deflected the path, as you can see, before transiting the lung and striking the spine. Ultimately it remained in the body and was sent to Dr Hewson."

"The injury pattern of a bullet is called terminal ballistics." Hewson stepped in. "An intact slug that comes to rest in tissue generally aligns along the track which is what we see here. Short, high velocity bullets yaw more severely upon entering tissue, causing more destruction."

"Lung tissue exhibits a low density with high elasticity," said Abernathy. "So, the bullet travelled through with minimal disruption. In comparison the liver, spleen and brain can be very easily impaired. Fluid filled organs, bladder, heart, bowel etc., burst simply due to the pressure waves generated in the body by the passage of the bullet nearby – the projectile doesn't even need to physically touch the organ. Like this." Abernathy moved the scan again, zipping through the body. "Where Mr Elliott's bowel is effectively flattened, like a burst balloon. Yet here." More movement, to the right arm. "We observe a path through the muscle with little residual damage. I could show you more of these, but it's largely repetitive; varying degrees of trauma resulting from gunshot wounds.

THE BLUE CODE

"In terms of the timeline – Mr Elliott was shot while upright, arms out to protect himself, before he fell back onto the seat, his head resting against the door. The gunman carried on firing as Mr Elliott was moving backwards, causing the shoulder wound and punching the holes in the door."

"Again, witnesses describe one, long burst from Draganov," said Crosse.

"Mr Elliott's left leg, bent at the knee, and left arm both hung in the footwell. Cause of death was a disruption of the heart; he basically bled to death."

"Very comprehensive, doctor," said Crosse.

"I have a report prepared which I'll send straight after this call ends."

"Thank you."

"I'd like to also take some time to discuss the body in the hole."

"Sure, we'll stay on the line."

"Before you do, can I have a moment to give you some information on the pistol found near to Draganov?" asked Hewson.

"Go ahead," said Crosse.

"The handgun is a PM, known as a Makarov, a standard Soviet military semi-automatic service sidearm." Hewson flicked a photo on-screen of a short, stubby barrelled black metal weapon with a brown handgrip. "It was issued to NCOs, police and tank and air crews. Although replaced by the PYa in 2003 there are still high numbers of them circulating in Russia and former Soviet states.

"I test fired the pistol myself, it's relatively heavy because of the blowback design, then analysed the spent shells. They're a .380 cartridge. I can tell you that the handgun has not been used in any other shootings. At least not in the UK. So this is a dead end, unfortunately. However, at least it's another weapon off the streets."

"Is that everything?" asked Crosse.

"If you don't need me for anything else, I'll depart," said Hewson.

"No, we're done, Doctor Hewson." Crosse nodded. "Thank you very much, most helpful."

"You're welcome." Hewson gave a brief wave, then he was gone and Abernathy alone occupied the screen.

"Alright." The pathologist focused her vision elsewhere for a moment before she clicked and a scan image came up on screen, a two-dimensional, greyscale photo of a squashed circle marked by a thin white line inside which were several black or white shapes.

"I need to complete my evaluation, but I felt letting you have this information as early as possible might help. After you all departed I had Magnetic Resonance Imaging and Computed Tomography scans performed on the unidentified burial. An MRI is basically a very large tube with a circular magnet around the outside which directs radio waves at the target. In comparison, CT uses X-rays. This, I believe, displays the probable cause of death."

"What are we seeing?" asked Pennance.

"It's a section of the skull and neck. Here," Abernathy moved the mouse arrow around a semi-circle at the top of the photo, "is the victim's jaw. And in the centre," another mouse move over what seemed like an inverted U, "is the hyoid bone. It should be one continuous structure, but it isn't." One side of the U stuck out at an angle.

"He was strangled," said Crosse.

"Not necessarily." Abernathy shook her head. "The damage indicates a pressure to the neck."

"It's obviously murder," said Shapiro.

"Why?" asked Abernathy.

"Duh, because he was found in a hole!"

"The interment was to conceal the body," said Pennance.

"Correct," said Abernathy. "For example, the victim may have committed suicide, say placing a rope around his neck which led to the broken hyoid. Then somebody else put them in the ground – which is not a murder."

"Can you tell if it was self-inflicted?"

"Given the decomposition of the corpse, the tell-tale signs like ligature marks aren't visible."

"Well, fuck-a-doodle-dandy." Shapiro lifted his eyes up to the ceiling.

"I also carried out other analyses." Abernathy seemed unaffected by Shapiro. "Inspector Pennance pointed out some colourations on the victim's arms that he thought were tattoos. It turns out, he was correct."

Several images came up on screen of what seemed to be mixed-up artist's colour palette. "The quality isn't great, I'm afraid."

"Is that a bird?" asked Pennance.

"An eagle I'd guess." Jansen stood, walked over to the screen and leaned in. She pointed at some letters. "Does that say Brenda?"

"You've better eyesight than me," said Crosse. "What do you think, Ed?"

Shapiro frowned, then peered at the screen. "What the –."

"Is there something?" asked Crosse. "Do you recognise the image?"

Shapiro blinked, glanced at Crosse with wide eyes before his eyebrows dipped deeply. "How the hell are we supposed to learn anything from this kind of information, Nick?" Shapiro waved an arm towards the photos.

"The doctor's doing her best, I'm sure," said Crosse.

"It's fucking useless!" snapped Shapiro.

"Thanks for the vote of confidence, Inspector," said Abernathy.

"Well, come on! The hyoid scan was great, but a pathetic swirl? We're trying to solve a murder here, not look at some kid's dot-to-dot scribble. This is a total waste of time. There's a proper investigation to get on with."

"Doctor?" asked Crosse.

"I was going to say before Inspector Shapiro went up like a firework – there are several other methods to evaluate both the design and the type of pigment used including X-ray fluorescence spectroscopy, attenuated total reflectance-Fourier transform infrared (ATR-FTIR) spectroscopy, and scanning electron microscopy-energy dispersive spectroscopy (SEM-EDS). However, I don't have these facilities at the hospital and would need to send them to an external laboratory. May I go ahead, Chief Inspector?"

"Seriously, Nick," said Shapiro. "Why bother?"

"Will it help ID the victim?" asked Pennance.

"Probably," said Abernathy.

"I bet it costs," said Shapiro. "A hell of a lot, right?"

"That's why I'm asking."

"Do we have the budget to pursue potential fantasies?"

"It could be valuable."

"How certain are you this will lead to meaningful information?" asked Crosse.

"Thirty to forty per cent," said Abernathy.

"There you go!" Shapiro threw his arms up in the air. "The definition of an utterly wild goose chase."

"I'll have to discuss it with Malik," said Crosse. "That's the best I can do."

"Understood," said Abernathy. "If you don't need me any longer?"

"No, I –," said Crosse, but Abernathy was gone well before he finished, cutting the connection. "Nice one, Ed."

"We shouldn't be having to deal with half-formed theories, Nick," said Shapiro. "Abernathy was well out of order."

"She's trying to help," said Jansen.

"Who asked you, pancake?" Shapiro rounded on Jansen. "You should leave the proper detecting to the men who know what they're doing."

Pennance slapped an open palm onto the table. "Shut up, both of you!" The pair stopped, turned to Pennance. "We're trying to solve a murder here and your constant digs at Jansen don't help anyone, Shapiro."

"What the hell has it got to do with you?" Shapiro's face twisted into a snarl. "I've about had enough of you sticking your nose in where it doesn't belong." His hands closed into fists.

Crosse leapt to his feet, body blocking Shapiro. "Calm down, Ed!"

"I'm trying to help," said Pennance. "Believe you me, I'll happily leave as soon as I can."

"There's the door," Shapiro pointed, leaning past Crosse.

"Pennance isn't going anywhere for now," said Crosse. "He's right."

Shapiro stood nose to nose with Crosse. "So, you're on his side now, Nick?"

"I didn't say that."

"What happened to 'We're both in this together'?"

"We are. Nothing's changed."

"Yeah, course." Shapiro snorted. "Your ambition's still as big as ever. I need a smoke." He left, slamming the door open into the wall.

Crosse wiped a hand across his face.

"Is that normal for him?" asked Pennance.

"Surprisingly, no," said Jansen.

Crosse stood. "I'll have a word and get him back on track."

"Good luck with that," said Pennance.

Once the door closed behind Crosse, Pennance said, "I don't know how you take all that crap from him."

Jansen lifted her shoulders. "Just part of being a woman in a man's domain. If I launched at every little slight, I'd go mad. Is it any different at the NCA?"

Pennance considered that for a moment. "Probably not."

"There you go."

THE BLUE CODE

"Where will Crosse and Shapiro talk?"

"Outside, at the hut, I reckon. Where all the nicotine addicts huddle."

"Can I see?"

"Sure."

Jansen led Pennance through the office, then up a set of stairs. On the landing, windows overlooked the car park. Crosse and Shapiro stood either side of a bus shelter, a man in a short-sleeved shirt between. Shapiro sucked furiously on his cancer stick, shoulders hunched.

Soon the gooseberry in the middle left and Crosse, e-cig in his fist, closed in on the DI, waving his arms like a banshee. Shapiro took the blast, arms crossed.

"Shapiro will be miserable after this," said Jansen. "Frankly that's when I prefer him. It's when he's happy that's he's the worst because he'll have had a win on the horses. Shapiro thinks he's bulletproof and behaves like a dick. Until the next race. All in one long, repetitive cycle."

"Shapiro has bad luck, then?" asked Pennance.

"Bad judgement, more like." Jansen scowled. "You said I should do something about Shapiro's attitude. Well I did, once. I reported him to Crosse."

Crosse now lit an actual cigarette.

Jansen said, "Crosse told Shapiro and since then all Shapiro has done is niggle away at me. That reference to me and him sleeping together?"

"I don't remember," lied Pennance.

"Never happened. It's just Shapiro, pushing away. That's why I don't react anymore. The job's hard enough as it is."

"I'm surprised at Crosse."

"The DCI is a half-decent guy and reasonably capable, but he needs results to keep the Super off his back. This case, it's bigger than anything Crosse has investigated, I'd bet. Shapiro produces, so the rest of us just have to live with the DI and all his idiosyncrasies. One rule for Shapiro, another for everyone else." She faced Pennance. "And to answer your earlier question; Shapiro is rarely this bad. Something's got into him."

Crosse patted Shapiro on the arm. Shapiro pulled away.

"Did you see that?" asked Pennance.

"What?" Jansen returned her attention out the window.

Crosse's phone must have rung because he dug around in a pocket and raised the handset to his ear. Shapiro, out of Crosse's eye line, left the smoker's paradise and took the long way back to the station, disappearing out of sight beneath Pennance and Jansen.

"Shapiro's slipping away," said Jansen. "Crosse won't be happy."

Done with the call, Crosse glanced up, obviously expecting to continue with his sergeant, and performed a double take. He stepped out of the shelter, realised Shapiro had gone, and threw his hands up in the air.

"The tattoos," said Pennance. "They set Shapiro off."

"What makes you think so?"

"Because he recognised one or more of the patterns. He wasn't bothered until then. He pushed Crosse hard to not take up any further analysis and won."

"So, he could be aware who the burial victim is?"

"Maybe."

"Why not say something?"

"You know him better than me. What do you reckon?"

"I've genuinely no idea. This is extreme, even for Shapiro."

"Then we'll have to find out. We need that analysis done."

"I doubt Crosse will even call Malik to discuss the tests. Crosse isn't exactly a risk taker."

"Maybe I can do something about that." Pennance found Abernathy's business card, dialled her number, watched closely by Jansen.

When Abernathy answered, Pennance said, "You stated in your presentation that there were several methods of determining the tattoos on the burial victim?"

"That's right."

"Have you sent off for the testing yet?"

"Yes, but I was about to call the lab to cancel. I've worked with DCI Crosse long enough to know it's pointless waiting for him."

"Forget about that. Start the process. The NCA will pick up the tab."

"Oh, okay. If you're sure?"

"Absolutely. I'll get you the budget details shortly from my boss."

"I'm on it, thank you, Jonah!" Abernathy rang off.

"Done," said Pennance.

"Crosse will be pissed," said Jansen.

"He won't when his Super is patting him on the back for making an ID." He speed-dialled Meacham's number.

"It's your funeral. 'Til then let's go and see a man about some data." Jansen shoved a hand in a pocket before withdrawing, car keys dangling between fingers. "We'll take my car."

"Again?"

"You love it."

"I definitely wouldn't put it that way. We need McAlaney, too," said Pennance. Meacham answered. "Hello, ma'am. I need your sign off on something. It's probably going to be expensive."

Twenty Eight

The PA showed Pennance, McAlaney and Jansen into Naughton's office, which was more than three times the size of the space Pennance shared with Hoskins and two other detectives at the NCA. Naughton, in jeans and a company-branded polo shirt, the logo a large 'O', emerged from a standing desk and six monitors.

Large windows delivered a view over flat fields. In fact the whole building, a purpose-built facility on Ermine Street just north of Huntingdon, was clad in glass, inside and out, absorbing light like a dull crystal.

Naughton hiked across the floor to greet them. Naughton raised Jansen's hand and kissed the back of it before releasing. "Always a pleasure, DS Jansen."

"Likewise." Colour rose on Jansen's cheeks as Pennance lifted an eyebrow at her.

"You remember Connor." Naughton indicated O'Shea who, dressed identically to Naughton, sat on a large U shaped black leather sofa in the centre of the room. O'Shea waved nonchalantly in greeting, not bothering to rise.

"It's a little bright in here, right?" asked Naughton.

"Maybe," said O'Shea. "If you think so."

"I do." Naughton pulled out his phone, tapped the screen a couple of times and the light level dropped by half. "Electrochromic glass."

"Okay," said Pennance.

"It's an electrically controlled coating which changes tint," said McAlaney.

"I don't think we've met before." Naughton seemed to properly notice McAlaney for the first time.

"Unlikely." McAlaney glanced around the room, not meeting Naughton's fixed gaze until he gave up and settled beside O'Shea.

"Coffee anyone? It's decaf." A large, burnished steel pot rested on a table encompassed by the sofa.

"No, thanks." Pennance saw no point in coffee without actual coffee in it.

"Nor me," said Jansen.

"Water, if you have it?" asked McAlaney.

O'Shea poured a cup for himself as Naughton tapped again on his phone. A few moments later the PA entered again carrying a condensation-stippled beaker which she offered to McAlaney before leaving.

"Now," said Naughton. "How can I help you?"

"We're taking up your offer from yesterday of showing us around," said Pennance.

"Happy to. By the way, you've no problem Connor being here I assume?"

"None at all. This is just informal."

"Good, good." Naughton grinned. "While I'm very glad to extend my hospitality I'm afraid there's not so much to see. It's just banks of servers and people in offices. All the best bits are tucked away inside them."

"Even so, I'd appreciate it."

"I guess there's no harm," said O'Shea.

Naughton stood, stuck out a hand for McAlaney's drink which he placed on the table.

THE BLUE CODE

O'Shea held the door open, allowing Naughton to lead the detectives along a walkway overlooking the reception area – an atrium sporting several very large and very green tropical plants – partitioned by a waist-high glass barrier. Pennance felt like he was in an upmarket hotel. Naughton paused beside an entrance. Seconds later came a metallic click from nearby and Naughton pushed the door open.

"Facial recognition," said Naughton.

"Do we need to be scanned?" asked Pennance.

"You're with me." Naughton held back the door for them to pass through. "So you're golden."

Beyond, in a large, open plan area dozens of people sat at desks, most with headphones on, the dominant sound the tap-dancing of fingers on keys. Nobody spoke.

"Lots of American companies have a pod structure in their offices," said Naughton. "Everyone behind their little walls; together, but not. So in here we've electrochromic glass dividers, in case someone wants some privacy. It's all individually app controlled on phones provided by the company." Nearby the wall around one of the desks darkened. Naughton held out an arm, smile of accomplishment on his face. "Ah, would you look at that, perfect timing."

"What happens in here?" asked Pennance. "Please assume I know nothing."

"You don't," said McAlaney. Pennance wondered whether she was spending too much time with Hoskins.

"This is where we computationally process and analyse data," said Naughton. "Like audio and visual files, internet clicks, log files, social network posts, emails, medical information etc. for businesses and bodies all over the world. Right from this building."

"You don't need to be on-site?"

"Nope. That's the power of our inter-connected world."

"It's amazing," said O'Shea.

"These people here," said Naughton, "are the most important assets we possess. Skilled operators are the key."

"Not computers?" asked Pennance.

"They're just dumb instruments. It's the hands and the brains behind them which make the difference. And how we slice and dice the files." Naughton hiked a thumb over his shoulder. "Let's show you our brawn." Naughton took them back through the door then down the sweeping stairs onto the ground floor. He paused again briefly outside another entrance at another facial recognition scanner.

Pennance entered a darkened area. Moments later lighting flickered on revealing a corridor a couple of metres wide.

"This is our architecture," said Naughton. "Our systems fill our entire ground floor. We have fire suppression facilities built in." He pointed to a vent above. "But in case of any issues we have a backup at a second site."

Through yet more glass to both sides stood banks and banks of tall electronic equipment. Pennance wanted to press his face up against the barrier. It was like something out of a movie – dark, matt metal, flashing indicators and a low pitch hum he had to be imagining.

"Very impressive," said McAlaney.

THE BLUE CODE

"It is, right?" Naughton flashed a schoolboy grin. "We have our own proprietary processing engine that's like nothing else on the market."

"Could you elaborate?" asked McAlaney.

"Not without you signing a highly extensive non-disclosure agreement," said O'Shea.

"Unless you want a job at Obsidian," said Naughton. "Then you get access to the lot."

"I might be persuaded," said McAlaney.

"Of particular interest to Obsidian is predicting human behaviour and interactions."

"That sounds somewhat Big Brother to me," said Pennance.

"Certainly, if done in the wrong way. But ultimately all I'm motivated by is delivering insights to our customers to drive enhanced business decisions and strategies." Naughton spread his legs and pressed the fingertips on both hands together. "Think of your HOLMES system. How much information is stored in there? Suspect photos, licence plates, fingerprints, witness statements, and so on. Billions and billions of characters relating to cases. How do you effectively scrutinise it?"

"That's the purpose of HOLMES though, isn't it? As a management system."

"Correct, but how easy is it to use?"

"It could be better," admitted Pennance.

"Much better," said McAlaney.

"Many organisations, like the police, just aren't *capable* of getting maximum value from what they hold – either because of time or resources," said Naughton. "I know for a fact the police have lots of dark data – that's information that's just pushed to one side and not assessed – which could be helping you catch criminals so much faster, just by efficient accessing of pre-existing knowledge. Think of that, Jonah!

"I mentioned data slicing earlier. Most companies use the Five Vs to characterise their information. Like Volume, Variety, Velocity and so on. A very few use ten. More attributes means greater granularity and greater depth. At Obsidian we have *thirteen* Vs and we're testing a fourteenth right now. More will follow in the future, I guarantee it. On top of that we incorporate machine learning and artificial intelligence to process, analyse and model the data in real time which we then give access to the originator for them to utilise immediately. There's nobody better at this than Obsidian. What we do is righteous, Jonah. I truly believe that."

Pennance reckoned he did.

O'Shea put his hand on Naughton's shoulder. "Maybe we should head back to your office?"

"Good idea," said Naughton.

In the atrium reception Naughton's PA was waiting. "I'm sorry, Kai, but your next appointment is here."

"I'll be up momentarily." Naughton then shook all their hands again, although this time he avoided kissing Jansen's. Naughton said to Pennance, "Obsidian can, and is, truly making a positive difference to society. Just remember that." Then the PA led Naughton away. O'Shea nodded before following.

THE BLUE CODE

***

Nobody spoke until they were in Jansen's car, heading back towards Huntingdon on Ermine Street. The plan was to drop off McAlaney at the station before going to see Ferrensby's mother at the home.

"What did you make of that?" asked Pennance.

"He's a true believer," said Jansen.

"Bordering on the zealot," said Pennance.

"Very impressive facilities," said McAlaney.

"Interested in Naughton's job offer then, Ava?" asked Jansen.

"No." She paused briefly. "There was something about that place I just didn't like."

Twenty Nine

Retirement homes were maybe Pennance's worst nightmare. It wasn't the indefinable, penetrative odour of decaying bodies and boiled vegetables. Or the pervading silence and the feeling of life on hold.

No, in Pennance's experience, from visiting his father years ago, they possessed the undertone of a knacker's yard, without the mercifulness of a quick end – Death may be inevitable, but sometimes He dawdled. At his father's home, residents either shuffled around or sat in common rooms not talking to each other, the TV blaring. There was certainly no merriment, just the pervading smell of long-boiled cabbage. All of which, Pennance reckoned, must gnaw into the souls of the far younger carers, like a burrowing worm, seeing first-hand what awaited them when it was their turn.

However, the facility where Jansen brought Pennance confounded and confused his expectations. Access to the light and airy reception area was via electronic sliding doors which allowed the sound of laughter, but no stench, to drift out. Inside, a large, overhead skylight nourished several flourishing pot plants with dark green leaves in a similar, though far less grand, fashion to Obsidian.

A waiting staff nurse, wearing a pale blue starched uniform, joyous eyes and her hair pinned up, threw them both a wide and genuine grin. Pennance started to reach for his warrant card, however the nurse held up her hand. "ID isn't necessary. We see Keri quite regularly. She weaves some stories! Although I'm never sure if she's telling the truth, or not."

"All part of the game," said Jansen.

The nurse tapped a badge on her chest. "I'm Amy, by the way."

"You have a relative here?" asked Pennance.

"Nothing like that," said Jansen.

"Since our residents heard we had not one, but *two* police officers coming today, there's been quite the buzz of excitement, let me tell you," said Amy. "They do love an appearance. We've a Zumba class on at the moment and an alpaca visit later, although they're nothing compared to true crime experts."

"Unfortunately we're here on official business," said Jansen.

"That's a shame." Amy's smile dimmed several watts. "Maybe you can stay after you're finished? I'd like to hear again how you rugby tackled that burglar."

"We'll see."

"Who are you here for?"

"Sadie Ferrensby, and I know the way."

"If you need anything, there's a call button next to every bed, just press it and me or someone else will be with you shortly." Another flashing grin and Amy was gone.

"Stories?" asked Pennance.

"I used to visit my grandmother. A few years after she died, when I was in uniform on probation, I started coming again. I didn't mind who I spoke to." Jansen led Pennance along a cornflower blue corridor which had bright photos spaced out evenly between open doorways. "It was a way of releasing some pressure of the job."

Pennance glanced inside a room, saw a resident in a chair looking out the window, listening to some music; jazz by the strangled trumpet.

"It helped me as much as it helped them," said Jansen. "So, I just carried on. I come once or twice a month."

In the next room a man lay in bed, legs crossed at the ankles, and he raised his hand in greeting.

Pennance nodded back as his phone buzzed. A text from Meacham. "My boss has given the go-ahead for Abernathy's tattoo analysis." He started to tap out a message to the pathologist.

"That's good news."

And fortunate, as Pennance had already given Abernathy the go-ahead.

Jansen paused inside the entrance to the next room. "Hello, Sadie."

"Oh, for feck's sake! What are you doing here?" The tone was akin to a screech, the Northern Irish inflection unmistakable.

"Mind if we come in?"

"We? There's more than one of you. Jesus, Mother and Mary!"

Jansen entered Sadie's room, Pennance following. A bed was pushed against one wall, a large wooden crucifix above. Opposite, so they were directly in Sadie's eyeline, hung a multitude of photos in frames. Positioned centrally was a huge print of Ferrensby in a t-shirt surrounded by long grass and his arm draped around a woman, shading his eyes with a hand on a sunny day along with maybe thirty others of various sizes arranged around the circumference.

In front of the window, offering a view into a central courtyard garden, stood a table and two armchairs; both were occupied. One by a woman with lank, bunched-up silver hair wrapped in a thick dressing gown and a scowl, presumably Sadie. A slim middle-aged woman perched on the edge of the other, her yellow cardigan bright to the point of being painful, hands clasped in her lap. It was she beside Ferrensby in the big print, although maybe a decade older. Hair cut shorter now, cheekbones made all the more prominent by her sunken face.

"Come in pairs, do you now?" Sadie's expression twisted into daggers. Her forehead was a row of deep grooves, as if flowing water had carved into rock. More lines round her pinched lips and narrowed angry eyes, like she'd spent her life disapproving of somebody or something. Maybe everyone and everything.

"Ma!" The younger woman of the two flashed a glare at Sadie, stood, smiled, held out her hand. "I'm Jacqui, her daughter."

"Obviously." Sadie tutted. "I know you're Jansen 'cos you're always traipsing round here, but who the feck are you?"

"DI Jonah Pennance," he said.

"Jonah?" Sadie reached for a small gold cross hanging from a chain around her neck. "The disobedient man who's punished before seeking forgiveness." Sadie waved away Pennance's ID. "That's a rare name for a kid to suffer."

"My mother was drunk most of the time."

"Hmm." Sadie peered at Pennance, interested now. "Park your arse, young fella. You're causing a crick in my neck." She directed him to Jacqui's chair, demoting her daughter.

"I'm not really young anymore, Mrs Ferrensby." Pennance took the empty seat.

"It's Miss, never married. The offspring have *my* name, not the fathers'. I dumped them both, the pair of wee, useless bastards."

"At least Da tried to be there for us all, Ma."

Sadie snorted then shook her head, like her ex was an irrelevance. "The only good to come out of all that squelching around was Matthew."

"I'll sit on the bed, shall I?" Jacqui perched on the very edge, legs at a sharp angle, staring at her feet on the floor while Jansen positioned herself behind Pennance, arm leaning on the backrest.

"It's my feckin' room," said Sadie to her daughter. "And no farting, I have to sleep there."

"For God's sake," muttered Jacqui, eliciting a cackle from Sadie. Jacqui turned to Pennance. "I'm sorry."

"Don't go apologising for me, young lady. I'm sure the copper has heard far worse."

"Occasionally," said Pennance.

"What are you here for?" All eyes were on Sadie and that's how she seemed to revel in it. "Has Jacqui fecked something else up?"

"Actually, Mrs Ferrensby," said Jansen. "It's your son, Matt, who we'd like to know more about."

"Be minding yourself, sergeant. It's Matthew." Sadie nodded at Pennance. "Why are you interested in my son?"

THE BLUE CODE

"Background for an investigation DS Jansen and I are working," said Pennance.

"Jesus and Joseph, but you people can't speak straight these days." Sadie threw her arms up in the air. "I mean, why use one word when ten will do?" Sadie turned to Jacqui. "Am I right, girl?"

"Yes, Ma."

"Matthew's a good boy; I'll tell you that for free. He's blundered a few times over the years, but haven't we all?" Sadie flashed Jacqui with a barbed glance.

"Any mistakes you'd care to mention?" asked Pennance.

"Working all the time for one. Too interested in grafting to get himself a girlfriend; so he's not given me grandchildren yet."

Jacqui blinked. "You've got grandchildren, Ma," she said. "Mine."

"They don't really count." Sadie waved Jacqui away who went back to staring at her shoes, maybe hoping the ground would swallow her. The grind of Jacqui's teeth was palpable. Sadie continued, "Matthew needs to have kids, so he can carry on the family name. You took your husband's, speaking of errors."

Jacqui shifted as if she was sitting on a landmine, ready to explode.

"Have you heard from Matthew recently?" asked Pennance.

"Not so much."

"He normally calls you every day, Ma," said Jacqui.

"He does not." Sadie's frown deepened.

"What is Matthew's job?" asked Pennance.

"He loves cars, been driving for as long as I can remember. He used to compete in karts. Now he's a chauffeur for the rich and famous."

"Like who?"

"I can't recall." Sadie cast her eyes away. "My mind's not what it was."

Pennance doubted that and, from Jacqui's upthrust brows, so did she. "Nobody famous lives in Huntingdon, Ma."

"What about the ex-Prime Minister?"

"I'd be amazed if Matt has been within a mile of John Major."

"Matthew," said Sadie. "My Matthew he drives *proper* people. He has a suit and everything."

"Do you know Logan Elliott?"

"The man who was shot yesterday?" Sadie narrowed her eyes. "Why would I?"

"Matthew was in Mr Elliott's car and Matthew walked away immediately before the murder. Like he had prior knowledge of what was coming."

"I don't believe you." Sadie pushed her shoulders back, tilted her head away from Pennance.

"We have witness statements."

"Then they're lying."

"I've spoken to some of these people myself."

"So feckin what?"

"Ma," said Jacqui.

Sadie turned to her daughter, twisting in the chair. "He can't come in here and condemn my Matthew."

"I haven't accused your son of anything, Mrs Ferrensby," said Pennance.

"Alright, then." Sadie huffed, pulled the dressing gown tighter about herself. "That's good."

"Are you aware your son has a police record?" asked Jansen.

"For what?" Sadie now focused laser beam eyes on Jansen.

"He was a getaway driver on bank raids. I arrested him myself several times."

"Did it go to court?"

"No," admitted Jansen.

"Then he's not a criminal, is he, Sergeant?"

"Depends on your perspective."

Sadie's mouth drooped even further and her expression set hard as concrete. "I reckon you can both feck off now."

"We aren't finished," said Pennance.

"You may not be, but I am." Sadie settled back in her chair and closed her eyes, then began to fake snore.

There was clearly no point continuing, so Pennance rose to his feet, dug out a business card from an inside pocket and dropped it on the table beside Sadie. "In case you think of anything of actual substance, Miss Ferrensby." Sadie carried on wheezing.

"I'll show you out," said Jacqui.

Pennance glanced over his shoulder as he left the room. Sadie had one eye open and was reaching for Pennance's card until she realised he was watching and went back to feigning sleep.

Jacqui led Pennance and Jansen towards the reception area before stopping at a distance she presumably believed out of earshot. "I'm sorry about that." Jacqui clenched and unclenched her fists.

"It's no problem."

"Ignoring Matt's shady history *is* a problem, Inspector. My ma, she makes me want to bloody scream." Jacqui bared clenched teeth. "You don't know what it's like putting up with her."

"I'm told parents often think the best of their children."

"And all the stuff she says about my kids."

"I'm sure she doesn't mean it," said Jansen.

"Oh, I know mine are little bastards." Jacqui gave Pennance a fast glance, put the knuckles of her fist between her lips briefly. "Oh my God, I'm sorry, that just came out." She ran a hand through her hair then shook herself, like she was physically moving on. "Matt, he was always the golden child, even though it was an open secret what he got up to in his 'job.'" Jacqui threw out some air quotes. "*That* was why my da left. Because he tried to tackle it. When the choice was between Matt and Da, *he* got the boot." Jacqui propped herself against the wall. "And Ma is cracked if she thinks Matt will give her grandchildren, unless he uses a surrogate or adopts, because he's gay."

"I wasn't aware of that," said Jansen.

"It's very unlikely you would be, Sergeant. Matt kept the fact totally quiet. Only a handful of the very closest friends and family know and they're sworn to secrecy. He doesn't want to affect his chances of getting work. So, he plays it macho."

THE BLUE CODE

"You and your mother disagreed on how often Matt contacts her," said Pennance.

"Matt rings her all the time, wherever he is. They're always talking."

"But not for the last few days?"

"So she said, which is totally out of character. Ma has seemed more agitated. I mean, she's always like a firecracker ready to pop, but at the moment..."

Pennance's phone and watch notified him a text had come in. Hoskins. "Give me a bell when you get chance. V."

Jansen took over. "Does Matt have a partner?"

"Apparently so, but I've no idea who he is. Matt's never introduced me to anyone and he's not mentioned a name or even given a hint of a description. As I said, Matt is very private about his sexuality; even with me. There's someone else you can talk to, though. Lesia Duschenko, Matt's best friend from school. I can call her if you want."

"Sean Ingle's ex?" asked Pennance.

"Yes, how did you know?" asked Jacqui.

"Can I have her address?" asked Jansen.

"Sure, if you've something to write it down with?" Jansen handed over a pen and one of her business cards which Jacqui scrawled on the back of before getting her phone out. "I'll call Lesia now."

"Thanks."

"Just find my brother," said Jacqui.

***

As Jansen started her car engine Pennance dialled Hoskins.

"Yo," said Hoskins. "What do you want?"

"I got a message from you to call," said Pennance.

"Oh, yeah." Hoskins was chewing on something. "I've been looking into that file from the estate agents with your friend, Alasdair Tremayne."

"Zinke."

"Uh-huh." Hoskins audibly swallowed. "We know what owns the house, but not who."

"I don't understand."

"I mean, River Road belongs to a business based in Delaware."

"America?"

"It's a well-known tax haven. Like The Cayman Islands or Luxembourg. And the company, Longshot Ventures, is registered there. It's a shell corporation, Tremayne traced it through the bank account details Zinke provided."

"Which means the actual ownership is concealed."

"Right."

"And we can't find out who they are."

"Maybe, maybe not. Tremayne is still scrutinising the details and I asked Esmie to see if she could help."

"You rang Quant?"

"Sure. Why not? The resources she can access are vast. We may as well use them."

"I suppose."

"Anyway, just an update. We're not done yet. We'll find out who's behind Longshot."

"What was that about?" asked Jansen when Pennance disconnected.

"I'm not sure yet." Pennance placed another call. "Mr Zinke? It's DI Pennance."

"Hello, Inspector. What can I do to help?"

"Have you heard of the name Longshot Ventures?"

Zinke didn't answer for a moment. "They're an entity who own several properties I rent out on their behalf."

"Could you look into them for me? Tell me about their portfolio, and so on."

"Is this all part of the same investigation we discussed earlier?"

"Yes."

"Then of course, Inspector. Happy to help."

"Thanks."

"I'll call when I have something for you." Zinke disconnected.

"Are you going to tell me what's going on now?" asked Jansen.

"I wish I knew," said Pennance.

Thirty

The address turned out to be a new build block of terraces, crammed between existing, much older properties, constructed of unsympathetic brick. The interlopers had made an effort to individualise their properties – front door, painted window frames, trees, hanging baskets, plants on climbing frames and in pots.

Except one.

Lesia's house couldn't have been plainer and less remarkable, probably looking the same the day the workers had walked off-site. Unlike the neighbours, concrete replaced the front garden, creating a second space where a fifteen-year old red Ford Fiesta was parked. A curtain flickered in the neighbour's house. A shadow of a person, there for an instant and gone.

Pennance leaned on the bell and the door was opened by a waif of a woman – under five feet, and slim, blonde hair – verging on bleached and washed out. She wore a white tracksuit, the top zipped up to her neck.

"Miss Duschenko?" asked Jansen.

"Lesia." She stepped out of the way. "Come in." A narrow hallway, stairs stretching up one side, a doorway opposite and another at the end of the hall. Walls painted, Pennance realised, in the same buttercup yellow that he'd seen at Huntingdon station. Stale cigarette smoke lingered.

It felt tight and claustrophobic with three of them packed in and Pennance was glad when Lesia led them into a living room. One reclining chair in leather which probably vibrated, given the cable which sneaked to a wall socket. A huge TV and a games console in front and a small table to one side with an ashtray on top. Then, a large, framed photo on a wall that had been popular in the 70s – a female tennis player hitching her short skirt up, part-revealing her backside.

Lesia sat on the floor, crossed her legs like a yoga pose, leaving the recliner for Pennance and Jansen to fight over. Lesia said, "Jacqui called, she told me you wanted to talk about Matt."

"I understand you two are friends?" Pennance shook his head at Jansen's unspoken inquisition, then she flopped down into the seat's embrace.

"We've known each other since school."

"Matt's missing and we're trying to figure out where he could have gone."

"I can't believe he'd be involved in someone's murder. I mean, he's been in trouble, but never this bad."

"What's he like?"

"His addiction and his ignorance of it defines him. Everything he does and says is motivated to feed his craving."

"Drugs?" asked Jansen.

"Gambling." Lesia straightened out one leg. "If something moves, Matt will bet on it – football, rugby, dog fighting, cock fighting, even the toss of a coin. Horses are his thing, though. He'll spend hours poring over form. Unfortunately, his only true skill is in losing. Over all the time I've known him he's spent more time in debt than out. Which means he's always being chased for cash. He's borrowed from me several times.

"We shared a house for a couple of years when I moved out from home. Most days someone was at the door. They used to ring the landline, too, 'til we had the phone taken out. Often, Matt made me answer. I had to say he wasn't in. Or they'd have a word when I was in a pub, and I'd relay back whatever threat they'd made. I was really worried they'd come for me eventually, so I went back home."

"This is your mother's house?"

"No, my partner's. We started seeing each other recently."

"You and Matt are still friends?"

"Too much history to give up that. We message regularly, talk on the phone most weeks. Occasionally we bump into each other around town. He's not changed much."

"When was the last time you spoke with him?"

"He rang about three weeks ago. Said he had a job, a big one which would pay off all his debts. Then he could give me what he owed me, too."

"What did you think?" asked Jansen.

"I didn't totally believe him, I wanted to, but there's no way Mercer would wipe his slate clean. Once that man has his fingers into you..." Lesia shuddered.

"Mercer is Matt's bookie?"

"Of course." Lesia wrinkled her nose. "Who else would it be?"

"We met with Sean Ingle earlier. He said he dealt with Mercer too."

"Around here everyone has some kind of connection to Mercer. Take me, besides my choice in friends and partners, I used to work in Mercer's shop when I was a kid."

"This job Matt mentioned, was anyone else on it?" asked Jansen.

"He didn't name names, only that several others were getting the same deal."

A key went in the lock then Shapiro appeared in the doorway. "Why are you in my house, Pennance?"

"He's your partner?" asked Pennance.

"Last I looked there's no law against it," said Shapiro.

"Wow." By the wide-eyed expression on Jansen's face, this was clearly a surprise to her.

"They're asking about Matt," said Lesia.

"Ferrensby?"

"We're friends."

"Really?"

"You didn't know?" asked Pennance.

"We don't talk much, if you know what I mean." Shapiro winked.

"Ed!" said Lesia.

"How did you two meet?" asked Pennance.

"Blind date," said Shapiro. "Lesia instantly fell for my charms."

"Not at Mercer's then?"

"Sorry?" asked Lesia. "Ed, what does he mean?"

"Your boyfriend likes a little flutter, right Shapiro?"

"He's talking out his arse," said Shapiro.

"Am I?"

"Tell me you're not." Lesia stood, went over to Shapiro. "Not with Mercer, please." She searched his face.

"*Pfft*. It's nothing." Shapiro wafted a hand. "Just a little fun, blowing off some stress. A few quid here, a few quid there. Nothing major."

"You know what that man's like." Lesia ran a hand over her face. "What he did to me."

"Won't be happening again." Shapiro gripped Lesia's forearms, Pennance and Jansen forgotten. "I'm here to protect you. I'm the law."

"Oh my God." Lesia shook Shapiro off, then made for the stairs. "How the hell do I keep ending up with men like you?"

"What does that mean?" Shapiro followed Lesia. She began to run upstairs. Shapiro shot out a hand, grabbed hold of her ankle through the banister spindles, causing her to trip and fall forward. She spun around, kicked at Shapiro until he loosened his grip and she wriggled free, continuing her dash.

"Les!" said Shapiro. A door slammed loudly in reply. He moved to the bottom step, called up again. Someone from next door hammered on the wall. "Fuck off!" Shapiro banged back in response. "Les!" shouted Shapiro once more.

"I don't think she's interested," said Pennance.

"What the hell have you done?" Shapiro turned to Pennance, pushed his shoulders back.

"I just asked a couple of questions. The rest was all you."

Shapiro bounded up the stairs, hammered on the bedroom door and rattled the handle. "Let me in, Les."

"Leave me alone!" she shouted.

Then came a loud crash and a screech. Pennance took the stairs two steps at a time, Jansen close behind. A door hung off its hinges. Inside the room Lesia and Shapiro faced off, either side of a bed. A whole wall was mirrored wardrobe doors, one of which was open and a bag on the floor was part-filled with a jumble of clothes.

"We can work this all out, Lesia."

"There's nothing to discuss, we're done," she said.

"You don't mean that." Shapiro shook his head.

"I can't abide liars. You didn't tell me you were gambling."

"Strictly that's not lying."

"I'm not having Mercer's men at me again."

"I've already told you, that's not going to happen!"

"Bullshit, Ed." Lesia hefted the bag. "Get out of my way."

Shapiro didn't budge. "You're not leaving."

"Inspector Shapiro," said Pennance. "Do as she asks."

"This is my house; I give the orders."

"Sir!" Jansen tried to get herself in front of Shapiro.

"Shut it, bitch." Shapiro shoved Jansen into the wall opposite.

Lesia lunged then, lifting a knee hard and fast into Shapiro's groin. He sagged to the floor, clutching himself and groaning. "Goodbye, Ed." Lesia stepped over him and Pennance moved aside, allowing her to dash down the stairs. She grabbed a set of keys from a hook behind the front door and ran. By the time Pennance was outside, Lesia had the Fiesta's engine going.

The curtain twitching neighbour, an elderly man sporting a suspiciously black hair, came out as Lesia reversed away at speed. As the red Fiesta accelerated away Jansen joined them, rubbing her shoulder. Stop lights flared briefly before Lesia took the corner and was out of sight.

"Poor girl, I hope she doesn't come back this time," said the neighbour.

"This has happened before?" asked Pennance.

"I hear them fighting all the time. Hard not to with how thin the walls are." He scratched at his rug. "If I'd have known what he was like I'd have bought somewhere else." Then he retreated inside.

"I'll go talk to Shapiro," said Pennance.

"I think I'll wait in my car," said Jansen.

"Fair enough."

Shapiro was in the kitchen, pouring himself a vodka measure. The bottle was iced, straight out of the freezer. "Are you here *just* to screw things up for me?" Shapiro knocked back the glass, snarled as the alcohol hit his throat.

"You seem to do fine by yourself," said Pennance.

"Maybe." Another shot went down. "I don't know." Shapiro offered Pennance the vodka.

"I don't drink much."

"Why doesn't that surprise me?" Shapiro ditched the glass and took a pull straight from the bottle. "I do know it's going to cost me to get her back. I'll have to buy something big and expensive. What do you reckon?"

"I reckon she needs space."

Shapiro raised his hands. "Why do I care what you think?"

"What's Mercer got on you?"

"Pennance, you see conspiracy everywhere." Shapiro wiped a hand across his nose. "You haven't a clue how it works around here. Not that you care, you'll be gone soon,

THE BLUE CODE

back to London. I've got to keep living in this town. There are rules to play by, rules you wouldn't understand."

"Why don't you enlighten me?"

"Get the fuck out of my house off, Pennance."

Thirty One

Jansen leant against her car, mobile to her ear. She beckoned Pennance over, then held the phone out flat between. "Say that again Mr Zinke." The estate agent. "I just put you onto speaker so Inspector Pennance can hear you, as well."

"Oh, good. Hello, Inspector." Zinke tinny and distant, like he was speaking from a metal dustbin. "You may recall when you were here earlier, I said we rented out both residential and commercial properties?"

"I do," said Jansen.

"Well, I have an admission to make, and an apology on behalf of my company. We have two offices in different locations. Ordinarily the records would be centralised on our computer system, but somehow, and this is why I'm calling; there's a connection we may have failed to make." Zinke coughed. "As well as the house, the Carnforths looked over another facility, a warehouse. It might be nothing, but I thought I'd let you know."

"I don't see how it's relevant."

"Well, I checked the ownership of the unit – it's Longshot Ventures, the same as River Road."

"When can you meet me us there?" asked Pennance.

"As soon as you wish."

"What about now?"

"That's the absolute least I can do."

"Where are we going, Mr Zinke?" asked Jansen.

"It's the old RAF base in Graveley."

***

THE BLUE CODE

The hamlet of Graveley felt far from civilisation – flat, featureless fenland and a road absent of vehicles. Though dusk was approaching, the failing light made the landmark Zinke had told them to look out for even more obvious – a cluster of tall wind turbines like silent sentinels guarding a huddle of blocky buildings.

The turning, a pathway of cracked cement, was blocked by a large Jeep. Zinke stood at the back bumper, waving. As Jansen drew up she lowered the window and a windswept Zinke leaned one arm on the sill. "Officers, if you'd care to follow me, the unit is over on the far side of the property."

"Lead away," said Jansen. Zinke patted the bodywork then used the same hand to flatten his hair as Jansen flicked the switch to raise the window again. Zinke got inside his car, exhaust spewed out of the pipe and then his brake lights flicked on. He rolled along the track, Jansen giving him a few feet of clearance.

Bypassing a large cast concrete construction several storeys high, Zinke immediately turned across an apron which appeared conjoined to the building, like all the material had been poured in one long, continuous flow although it was in a poor state, crumbling underfoot, weeds bursting through cracks. Large doors barred an entrance which Zinke ignored, aiming his Jeep tangentially over the flat and towards a dark shape on the far side.

Zinke halted and Jansen drew up alongside, switched off the engine. Pennance stepped out and pulled his jacket tight about him, the wind's chill fingers caressing him. For a moment, Pennance felt all alone in the world.

The estate agent broke the spell by brandishing a bunch of maybe thirty keys. "This way." He led them to a building shaped like a corrugated tube cut in half beyond which the ploughed dirt stretched away on all sides until they met with greying sky.

"What is this place?" asked Pennance.

"Was, Inspector," said Zinke. "Used to be a World War Two air force base. Lots of them were thrown up quickly in the late 1930s and early 1940s, maybe fifteen in Cambridgeshire alone and more over into Essex."

"That many?"

"The land is perfect, hardly any hills to get in the way of take-off, and the distance into Europe not so far. Hurricanes launched from here 75 years ago, just think of that. Those beautiful killing machines swooping above us. When the war ended most airfields were abandoned – there's only a handful left now. Duxford is a museum, there's Cambridge airport just off the A14 south of the city and Alconbury to the north which was to close but has had a stay of execution while the Yanks decide what to do with it.

"Anyway, the farmers whose land it was in the first place mostly got to reclaim what they'd given up for the effort against Hitler and inherited the air force buildings. Some got knocked down, others were re-purposed. We've been responsible for renting this one out for nearly thirty years, which isn't so easy a task these days." Zinke stopped in his tracks and swore before pointing for Pennance's benefit. Access to the building was gained through a pair of floor-to-ceiling sliding double doors painted in a flaking racing green. Frosted glass was inserted about two thirds of the way up, above head height. Zinke directed his ire towards the heavy padlocks and chains looped between rugged looking handles.

"Not one of yours?" asked Pennance.

"It damn well isn't." Zinke rattled the chains like Marley's ghost before pulling out a phone and placing a call. He tapped his foot while waiting for it to connect. "Ah, Elaine, it's Adam, where's Saxelby today?" A pause. "Okay, good, get him out to Graveley, quick as you can." Zinke listened briefly, waved a hand. "I'm not interested, whatever he's doing, make him drop it. I don't want to keep the officers waiting any longer than I must. It's bloody parky." Zinke threw Pennance a weak grin which Pennance felt obliged to return. "Thanks."

Zinke disconnected, slid the mobile back in his pocket. "Saxelby is one of our contracted handymen. He also happens to be a rather proficient locksmith. Fortunately, he lives in Hilton, a village about three miles northeast of here, so he won't be long. He just needs to jump in the van. Five minutes maximum if he moves his arse, officers. Sorry again."

"You weren't to know," said Pennance.

"So no-one rents the building right now?" asked Jansen.

"Supposedly not. I left the damn folder on the passenger seat. Hang on a second." Zinke trotted back to his car, leaned into the back and returned with a folder which he flipped open. A wind gust caught the piece of paper inside, blowing it out of Zinke's grip. He scampered after the errant document, almost grabbing it twice before some unseen hand tugged it away from him. Eventually he literally cornered the page outside the building before returning to Pennance and Jansen.

"Bloody elements out here." Zinke clicked a button on his car keys and headlamps came on. Zinke brushed some dirt off the document, clamped tightly down now, and ran a fingertip down the printed words briefly. "The last occupant moved out over six months ago. Longshot Ventures has owned the property for more than a decade. Like River Road, it's not currently available." Zinke stared up along the track, shifting from side to side like he was looking past an obstruction but there were none. "Where is he?"

"It's only been a few minutes," said Pennance.

"Even so."

"I'm going to have a walk around."

"Be my guest."

"I'll come too," said Jansen.

"And I'll wait here." With another gust of wind Zinke hugged the paperwork to himself. "Or maybe in the Jeep."

Pennance and Jansen headed in the opposite direction to Zinke. Then they parted ways, tracking along separate sides of the building, which was perhaps thirty feet long. The curved corrugated roof reached down to within a couple of inches of the floor. The material was spotted with moss patches, despite a probable high asbestos content. The concrete base extended a few feet or so all around the building, giving Pennance a narrow path. Weeds pressed through cracks, forcing him to take care where he placed his feet.

At the far end a haphazard pile of pitted, rusted engine parts, from a tractor or maybe even a plane, Pennance didn't know, leant either side of a solid wooden door in the brick wall which capped the tube shaped building off. No windows to peer through.

Jansen rounded the corner. "Anything?"

"Just junk." Pennance tried the door handle which was welded tight. He brushed brown metal flakes off his hand.

"Go back?"

"May as well."

Zinke was in his car, leaning back against the headrest, eyes closed, jaw working while he chewed, some music faintly playing. Pennance lightly tapped on the glass. Zinke wound down the window, allowing the melody to leak out. "Vivaldi. If the gum doesn't quite do the job then a bit of classical takes me somewhere else. Saxelby should arrive any moment."

"Now, I'd say." Jansen pointed up the track, towards a silver painted van bouncing across the apron, ploughing straight through the potholes at speed.

Zinke got out, watched Saxelby's progress briefly. "That's embarrassing." He shook his head. "You must think we're country bumpkins around here."

"Not in the slightest," lied Pennance.

When only yards away Saxelby braked sharply, causing his van to slew almost forty-five degrees and revealing sign-written text on the side which said, "'andy Andy Tools of the Trade."

"The H is deliberately dropped." Clearly, Zinke had felt the need to explain this more than once. Zinke grabbed more gum from his car.

After killing the engine, Saxelby popped the door and leapt down out of the driver's seat, ready for action. "Where's the emergency?" Saxelby, in a grey boiler suit and his dark hair carefully spiked with a wet-look gel, even pounded a fist into his open hand.

"Get your tools, Andy." Zinke sounded like his batteries were draining fast.

"Roger that." Saxelby cut off the salute he was part way through when he caught the expression of distaste on Zinke's face.

Pennance fell into step beside Zinke, Jansen pausing for Saxelby. "This is what comes of employing your son and his friends, Inspector." Zinke tossed a piece of gum into his mouth, then followed up with a second.

"I haven't got kids," said Pennance.

"Sometimes, I wish I didn't too." Zinke paused beside the doors, pointed at the padlock as Saxelby bounded up. "Can you deal with these?"

"Quick as a flash," said Saxelby.

"Holy Houdini, Batman," said Pennance, drawing a strained groan and a shake of the head from Jansen.

Zinke chuckled. "I like it."

"What?" Saxelby frowned.

"Never mind," said Zinke. "Just do your stuff, please."

Saxelby knelt, placed his toolbox on the ground, opened it and went to work. "That's one." Saxelby raised a padlock to show Pennance and Zinke before he tossed it and the chain away.

"He might be a showman, but he is capable." Zinke spoke loudly enough for Saxelby to hear; the locksmith simply grinned briefly over his shoulder.

THE BLUE CODE

Saxelby stood, second padlock and chain in his hand. "All yours."

Zinke put his key into the hole in the door, twisted. Then he grabbed a large handle. "Would you take the other, Inspector?"

The metal was smooth in Pennance's palm. He wondered how many others had done the same over the decades. Then Zinke tugged and Pennance followed suit, the large square of wood moving easily on well-oiled rollers, barely even a squeak, until it hit a stopper. Zinke made to enter until Pennance put out a hand and held him back. "Stay here, please."

"Perhaps I should get more gum?"

"No harm being prepared, sir." Jansen offered nitrile gloves to Pennance.

Pennance stepped over the threshold. The light from outside only reached in so far, shadows deepening from about halfway along such that he couldn't pick out any shapes through the blackness.

Overhead, strip lights hung down from chains. Pennance found the switch in the obvious place and he clicked it down. The bulbs flickered on, one after the other, vaguely filling the space. A large tarpaulin covered a hump at the far end.

Pennance said to Zinke, "Was that here when you rented it out?"

"I've no idea."

"Check, please," said Jansen.

"Can you pay me now?" Saxelby held out a card machine.

"Really, Andy?" said Zinke. "We keep you on a retainer, remember?"

"Yeah, but this is extra, surely? There's the petrol for starters."

Pennance shifted his attention away from the negotiation and headed for the shape, Jansen close behind.

"Jonah." Jansen had paused, squatted down.

Pennance joined her, shifting slightly so his shadow no longer fell on where she'd pointed. A splat of liquid, dark brown. "Dried blood?"

"Looks that way."

At the tarpaulin Pennance grabbed a corner. "You take the other." When Jansen was ready he said, "Go."

Underneath was a car, which had been driven straight in – grille pointed at the far wall, boot to the entrance.

Between them Pennance and Jansen dragged the heavy and brittle tarpaulin off. Pennance said, "How did witnesses describe the car at the supermarket?"

"Big and silver."

"And four concentric circles on the grille."

"An Audi."

"Like this one."

"I'll call Crosse and CSI," said Jansen.

Pennance peered through the grimy glass; nothing within. Pennance tugged on the handle. Locked. The same with the boot.

At the entrance a silhouetted Zinke had his phone poised over Saxelby's credit card machine. And Jansen a few yards away, making a call. Maybe prioritising Crosse, maybe not.

THE BLUE CODE

"Try again," said Saxelby.

"There's no reception out here," said Zinke.

"Mr Saxelby," said Pennance. "I need you to open the boot."

"Who's paying?" said Saxelby.

"Just get on with it, Andy," said Zinke.

Saxelby pushed the card machine into the estate agent's hands, then picked up his gear. Beside Pennance, Saxelby bent over at the waist and examined the lock. "I'll need to drill."

"Go ahead," said Pennance.

"There might be an alarm."

"We'll just put our fingers in our ears."

The locksmith pulled out a cordless drill, changed the bit and got to work.

After a few moments of the high-pitched whine of metal on metal Saxelby stopped and reached forward.

"Leave it," said Pennance. Saxelby froze. "Step back, please." Saxelby did.

Pennance pushed up the boot and a pungent, thick odour escaped, coating the inside of Pennance's mouth and nose.

"Argh!" Saxelby reeled away.

Pennance grabbed Saxelby by the elbow and ushered him into the fresh air.

Zinke stared at Saxelby as the handyman leaned against the hut and retched.

"Look after him, would you?" asked Pennance.

Back in the hut Pennance ignored the stench, which was already seeping through the space, and peered closer into the boot. Two bodies were crammed inside, foetal like, a yin and a yang arrangement. The nearest corpse was a small and skinny man. A large, dark blemish marred his forehead. An obvious bullet hole.

An electric surge of recognition hit Pennance. Matt Ferrensby.

Pennance retreated, pulled one door after the other shut.

"What is it?" asked Zinke.

"You're going to need plenty of that gum," said Pennance.

Thirty Two

Night had seized hold of the Cambridgeshire countryside. An owl in a nearby tree told Pennance so via a mournful hoot. However, in this one little corner of barren landscape the darkness was temporarily held back by the technology of man. Crime scene technicians had set-up several of their powerful spotlights on tall stands, flooding both the exterior concrete apron and hangar interior.

Abernathy, as the attendant pathologist, and white-suited CSI technicians, led by the CSM, Thriplow, worked the scene inside the hangar, scouring the floor and crawling over the vehicle like beetles. For a brief instant a bright flash washed out the Audi as a technician snapped a photograph into the boot, capturing the dead men's embrace forever in digital format while a ragged row of uniformed cops progressed slowly and steadily in measured steps across the concrete apron, gaze down cast, seeking anything out of the ordinary.

Pennance leant against the bonnet of Jansen's car, now parked in the lee of the large block building. Jansen herself worked beside Shapiro inside the hangar, leaving Pennance to contemplate the scene and little else. Zinke sat in his car, classical music cranked up, smoking furiously. The wail of violins easily carried, despite the windows being closed tight, holding in the self-imposed nicotine smog.

CSI vans were arrayed along the track from the road, with Crosse's vehicle at the rear which, as far as Pennance was concerned, is what you got when you arrived last.

Right now, Crosse was walking away from the hangar, pushing down the hood of his evidence suit, peeling off one nitrile glove after another then positioned himself beside Pennance. "What a bloody mess." Crosse nodded towards the estate agent who stuffed a fresh cigarette in his mouth, lit it with the stub of the one he'd been sucking on seconds ago. "He's not happy."

"Zinke doesn't do stress," said Pennance. "And we weren't expecting to find corpses."

Crosse pulled out an e-cigarette and took a quick draw before expelling liquorice-smelling air. "I fancy a proper smoke myself. But the missus would smell it a mile off, she's got the olfactory senses of a fox."

"You're married?"

"Recently started seeing someone new. She's not police like my ex. I'm trying to keep my two lives totally separate this time."

"Fair enough." Pennance respected Crosse's choice. Not one he'd made himself.

"As you thought, one victim is Matt Ferrensby. The other is James Haigh, a nobody who was briefly a somebody. Won a cool £1.2 million on the lottery. Bought a house, a car and a Thai bride. She left the moment the money did."

"Haigh spent it all?" said Pennance.

"Spent and gambled. He liked the gee-gees."

"Ferrensby bet, too."

"Lots of people do." Crosse shrugged. "Abernathy won't be drawn on cause of death but it's clearly a single bullet through the brain."

"Brutal."

THE BLUE CODE

"And damn frightening, I would think. From blood spatter Thriplow reckons both men were shot inside the trunk."

"Good God."

"I don't think there's anything holy about this murder, DI Pennance."

"How long have they been in-situ?"

"Abernathy reckoned at least a day but won't be more exact that that."

"So, potentially soon after Elliott's shooting?"

"Could be." Crosse shrugged. "We've found a gun as well, a Kalashnikov. Maybe Draganov's. I'm having it couriered to Hewson at NABIS."

"What about the car?"

"The plates are fake, taken off a car in Liverpool months ago. I've had people checking the local CCTV network. Whatever route the Audi took to the supermarket wasn't past any cameras so there's no way of determining the start point." Crosse exhaled more smoke. "Sometimes there's too many eyes on us. Others, not enough."

"You've been busy."

"It's murder, what do you expect?" Crosse frowned. "Also, Abernathy told me that someone who's a pain in the arse authorised the analysis on the markings found on the burial."

"You're welcome." Pennance's mobile rang. "Sorry, I need to take this."

"Hi Jonah, this is Alasdair." Tremayne, the forensic accountant. "I've continued looking into Longshot Ventures."

"I've got the SIO, DI Crosse, who's leading the case with me," said Pennance.

"He'll want to hear this. Go onto speaker, please."

Pennance did so. "Alright, Alasdair."

"Okay," said Tremayne. "It's taken quite a lot of effort but I've been tracing ownership of Longshot Ventures. The Directors are a Felicity Ratliffe and Wayne Mercer. Do those names mean anything to you?"

Crosse blinked then said, "Bloody hell." He began tearing off his evidence suit. "I've got him. I've finally got Mercer!"

"This isn't enough," said Pennance.

"Oh. It's plenty, what with Dr Abernathy's scan results. Those markings on the burial, they were tattoos after all and the database matched them to one Howard Epstein."

"I don't know who that is," said Pennance.

"He's the connection we've been waiting for."

"Can somebody tell me what's going on?" asked Tremayne.

"We're going back to the station," said Crosse, "to round up the troops then hit Mercer. We're taking him down. Tonight."

Thirty Three

Crosse nudged his Porsche through the arch and into the courtyard, pulling up a few yards away from the window of Mercer's bookies. He left the engine grumbling, drummed his fingers on the steering wheel. "You wouldn't believe how long I've been waiting for this."

"Then let's go." Pennance opened the passenger door, glanced up at the cameras above the entrance. Mercer would already be well aware of their arrival.

Crosse lifted a radio receiver to his mouth. "All units, wait for my command."

A crackle in response, then Jansen: "Yes, sir."

Besides Jansen, Cairns from Digital Forensics, three CID officers and four uniform were split across a van and two squad cars, parked up on several streets in the surrounding area. Should Mercer bolt, they would be ready. Crosse let the Porsche's engine die, slid out of his seat.

Pennance waited because this was Crosse's moment. Crosse stepped over the threshold into Mercer's and paused, hands down, loose. Like a gunslinger, awaiting the draw. Crosse deliberately left the door gaping, allowing the wind to filter in, and Pennance made no move to close it.

Ratliffe occupied her accustomed position behind the counter, her neck bent, eyes down, dealing with a grey haired guy in a stained raincoat. As Crosse and Pennance arrived at the counter the old guy scooped up a brown envelope, a sheaf of banknotes visible, and shoved it in an inside pocket.

Crosse placed his hands on the counter, while Ratliffe scribbled in the ledger.

Without pausing in her work Ratliffe said, "What do you want?"

"A word with your boss." He tilted his head at the hidden door. "Open up, would you."

"Have you got a warrant?"

"Do I need one for a friendly chat?" Crosse reached inside his jacket, extracted a folded piece of paper, slid it through to Ratliffe. "But as you ask so nicely, yes I do."

The door lock clicked, Ratliffe not bothering to read the document which Crosse retrieved. "Thank you very much."

Crosse climbed the stairs, emerging through the hatch ahead of Pennance. The birds chirped loudly, flitting frantically from perch to perch, like there was danger close by. Even the parrot hopped from foot to foot.

"Chief Inspector Crosse." Mercer sprinkled some fish food into one of the tanks. "Always a pleasure. How's that new girlfriend doing?"

"None of your fucking business."

Mercer chuckled, pointed to the guest chairs and sat himself. "Take some weight off those flat feet, officers."

"I'm here to talk about Howard Epstein." Crosse dropped the warrant onto Mercer's desk beside the branded mug with the black O which Pennance now recognised as Obsidian's logo. Suddenly, the birds fell silent.

Mercer used his fingertips to pull the warrant over to him. "Who's he?"

"One of your customers."

"Don't believe I know him."

THE BLUE CODE

"He's a general low-life. Minor drug dealer, occasional shoplifter, regular drinker and had a gambling habit."

"Had, Chief Inspector? Is he reformed?"

"Epstein was feeding us information on your operation, until he disappeared a couple of weeks ago."

"Maybe he fell in the river, pissed up?"

"Actually, he was discovered several days ago in a shallow grave, probably strangled," said Pennance. "He'd been buried for a couple of weeks."

"My commiserations to his family." Mercer tossed the warrant back onto his desk. "Well, if I can help solve a crime, I'm happy to help. Though there was no need for this." He waved at the legal paperwork.

"Just before his death Epstein made a call from your premises," said Crosse. "Then he travelled from here to a large house on the edge of Brampton, not Epstein's kind of place at all. Far too nice. Epstein wasn't qualified to drive, and there weren't any buses running. We checked with all the taxi firms, and nobody took a fare from anyone matching Epstein's description. Which means he was driven there."

"Okay, great. Access CCTV, there's enough of it around." Mercer, in front of his own bank of monitors, steepled his fingers.

"As well as Epstein we also found a rather imposing Bulgarian hitman by the name of Alexis Draganov in the living room. He'd been stabbed to death. Draganov, we now know, shot Logan Elliott to death earlier in the day."

"Have you heard of Longshot Ventures?" asked Pennance.

"Isn't longshot a gambling term?" Crosse turned to Pennance. "Basically, a risky bet with a potentially huge payoff."

"Longshot is a shell company," said Pennance.

"Usually employed by shifty bastards to hide cash from the taxman."

"*Vive la resistance*," said Mercer.

"The property where Epstein was found is owned by Longshot Ventures," said Pennance.

"And so is the old Graveley air base. Where two men were murdered." Crosse tossed a photo of Ferrensby and Haigh lying dead in the Audi's boot onto Mercer's desk.

"Elliott's driver, one Matt Ferrensby, and James Haigh who, we believe, took Draganov to and from the Elliott hit."

"Aren't both of these men clients of yours, Wayne?" asked Crosse.

Mercer said nothing, a half-smile playing across his lips.

"An NCA colleague, Alasdair Tremayne, is rather good at following financial trails," said Pennance.

"I like him," said Crosse.

"Me too."

"This Tremayne traced ownership of Longshot back to you, Wayne."

"Bullshit," said Mercer.

"He's able to employ the full resources of the NCA on his investigations," said Pennance. "If Tremayne says you own Longshot, then you do."

Crosse nodded at Pennance.

Pennance texted Jansen, 'Got him'.

Which got an immediate reply, 'We're rolling'.

THE BLUE CODE

"So," said Crosse. "That means we have Epstein travelling from this very building to where he and the man who shot Logan Elliott died. Along with a third property where two more bodies were found. All three locations are owned by Longshot Ventures, which in turn is owned by you."

"Circumstantial evidence, at best," said Mercer.

"Enough for me to get that warrant to search your property and to take you in for formal questioning." With a flourish Crosse produced handcuffs from a pocket. "Please, make it difficult for me, Wayne."

On the TV screen police vans and squad cars entered the courtyard – Jansen and her team.

Mercer, though, slowly stood and turned around. "You're making a huge mistake."

As Crosse ratcheted the cuffs around a wrist he said, "Wayne Mercer, I'm arresting you on suspicion of conspiracy to murder Howard Epstein."

Jansen's head popped up through the floor. "Want me to take him, sir?"

"No, that's my honour." Crosse led Mercer to the hatch and Jansen came into the office, out of Crosse's way. "Make sure you don't fall and break my neck, Wayne."

Shaking himself out of Crosse's grip Mercer said, "I've information I can trade. Other stuff I can tell you." The birds set to screeching again, the parrot bobbing on its perch.

"You're not wriggling away this time."

"Jonah." Mercer turned to Pennance. "Give me a minute, just listen."

"Why have you got a mug from Obsidian?"

"What are you on about?"

"The cup on your desk."

"You're just indulging him, Pennance." Crosse was having none of it. "Move it, Wayne. And don't worry about your pets, someone will look after them."

With Pennance leading, Mercer made his way carefully down, one step at a time, blinking as he emerged into his shop, Crosse following in his tracks. Ratliffe remained in place, observing, impassive.

A car engine came from outside, loud and large. A black Range Rover screeched to a halt outside the doorway, all four doors popping, men in suits spilling out from each.

"Whoa, whoa!" A PC blocked access to the shop. "What the hell do you think you're doing?"

The men surrounded the PC. A blonde guy reached into his pocket, showed the PC something before he backed away, allowing the quartet to enter.

"Who the bloody hell are you?" Crosse still held onto Mercer's arm.

"Looks like competition," said Mercer.

The blonde guy nodded at Pennance. "Pennance can tell you my name, DCI Crosse."

"This is DCI Leigh Fulton, City of London police," said Pennance.

"Me and my team are with the National Economic Crime Centre, an NCA task force."

"A mate of yours then, Pennance?" asked Crosse.

"Hardly," said Fulton. "We've been carrying out an investigation into Wayne Mercer."

THE BLUE CODE

"And operating on my patch without telling me? At least Pennance had the courtesy to introduce himself," said Crosse.

"Now you know who I am," said Fulton, "I'll be taking Mercer."

"I don't bloody think so, son, he's my collar." Crosse glanced around. "Where's Jansen?"

"Here, sir." Jansen emerged from the doorway to Mercer's office.

"The NCA takes precedence here," said Fulton.

"Oh, really? Have a look around, mate. There's a lot more of us than you already and I can easily add more bodies." Crosse's team not so subtly closed in on Fulton and his men, shifting forward a step. "Jansen, put Mercer in the back of the van." Crosse handed Mercer over, like they were passing a baton.

"You're making an error," said Fulton.

"Funnily enough Mercer told me the same just now." Crosse got up close to Fulton. "Look, pal. I don't know who the hell you are or what you're really up to. This is the first I've heard of your apparent case. So, if you think I'm just going to let anyone out of my custody to yours, try again. Mercer is being taken into my nick."

"I'll be talking with Director Quant."

"Like I care."

In the courtyard, Jansen swung open the van door, revealing a mini cage, the walls a metal grille. Jansen pushed Mercer inside, then slammed the door shut while Fulton dug out his phone and put it to his ear.

Crosse grabbed Pennance's arm and steered him outside. "Did you know about that lot?" Crosse leant on a wing of his Porsche and sucked on his e-cig.

"I promise you, no," said Pennance.

"Who the hell are they?"

"They're a specialised team focused on financial crimes. Ava found reports on the NCA server that they'd previously investigated Mercer. They were looking at potentially fraudulent accounts."

"So you *are* aware of them."

"Kind of, but not what they were up to right now. If my boss did, then she kept it from me." Pennance would be ringing Meacham as soon as he could.

"So we've both been stumbling around in the dark."

"Seems that way."

"How will your friends react to me keeping Mercer?"

"They're not my friends," said Pennance, "Fulton is my partner's boss. I don't like him so much, and the feeling is mutual. However, Fulton will be true to his word and he'll be shaking the management pole right now. At some point you should expect the NCA to have their fingers right into your investigation."

"Well, we'd better crack on then." Crosse pushed off the Porsche and held out a hand to Pennance. "I reckon we can operate on first name terms from now on." They shook. "So, let's see what we can find to keep Mercer locked up 'til he's old and incontinent."

Thirty Four

Mercer's was now closed. The door locked shut. The blind down on Ratliffe's booth. Curtains open in Mercer's office.

Crosse's entire team were fanned out, opening filing cabinets, drawers and cupboards, extracting piles and piles of paperwork to be sifted through in detail.

Cairns and McAlaney, seated side by side behind Mercer's desk, reviewed the CCTV footage while Crosse leaned over them. A laptop sat beside Cairns, lid open.

"Anything?" Crosse glared at the parrot when it squawked.

"I've not been at it long," said Cairns, "but it seems some of the footage from the dates you're interested has been wiped."

Jansen opened a desk drawer. She stepped back to allow a photographer to snap the contents in-situ before removing the items within and bagging them individually.

Pointing to the uppermost screen, Cairns said, "This is from out front." Pennance watched someone exit the shop and out of sight before the image dissolved into static. "There looks to be maybe half an hour missing. Possibly longer."

"What about the other cameras?" asked Pennance.

"I don't know yet," said Cairns.

"Give him a chance," said Crosse.

"Hello, what's this?" Jansen paused in her search, gloved hands on hips.

A phone nestled in the bottom drawer. Cheap and not smart.

"A burner." Crosse stating the obvious. "Cairns?"

The Digital Forensics technician powered up the phone, checked the number on screen before pulling over his laptop and tapping away.

"It's the same one that followed Epstein to River Road," said McAlaney.

"She's right," said Cairns.

"Absolutely brilliant." Crosse did his over-enthusiastic hand-rubbing thing then moved to Mercer's coffee machine and started looking for an on switch. "You'll be on your way to that there London before you know it, Jonah."

"It feels like we've still a lot of unanswered questions." Pennance lifted Mercer's mug. "Like, who hired Draganov, and why?"

"Yeah, but there are always unknowns." Crosse pressed a button and the machine began to chug. "Bloody hell, where are the cups?"

Pennance's phone rang. He moved away into a corner before answering. "Ma'am, thanks for calling me back." Crosse still hadn't found a receptacle and coffee was spilling out of the spout.

"Sorry it took so long. I've been in with Quant," said Meacham. "There's some angst in the building over Fulton's treatment by Crosse. Quant is onto Malik right now."

"Why didn't you tell me there was a second team operating in Huntingdon?"

"Because I wasn't aware. Quant didn't bring me into her confidence. She told me it was her prerogative to act how she wished. Our conversation on that aspect was extremely short."

"Sorry, ma'am."

"It's hardly your fault, Jonah," said Meacham. "Quant is very pleased with your work, by the way. She's delighted Logan Elliott's killer has been caught."

"We don't know for sure yet what Mercer's involvement is, ma'am."

"Even so, Quant is convinced. I'm expecting you'll be able to come home very soon."

"So I keep being told."

"That's what you want, right?"

"Sure." Eventually.

"Can you have a word with DCI Crosse? Advise him to let Fulton and his men in. It'll go easier for everyone."

"Crosse isn't really a laid back kind of guy."

"Try at least, Jonah." Meacham disconnected.

At Mercer's desk the phone Jansen had found was inside a clear plastic evidence bag and hooked up to the laptop via a cable. McAlaney worked away, watched by Jansen, Cairns and Crosse.

"Nick," said Pennance. "Have you got a moment?" Pennance moved beside a fish tank and Crosse joined him. Pennance said, "I've just had my boss call. Director Quant is on with Malik right now. Whether you like it or not, Fulton and his men will be on the case soon. I'd suggest its worthwhile letting them in yourself before being told."

Crosse pushed his hands into his trouser pockets. "That sounds like surrendering, Jonah."

"No, it's good tactics. If you resist the NCA could completely take over the case. Mercer would be theirs to close out. Surely you don't want that?"

"Not a bloody chance."

"Then talk to Fulton."

"You think it'll work?"

"Better to be in control of the narrative than having someone tell you."

"Typical Pennance," said Crosse. "Using thirteen words when just saying yes would have done." He grinned. "How about you negotiate on my behalf? As you're both NCA."

"Only I am; Fulton's City of London police."

"Same thing, though."

"Not really."

"Seems so to me – Londoners, entitled and operating on my patch."

Pennance sighed. "I can give it a try."

"Chop, chop then, Jonah."

"You're not my boss, remember?"

"Then let's be thankful for oversized mercies, eh?"

***

Pennance found Fulton in the back seat of the Range Rover, head leant back against the rest. "Hello, Leigh."

"Get in," said Fulton. "And shut the door. We don't want to be overheard by the locals."

"I guess it was you I saw outside Naughton's party and his office."

"And at the traffic stop yesterday when you arrived."

Pennance said, "So, you knew about me, but not the other way around."

"Seemingly."

"How long have you been monitoring Mercer?"

"On and off for about six months, but we've had a full team operating in rotation for two weeks now."

"Crosse isn't happy. He's been after Mercer a lot longer."

"I don't really care about the DCI's opinion. I assume he sent you to reason with me?"

"I'm here of my own accord. To find a way that we can all work together."

"Makes a change for you to provide balance, Jonah."

"Maybe something of Simone is rubbing off on me."

"How much do you know about Obsidian?"

"Naughton's company? He told me they mined big data to improve corporate decision making and I'm aware they have various civil service contracts."

"How about the fact that the NCA has been funding them for the last five years?"

"What? No, I wasn't aware of that."

"Big data is just one tiny aspect of Obsidian's actual intellectual property. Naughton's true focus is on the development of machine learning and computer vision algorithms and techniques."

"I don't know what that means," said Pennance. Not for the first time.

"Computer vision is a branch of artificial intelligence that trains the computer to understand the visual world by analysing camera data. So, it can be used to position locations and identify objects. By machine we mean computer and it teaches itself to improve each time, getting better at recognising items."

"Okay."

"Naughton's predictive algorithm package is called CINN." Fulton pronounced the acronym as 'sin'. "It stands for 'Criminal Intelligence Neural Network'. Its purpose is to forecast crime – where it'll occur and by who. We prefer to call it The Blue Code."

"This is fiction, surely?"

"It's absolutely true, Jonah, believe me. You know we're suffering an ever wider and increasingly complex range of criminal activity although we're not getting more cops on the street any time soon. We're overwhelmed. The theory is CINN allows police forces across the country to better focus their resource."

"Do you believe that?"

"The system relies on a heavy amount of monitoring, some of it potentially intrusive. Like scraping millions of photographs off social media and uploading them into a database, completely disregarding every privacy policy. Then using CCTV coupled with facial recognition software and accessing mobile devices to map people's movements. Bring in racial profiling, and your skin colour can be used against you. Once there's enough data all of this can be utilised as a predictive tool in advance or evidence gathering to make convictions more likely after a crime has occurred."

"This is unbelievable."

"Trust me, it's perfectly possible and it's already happening. The development of CINN has been conducted in great secrecy by Obsidian and in all likelihood the public won't know of it until long after the system is operational."

"Why are you telling me this?"

"Did Quant make you aware of CINN when you began the investigation?"

"No."

"Then that's a question you should be asking," said Fulton. Crosse wandered outside, e-cigarette in mouth and began puffing away. Fulton continued, "Logan Elliott and I were colleagues. One thing I can tell you for sure, he would never have been involved in something which was so clearly a breach of human rights."

"Is that what CINN is?"

"What would you call monitoring by the state? As a minimum CINN is an incursion into civil liberties."

"How is Mercer tied into all of this? It seems like a lot of effort to bring down a small town loan shark. Mercer's barely local, never mind national.

"Quant's orders – she wanted Mercer out of the way."

"But why?"

"I don't know," admitted Fulton. "Then there's the lawyer, O'Shea."

"He cleans up people's reputations."

"Yes, but in this case, whose?"

Pennance had been asked the same question just yesterday. "We need to talk with Crosse."

"Are you sure?"

"Do you trust my opinion?"

Fulton paused a long moment "No, but for some reason Simone does. And that's enough for me."

"Ah, my competition." Crosse blew a large stream of smoke through pursed lips as Pennance and Fulton walked towards him and put his e-cig away. "I assume you want something?"

"To be included in any and all interviews you have with Mercer," said Fulton.

"If you share all your intelligence on Mercer with me."

"That might be a challenge."

"Then we have a problem." Crosse rubbed a sleeve on an invisible mark on his Porsche.

"As much as we can," said Pennance, "Yes, you'll get the information." Pennance ignored Fulton's glare.

"And to speak with Mercer alone," said Fulton.

"Definitely not." Crosse shoved hands in pockets. " When you're there, so am I."

"Would you prefer me to just take Mercer back to London and cut you out entirely?"

"I'm up for a fight."

"I can make it happen. You know that."

"What about if I bridged the gap?" said Pennance. "Meaning I attend all the interviews."

"But you're both NCA," said Crosse.

"Not at all," said Fulton. "I'm City of London. I don't like the NCA. Far too much over-reach."

"But you're seconded to them."

"Orders." Fulton shrugged.

"That I get."

"I'm fine with Jonah being the connection between the cases," said Fulton. "One of his few positives is he doesn't lie."

"Not a fan?" asked Crosse.

THE BLUE CODE

"No."

"I've worked with worse." Crosse crooked a finger at Fulton. "You've got a deal." He turned and walked towards Mercer's. "Come and see what we've found so far."

***

Upstairs, in Mercer's office, Fulton paused for a moment, taking the surroundings in. The parrot raised his plume, stuck out his tongue and hissed at Fulton. Maybe there was something redeemable about the bird.

"This is Cairns," said Crosse. "Digital Forensics."

Fulton nodded at Cairns, then McAlaney. He said, "Ava."

"Chief Inspector," said McAlaney.

"They've been working on a burner Mercer left lying around," said Crosse.

"Very careless," said Fulton.

"We're done with the phone," said Cairns. "It's only been in use for a few weeks. There are three other numbers it's been in contact with, all untraceable. One we've already identified as Epstein's. Another we don't recognise. But the third, this one," Cairns tapped his laptop screen, "was also called by Epstein several times including on Epstein's final day."

"We need to find out whose number that is," said Crosse.

"Agreed," said Fulton.

"Well done. Get the phone off for forensics. I'm sure Mercer's grubby digits will have been all over it." Crosse rubbed his hands together.

***

Later, Pennance watched Mercer being bundled out of the police van. Mercer blinked under the harsh spotlight and the glare of multiple police officers. It seemed that the whole station had turned out to witness him being brought in.

Mercer bowed to his audience before Crosse grabbed his upper arm and hustled him inside to be booked in.

"It's weird seeing him outside the shop," said Jansen.

Pennance's phone rang.

"Inspector Pennance?" asked Lesia. "Is it true that Mercer has been arrested?"

"News travels fast in this town."

"Can you come around here? I need to show you something."

"What is it?"

"No, you've got to see it. Now, please, it's important."

Thirty Five

Pennance knocked on the front door of the address Lesia had given him – not Shapiro's house – just a few streets away from Melody's B&B. Behind, Jansen's car engine ticked as it cooled. A lock turned and several bolts drew before Lesia opened up a crack.

"Come in." Lesia widened the door for them to enter.

At the end of the hall, in an open entrance way, stood a much older woman who wore an obvious wig and a house coat. Her cheeks were sunken and deep, dark circles beneath her eyes.

Lesia glanced along the road before closing and securing the door. Then she said something in a language Pennance didn't know to the older woman who nodded in reply before shuffling slowly out of sight.

"This is my mama's house," said Lesia

"Is your mother okay?" asked Pennance. "She doesn't look so good."

"She's just tired, she hasn't been sleeping."

Pennance thought it more than that. Lesia's mother appeared deeply unwell.

Lesia led Pennance and Jansen upstairs and into the first room off the landing. The curtains were closed and the overhead light illuminated a single bed with a line of teddy bears up against the pillow. A couple of boy band posters, manufactured groups Pennance would never listen to, were stuck on the wall above a desk and chair. Then a flat head screwdriver and some screws obviously out of place on the flowery duvet.

"Ed had asked me to keep something for him." Lesia rolled back a rug from stripped floorboards before she reached for the screwdriver and levered up a board maybe a foot long with holes in each corner where the screws would have been. "I haven't touched it."

"When was this?" asked Pennance.

"He's opened the hole several times since we met. Last time was a couple of days ago. Ed told me not to not say anything to anybody and to trust no-one. He was very insistent. He grabbed me by the arms and shook me." Lesia raised her arms, crossed them, gripped her biceps. "Since I left Ed's yesterday it's been on my mind. He's called me several times. I haven't picked up. I'm afraid he'll come over."

Jansen squatted above the gap and pulled on nitrile gloves. "Take a look at this."

A black plastic folder pushed into the space between two beams.

Jansen pulled the package out as Pennance got gloves on too. Inside were three identical packages – A3-sized bulky, brown paper envelopes. And then a padded envelope half the size of the others. Jansen shook out the contents of the uppermost package.

Bundles of banknotes, each tightly bound by an elastic band, hit the floor. Jansen picked a couple up, riffled through them like they were packs of cards. All were grouped together into tens or twenty's. The other two packets also contained cash. "There could be twenty or thirty thousand pounds here."

THE BLUE CODE

"Easily," said Pennance.

Jansen turned her attention to the final envelope which itself contained three items. The first was an Irish passport. Shapiro's photo was on the back page, the issue date just over a year ago and the name was Cormac Byrne.

Pennance took the travel permit. "Very good quality."

The others were a no-frills burner phone and a brand new smart phone.

"We should get these to Digital Forensics," said Jansen.

"Let's take a look for ourselves first." Pennance held down the burner's power key until the screen lit up and the handset vibrated. He went to the call list – empty. Either none had been made or the details had been deleted. "How do you find the number on these things?"

"I'll have to Google it." Jansen did so. "Type hash, then four zeros and hash again."

Pennance tapped away at the keypad, and the number popped up on screen. "That's the same as on Mercer and Epstein's, right?"

"I think so, yes," said Jansen.

Now, Pennance switched on the smart phone, more like a mini-tablet given the size of it in his palm. The manufacturer's logo came up before a screen-lock kicked in requiring either a password or a face ID. However, Pennance didn't need to crack the code because the screensaver photo told him all he needed to know.

Elliott and Olivia, sharing a glass of fizz. On a dead man's mobile.

"We need to tell Crosse," said Pennance. "His favourite officer is dirty."

Thirty Six

Jansen opened the door to reveal Crosse leaning at an angle, one hand on the wall like he was propping up the house, rather than himself.

"What the bloody hell's going on, Keri?" The first time Pennance had heard Crosse use Jansen's first name. Maybe he was softening. "This had better be good."

"Best we talk inside, sir."

"If you insist." Crosse stepped in.

"It's about Shapiro," said Pennance as Jansen closed the door. "His girlfriend has just shown us several items he's been concealing here, including tens of thousands of pounds in banknotes, a fake Irish passport and two mobiles."

Crosse laughed. "This is a joke, right?"

"One of the phones," said Jansen, "belonged to Elliott."

"Horseshit, Sergeant."

Jansen held out the smartphone, now in a clear plastic evidence bag. She touched a button on the side, illuminating the photo of Elliott and Olivia.

Crosse took the bag, stared at the screen. "I don't believe it."

Pennance showed Crosse the burner. "It's the same number contacted by Epstein and Mercer's handset."

"This is a set-up."

"Everything was hidden under a floorboard upstairs," said Jansen.

"I want to talk with the girlfriend."

"Lesia."

"Whatever."

Lesia stood when Crosse entered her bedroom. "I'm DCI Crosse."

"I know who you are," she said. "Ed talks about you all the time. And I saw you on the news the other night. Outside a curry house."

"Right." Crosse focused on the hole in the floor and the screwdriver. "Sit down and tell me about you and Shapiro."

"We've been in a relationship for a few months, on and off." Lesia settled again onto a corner of the bed.

"Do you live together?" Crosse pulled out the chair from under the desk, leaving Pennance and Jansen in the doorway.

"No, I just sleep over some nights, when he's not working. I have some of my stuff there. Otherwise I'm here, at mama's. Ed isn't allowed to stay, which is why I go to his."

"How long has he been asking you to conceal things for him?"

"Not long, a few weeks."

"Did you know what he was giving you?"

"I never asked and he didn't tell me."

"Why would you let him?"

Lesia scooted back across the bed, leant against the wall and drew her legs up. "He scares me."

"You stood up for yourself last night," said Pennance.

"What does that mean?" asked Crosse.

"The Inspector and Sergeant spoke to me while I was at Ed's house yesterday. He wasn't there at first. When he came home he turned aggressive. I got upset, we argued and I wanted to leave. He wouldn't let me. Until I kicked him in the balls."

"Shapiro was well out of order," said Pennance.

"I was shaking like a leaf afterwards." Lesia glanced at Pennance. "I had to stop the car when I got around the corner and calm myself down. When we were first together he was lovely, but he'd have these bouts of anger these last few weeks, Ed said it was stress, and he's been on the verge of hitting me several times."

"What started your argument yesterday?" asked Crosse.

"Ed admitted he was gambling again. With Mercer."

Crosse stood. "I think I've heard enough, thank you, Lesia. We'll get you down the station for a formal interview. Otherwise, no contact with Shapiro – no calls, nothing, okay?"

Lesia nodded.

"Come on you two." Crosse pushed his way through Pennance and Jansen then descended, feet heavy on the stairs.

Outside, Jansen pulled the door to as Crosse headed onto the pavement to stand beside his Porsche parked behind Jansen's.

Pennance carried the evidence bags. "We have to lift Shapiro."

"Not right now." Crosse shook his head.

"You're kidding."

"Look, Jonah. I'm in a difficult position here. I was hand-picked by the Chief Constable to turn around Huntingdon CID. I specifically selected Shapiro and promoted him to inspector. If he's bent I'll be at the front of the queue pushing him into a cell. However, I want to be utterly certain and leave zero room for doubt. Right now it's her word against Shapiro's and he's police. Understood, Jonah?"

After a long moment Pennance said, "Alright."

"Thank you." Crosse opened his door. "Right, I need to see what's on this phone."

***

McAlaney and Cairns were waiting in the Digital Forensics office at Huntingdon police station, Cairns at his desk, McAlaney at his absent colleague's. Crosse carefully placed both handsets in front of Cairns but left his fingers on top of the package, holding it down.

"Before we start I want to impress upon you the need for total confidentiality regarding anything you find on these other phones."

"I signed a non-disclosure agreement on my first day," said Cairns.

"I want more than a piece of paper here, Cairns. You don't talk to anyone. Not Brooker, your missus, your mates down the pub. Not a sausage. Because it's your nuts and mine in a blazing fire if any piece of evidence comes out."

"Sure, I get it."

"You'd better." Crosse pushed the evidence bags towards Cairns, then lifted his hands away. "The burner first. Pennance reckons this is the phone that was called by Epstein and Mercer."

"Let's see." Cairns went over to the equipment on the nearby table he'd previously used. McAlaney scooted across in her chair before Pennance, Crosse and Jansen formed a rough semi-circle behind them.

Cairns wiggled a mouse, bringing the gear to life and connected the phone. He pressed a few buttons on the handset then looked up at Crosse. "Yep, it's the same."

"Crap." Crosse squeezed the bridge of his nose.

"Who does this belong to?"

"Nuts and fire, remember?"

"Oh, okay." Cairns tilted his head briefly. "I'll call him Rorschach."

"Or her," said Jansen.

"What?" asked Crosse.

"Cairns is assuming the phone owner is the man, it could be a woman.

"No, I meant, what's Rorschach?"

"A masked anti-hero in a graphic novel," said McAlaney.

"A comic then."

"No."

Cairns said, "Ava and I have been working on triangulating the position of all the phones to determine who was speaking to who and when." Cairns brought up a map showing Huntingdon hemmed in by the ring road and a river and lakes to the east. "If you remember, there were so many numbers the data was hard to sort through. However, now we can focus." Cairns tapped away briefly. "So, this number spends most of its time unreachable, only appearing on the network for very short periods when a call is made or received, before being powered down again.

"Seventeen days ago Epstein's mobile was called four times, each conversation lasting less than a minute." Cairns clicked his mouse and pins dropped onto the map. "The yellow pins are Epstein, the blue, Rorschach. Remember, at the time Epstein was moving across several locations." Cairns clicked and the pins disappeared. "The following day there were two calls, both from Epstein to Rorschach." Just the yellow pins appeared this time. "Notice anything interesting?"

"One is at Mercer's again," said Jansen.

"And from River Road," said Pennance.

"The call from near Mercer's came first, the second half an hour later," said Cairns. "Then I started working backwards, filling in some of the blanks. On day sixteen a call was made to Rorschach from Mercer's and occurred almost immediately after Epstein's call to Rorschach.

"Another call was made, from Rorschach to Mercer, just after the first on that day from Epstein. The phone used was a burner and it remained at Mercer's. Cairns clicked his mouse and now a red pin appeared. "That's Mercer." Then more yellow pins, tracing a route from central Huntingdon to River Road. "This is Epstein." Now red pins made their way from Mercer's converged at River Road.

"So, let me get this in order," said Pennance. "Epstein and Rorschach talk multiple times over two days. Mercer contacts Rorschach which then triggers another conversation between Rorschach and Epstein culminating in Epstein going to River Road and then, very soon after, Mercer arrives?"

"*Someone* from Mercer's, yes. The final time the burner was used was four days ago." Another mouse click from

Cairns and the blue dot for Rorschach's phone dropped onto the map.

"That's Lesia's address," said Jansen.

"What about a proximity search?" asked McAlaney.

"Good idea," said Cairns.

"We can see if there were any other mobiles close enough to each other to tether."

They waited while Cairns worked.

"There were three other phones near to Rorschach's." The details were up on Cairns' monitor. "Give me a moment to carry out a data-filter search, then I can tell you whose is whose."

"You don't need to." Crosse pulled out his own phone, scrolled through, then put the handset down on the desk. The number on-screen matched one in Cairns' list. "It's Shapiro's personal mobile."

"Rorschach is Shapiro?" asked Cairns.

"Bloody hell," said Jansen.

"So that directly connects Shapiro to the burner found at Lesia's," said Pennance.

"They were in the same location, at least," said Cairns.

"We can check any CCTV in the area," said Crosse. "What about the other handset?"

Cairns removed the smart phone out of the bag. "Now, this will take a little more effort." Cairns unplugged the burner, selected a different cable and connected Elliott's mobile. "I need to get around the security." Cairns tapped away for a few minutes, switching between phone and computer.

THE BLUE CODE

McAlaney took over briefly before sitting back. "Here you go."

A window on the monitor displayed the phone's contents. "There's some photos, plenty of calls in and out. We'll have to spend some time analysing any web traffic, see which sites were accessed and so on. There's also a data card." Cairns clicked on a folder. "We've two in a WMA format, meaning they're audio files, and an mpeg; a video."

"Play the video," said Crosse.

Cairns double clicked on the file, before expanding the new window to fill the screen. The opening few seconds was black, then came an occasional flash of white from the edges, like light was spilling through a curtain, before a man stepped back from the lens.

Pennance immediately recognised Logan Elliott.

"Is there any sound?" asked Crosse.

Cairns stabbed at a key. "Turned right up."

Nothing issued from the speakers.

Behind Elliott was an office, a desk nearest stretching away like an ice shelf, windows beyond, a chair behind the desk, another in front.

Elliott swivelled at something then walked away, glancing over his shoulder at the lens. He disappeared out of the shot briefly before re-entering. Elliott pointed to one of the chairs and his visitor sat.

Crosse reached out, hit pause, freezing the action.

The man facing Elliott was Shapiro.

Thirty Seven

Crosse thumped on Shapiro's front door, using the side of his fist. He paused briefly, listened, hammered again.

The next door neighbour came out of his house, the same man with over-dark hair from previously. "Thank God you're here at last! There's been a terrific racket from inside. Things being smashed and screams. The worst I heard since moving in."

Pennance turned the handle. The door wasn't locked. He pushed it wide.

"Ed?" Crosse paused at the bottom of the stairs, a foot on the lowest step. "Ed, are you here?"

"Thank you, sir." Jansen closed Shapiro's door on the neighbour craning to get a look.

It looked like a bomb had gone off inside the living. Curtains torn down, the rail snapped and dangling. The TV lay on the floor, screen smashed and the games console in pieces.

Shapiro sat on the recliner in a terry towelling dressing gown, hair tousled like he'd just got out of bed. "Evening all." He raised a glass of something dark and, Pennance guessed, alcoholic. Shapiro chased down the shot and poured himself another. "I'd offer you one but I think I broke all the other glasses."

"We just want to talk." Crosse sat on the arm of the chair while Jansen started to tidy up some of the debris. Crosse put out a hand and Jansen stopped her efforts.

"I can't go to prison, Nick. They'll kill me."

THE BLUE CODE

"I'm sure you'll be fine." Pennance patted Shapiro.

Shapiro twisted. "Get your hands off me."

"Show me your bicep."

"Why?" asked Crosse.

"Abernathy said whoever killed Draganov was clipped by a bullet."

"I'm many things." Shapiro stood. "But I'm no murderer." He revealed one arm, then the other. No wounds. Shapiro flopped back down. "I really don't like you, Pennance."

"Why, Ed?" asked Crosse.

"Look at him," said Shapiro. "He's an arsehole."

"That's not what I meant."

"I know." Shapiro just shrugged. "Just poor choices, Nick."

"You should have talked to me."

"I really couldn't." Shapiro necked another drink. "What was it in the end?"

"Several things – like identifying Epstein. He was your snitch at Mercer's."

"You guessed it was him when Abernathy put his tattoos up on screen," said Pennance.

"I shouldn't have reacted so much," said Shapiro.

"And Lesia," said Crosse. "She showed us everything you were hiding at her mother's."

"She's lying. I didn't give her anything."

"Passport, £31,000 in cash and two phones – your burner and Elliott's mobile," said Pennance. "I bet when the labs carry out their analysis they'll find Elliott's blood still on it. Along with your prints."

"The passport was issued in Ireland more than a year ago," said Crosse. "The photo inside is of you."

"It's not mine!"

"Where did the money come from?" asked Pennance.

"This is all crap!" said Shapiro. "I've been set-up."

"I don't believe you," said Crosse. "I can't. Because we found video footage on Elliott's phone of you and him meeting. What did you want from him?"

"Nothing," said Shapiro. "It's fake."

"There's a record of you visiting Obsidian's offices," said Pennance. "We checked."

"Jesus, Ed." Crosse put a hand across his face.

"It's O'Shea you should be picking up. O'Shea and Lesia. They're in it together," said Shapiro. "O'Shea's job is to protect his client and he did it perfectly. Did you know Lesia's mother has cancer? Suddenly Lesia can afford private treatment. How does she manage that on a shopworker's wage? I can tell you – O'Shea paid her to screw me over."

"Do you have any proof?" asked Pennance.

"It's just obvious."

"I've had enough," said Crosse. "Edmund Shapiro, I'm arresting you on suspicion of murder."

"You're wrong."

"Anything you say can be used against you." Crosse read Shapiro the rest of his rights before leading his inspector away.

Thirty Eight

Mercer stood tall and upright when he entered the interview room with his be-suited and bespectacled lawyer. Crosse pointed to a chair. Mercer sat in the adjacent one.

"Always with the games." Crosse settled in opposite Mercer, moving the file across the table with him.

"I could say the same." Mercer glanced up at the CCTV lens. Fulton and his team were in a room nearby, watching events.

Pennance faced Mercer's lawyer – waistcoat buttoned to the top, tightly knotted tie, pursed lips and narrowed eyes. Like he meant business and ate cops for brunch.

Crosse started the digital recording machine, waiting for the long beep. "Detective Chief Inspector Crosse and Inspector Jonah Pennance interviewing Wayne Arthur Mercer in the presence of Gareth McNair." Crosse then read off the time and date before focusing on Mercer.

"I give it an hour," said Mercer. "Before I'm out of here and McNair's filing a wrongful arrest suit against Cambridgeshire Constabulary. Again."

McNair placed his fingertips on Mercer's forearm and received a glare in response. McNair withdrew, but the message had been dispensed.

Crosse flipped open the folder, extracted a photo of Elliott lying on the back seat of the Merc and pushed it towards Mercer. "Two days ago," Crosse checked his watch. "Make that three as we've passed midnight. Three days ago, Logan Elliott was shot to death outside a supermarket."

Another photo went next to Elliott's, this one a mugshot. "The killer was Igor Draganov."

"My client has no knowledge of these heinous crimes," said McNair.

"Prior to the shooting Draganov was staying here." Crosse placed a third photo opposite Mercer, ignoring McNair's interruption. "A property on River Road owned by one Longshot Ventures. As we discussed in your office, Wayne, Longshot is a shell company, the ownership of which some very clever people at the NCA have traced all the way to you."

"My client disputes that," said McNair.

"Where, following a phone call from a concerned neighbour, Inspector Pennance here discovered two corpses – Draganov in the front room and Howard Epstein, who'd been buried in a shallow grave in the garden."

Two further photographs – Draganov face down and Epstein's half-chewed arm poking out of the ground. Mercer ignored both. "No comment."

Crosse continued, "Now, Epstein was somewhat decomposed. I won't inflict those images on you, Wayne, and it took a little time to identify him. However, what we did find was a mobile underneath his body that someone had rather carelessly left behind." Another photo. "You'll see it's a Nokia, what I'm sure you know we refer to as a burner."

"Where's this going, Chief Inspector?" asked McNair.

"Just bear with me."

Mercer said, "Let him spin his little irrelevant tale, Gareth."

THE BLUE CODE

"Thank you so much," said Crosse. "We'll come back to the phone shortly. Anyway, not long after Draganov's body was discovered two more turned up, discovered by Inspector Pennance again."

Crosse put down another photo. "Matthew Ferrensby and James Haigh – the drivers of Elliott's and Draganov's cars respectively, both killed by a single bullet to the head. While in a car boot."

Mercer stared at the half-painted wall.

"Their bodies were concealed on the old Graveley airbase. Which just happens to be owned by one Longshot Ventures." Crosse pointed to Mercer. "Your company."

"To repeat, my client disputes your apparent findings," said McNair.

"Ferrensby and Haigh were known clients of yours," said Pennance.

"The bloodhound speaks," said Mercer.

"I've been informed that men in your employ, Mr Mercer, demanded repayment of debts by Mr Ferrensby."

"My client has never threatened anyone with physical violence," said McNair.

"What about mental torture?" asked Crosse.

"I repeat, Mr Mercer has never caused harm to any of his customers."

Mercer held out his hands wide, expression like an angel; innocent.

"Another witness has informed us that you were instrumental in getting Ferrensby the job driving Draganov," said Crosse. "To pay off his debts. Haigh too."

"I resent your statement, Inspector," said Mercer. "I wouldn't have contributed to his death in any shape or form."

Crosse withdrew one last photo from the folder – another burner phone. "When we searched your office earlier this handset was found in your desk drawer."

Mercer flicked his eyes down, then up again. "I've never seen this before. Someone planted it."

"Are you saying my people are crooked, Wayne?"

"Everyone is."

"This is the call log." Now Crosse put a piece of paper before Mercer. "Showing the numbers dialled to and from your mobile."

Mercer bent sideways towards McNair.

Crosse added more documents. "These are call logs from two other phones, including the one found with Epstein. You'll see they match."

McNair picked up the pages and glanced them over. Mercer shook his head when McNair offered them to him.

"So, now we have four bodies, all found on property owned by you. Two of the deceased we know owed you money and were coerced into involvement in Elliott's murder to settle their debts. Then, add in the mobile communication on a device in your possession and I think, Wayne, I've finally got you."

"You're looking at the wrong man, Crosse, as always," said Mercer. "This isn't me."

"Then tell me who I should be after then, Wayne?"

That was when an alarm went off.

Thirty Nine

Crosse ran into the corridor, grabbed a nearby PC. "Stay here, keep the door locked and don't let either of those two out under any circumstances."

"Yes, sir."

Crosse trotted away, Pennance catching up within a matter of strides. "What's going on?"

"It's the custody suite alarm."

Using his key card, Crosse barged through several doors before they entered the custody suite, continuing until they reached the cells. One of the doors stood wide and a group of cops were bunched around the entrance. Crosse barged his way through, Pennance in his wake.

Shapiro lay on the tiled floor of a cell, eyes closed, his face turned dark. A belt was fixed around his neck. Jansen had Shapiro's shirt open, hands pressing on his chest repetitively until she paused, then bent over, pinched his nostrils shut between two fingers and blew into his mouth.

"Somebody turn that bloody racket off." Crosse had to shout over the alarm. One of the bystanders slipped away as Jansen switched back to pumping Shapiro's chest.

The alarm cut out.

"What the hell happened here?"

"I checked on him." A uniformed sergeant, his face pale as snow, beads of sweat glistened on his forehead. "And I found him like that, hanging off the doorknob. He was fine earlier."

"You left him with a belt?"

"He said his trousers would fall down otherwise. It was Shapiro, I thought it would be okay."

Crosse ran fingers through his hair while Jansen blew into Shapiro's lungs again.

"He'd just sat down." The sergeant was shaking now, his whole body quivering. "Shapiro could have stood up at any time if he'd wanted. But he didn't. He wanted to die."

***

Two paramedics in green uniform – a tall, thin woman and a short, stubby man – wheeled the trolley out of the station. Shapiro lay there, held down by straps, a drip connected to his arm, looking like he should have been in a body bag, rather than under a blanket.

"How is he?" asked Crosse as the male paramedic manoeuvered Shapiro.

"In a coma," he said, wheezing with the effort.

Shapiro was loaded into the rear of the ambulance. The male paramedic joined Shapiro and began hooking him up to a monitor. The woman held onto the door, said, "Does one of you want to join him?"

"Go on, sir," said Jansen.

"No, I need to stay here." Crosse turned to a pair of PCs standing nearby, watching. "Don't let Shapiro out of your sight. I'll get someone to relieve you soon as I can."

Then the paramedic shut the doors and, moments later, the ambulance pulled away, lights on but no sirens.

"Well done, Keri." Crosse watched the ambulance round a bend and pull onto the ring road. "You may have saved

THE BLUE CODE

Shapiro's life. Then, when he's recovered, we can make sure he goes down for what he did." Crosse rubbed his eyes. "I don't know about you two, but I'm knackered. Mercer can wait 'til the morning. Let's all get some sleep."

Pennance got a text then, from Meacham. 'Pack your bags, Jonah. You're coming home'.

Pennance should have felt like celebrating. But he didn't.

Forty

Pennance was dreaming about fly fishing when he was woken by a hammering on his door. He blinked in the darkness, wondered why his brain had picked a sport he had no interest in and had never done before the beating started again. Pennance staggered out of bed, opened his door. Found Hoskins standing in the corridor in a pair of green paisley pyjamas, illuminated by the laptop in his hands.

"What time is it?" asked Pennance.

"Dunno. 5am, maybe?"

"Couldn't it wait, Vance?"

"No." Hoskins pushed past Pennance, put the laptop down and flicked on a lamp before he sat. "I couldn't settle so I looked back over Alasdair Tremayne's analysis of Longshot's accounts. One of the company's earliest transactions was a land sale. I did a bit of digging and the price Longshot got was well below market value. They sold it off really cheap."

"So?"

"Do you recognise the location?"

Pennance tried to focus on the screen, sleep still in his eyes. He blinked and finally his lenses focused. "Ermine Street."

"Where Naughton built his offices. I didn't make the connection initially as I wasn't on your jaunt over there. Anyway, I rang Alasdair, he seems to sleep even less than me, and we went over Obsidian's accounts together. Obsidian got a loan to purchase land, then, not long after, the company received planning permission for the building and had the land re-evaluated – at a much, much higher multiple – that Obsidian then used to obtain investment from backers which was ultimately used to construct and kit out the building."

"What does this mean, Vance?" Pennance's brain was still foggy.

"Fraud, Jonah. All along, the land had a significant worth attached to it. By Longshot undervaluing it, so Obsidian's cost – their first loan – was reduced. Then when it was correctly assessed that meant Obsidian's business value was way higher and gave Naughton's backers, mainly Americans, a lot of confidence he had the cash to succeed. Silicon Valley start-ups typically operate a 'fake it 'til you make it' approach. It's all front and bravado to bring in the finance, then you work like hell to actually prove your product. Many fail, some don't. But without that initial injection none would get off the ground."

"Smoke and mirrors."

"And Naughton had learnt from the best," said Hoskins. "He got his kick-off funds."

"From Mercer." The mug on Mercer's desk.

"Then in came the NCA who presumably had no idea one of Obsidian's stakeholders was Mercer."

"And the investment was dirty money. Which really wouldn't look good."

"Right, and who gets brought in to sweep up?"

"A reputation lawyer."

"Bingo," said Hoskins.

Melody was leant against a counter, folded *Racing Times* newspaper in one hand, mug of coffee in the other, when Pennance entered the kitchen.

"Morning, Jonah. Breakfast?"

"No, thanks. I'd like to ask a favour."

"Sure."

"Can I borrow your car? I'm not going far and the NCA will reimburse you."

"No problem." Melody put down cup, reached inside a nearby drawer and fished around before holding out the keys.

"Thanks." Pennance nodded at the *Times*. "How much do you lose?"

Melody glanced at the newspaper. "These days, nothing. Reading it is just like being an ex-smoker and putting a plastic cigarette in your mouth. But once, nearly everything went – life savings, husband, most of my family. All I've left is this house, which is mortgaged to the hilt, and Keri."

"You borrowed from Mercer?"

"Keri tells me he'll probably die in prison, so today is a good day." Melody grinned. "Which I guess means you're going back to London."

"Yes, just something else to do first."

***

Pennance was waiting when Naughton arrived at Obsidian's office when Naughton drove his Aston Martin in, parking right next to the building entrance.

THE BLUE CODE

"Bright and early, Inspector!" Naughton wore the same get-up as when Pennance visited last – slacks and polo shirt.

"I remembered you saying you start every day at 6am."

Naughton showed Pennance through the atrium and up to his office. "Coffee?"

"I'll pass."

Naughton fired up his computer and focused on the screen. "Well done on cracking the case and getting your man."

"Have we?"

"So Crosse says. After Logan's death I've an opening. I think Crosse wants the job. He's going to be sadly disappointed."

"Although I'm sure you're pleased Crosse has got rid of Mercer for you."

"I've no idea what you mean."

"Longshot Ventures."

"You'll have to talk to Connor about all of that." Naughton tapped away at his keyboard. "Really not my field."

"How long has Mr O'Shea been your lawyer?"

"Hmm?" Naughton glanced up. "Oh, he's not really *mine*. I don't pay him."

"Who does?"

"We all work for the same woman, Inspector."

"What does that mean?"

"I think you know." Naughton glanced past Pennance. "Ah, speak of the devil!"

O'Shea entered Naughton's office. He paused on the threshold, eyes flicking between Pennance and Naughton. "Inspector Pennance, anything I should be aware of?"

"I'll let your client fill you in," said Pennance.

As Pennance trotted down the stairs to the atrium he sent a text. 'We need to talk.'

The reply came back almost immediately. 'Where?'

Pennance answered, then unlocked Melody's old Mini.

As Pennance drove away from Obsidian he glanced in the rear-view mirror. O'Shea stood in the entrance, watching.

Forty One

The temporary office was empty, Hoskins and McAlaney had already left, on their way to London right now. Pennance was perched on the corner of the desk where Hoskins had stretched out when the door opened.

"I hear you're leaving," said Jansen. "Come to say goodbye?"

"How's your arm? Don't tell me it's from exercising."

Jansen lifted a hand up, stopped. "I don't know what you mean." She leant against a wall, hands behind her.

"You were in the alley when Elliott was shot. Draganov saw you, so you had to take him out."

"That was Shapiro. Crosse has him down for it."

"Maybe not anymore."

"Shapiro was Mercer's eyes and ears in the station."

"Agreed, however he wasn't the only one. You helped Mercer too."

"That's not true."

"Your Aunt got into debt with Mercer. You worked out a deal with Mercer so Melody could keep her house." Jansen said nothing. Pennance continued, "Yet you were stuck under Mercer's thumb, until your dark knight on his charger came along – Connor O'Shea. You had a shared objective. Getting rid of Mercer.

"Then there's Lesia, conveniently revealing all of Shapiro's stuff, including the phone that you took off Elliott. Lesia's mother has cancer, I'd guess the waiting list for treatment on the NHS was too long, so money went her way for her to go private. But you needed someone to take the blame. Enter Shapiro."

"Who deserves all he'll get. Everyone does."

"You know I can't let this slide."

"What are you going to do about it?" Jansen pushed herself off the wall and crossed room. "So, toddle back off to London, Jonah because you can't prove any of it."

Jansen opened the door. "Hello, Keri." Crosse stood there, one hand gripping Lesia's arm.

"Want to bet?" asked Pennance.

Forty Two

Pennance had never been up to the top floor of NCA headquarters. Until now.

Quant's office was reached by passing through another office occupied by her administrator, a young man in a sharp three piece suit and centre-parted, slick hair. It was the administrator who showed Pennance in. A large, framed black and white photo of an unsmiling woman wearing a long out of date police uniform stared back at Pennance. He knew this was Edith Smith, the first woman to be granted powers of arrest back in the late 19th Century.

"Ah, Jonah," Quant rose, removing large, black rimmed glasses. "Thank you, Glenn." Quant came round from behind her desk. "We finally meet." She pointed at a sofa. "Please, sit. Do you want a drink?"

"I'm fine, thank you, ma'am." Pennance lowered himself into the furniture's soft embrace while Quant placed herself opposite him. The sharp fringe to Quant's grey hair was her only visibly severe characteristic. No power dressing for the Director – denim jeans and a blue shirt. "I read your report and I wanted to personally congratulate you on a job excellently done. It was highly important to me for Elliott's killer to be brought to justice."

"Team effort, ma'am. I couldn't have done it without Hoskins and McAlaney."

"And be assured, I'll be talking to them separately. However, it was you who led from the front and in your first investigation outside of London and under a lot of pressure from the top." Quant smiled and there seemed genuine warmth within.

"Just part of the job, ma'am."

"I don't agree, Jonah. You went the extra distance for the NCA and for me. I won't forget it."

"Thank you."

A knock at the door came – Glenn and his shiny hair poking through the gap. "Your next appointment is here, Director."

"Hold them a few moments, please."

"Yes, ma'am." Glenn withdrew.

"In your report you state it was Mercer who hired Draganov to kill Logan?"

The SIO, DCI Crosse thinks so, yes. Ballistics tests confirmed Draganov then shot the two drivers."

"What was Mercer's motivation?"

"We don't know yet, ma'am. Mercer is denying any involvement."

What about the inspector at Cambridge Constabulary?"

"Shapiro."

"Right. I understand he's still in a coma?"

"Yes, ma'am. The doctors say that even if he wakes he'll have a degree of brain damage."

"So he won't be able to fill in the blanks?"

"Unlikely. Shapiro seems to be the linchpin. Epstein, the man buried in the back garden, was officially Shapiro's snitch. But in likelihood Shapiro was a conduit, passing information back to Mercer."

"And what about the back-up drive with the algorithm that was taken from Logan?"

"It still hasn't turned up, ma'am."

"It's probably only important to Obsidian and Kai Naughton."

"I'm sure." Pennance accepted Quant's lie.

"And what about the lawyer?" Quant raised her eyes to the ceiling. "I've forgotten his name."

"Connor O'Shea."

Quant clicked her fingers. "Right."

"He had no involvement at all that I could see." Another untruth.

A knock came and Glenn was back once more. "Your appointment, director."

Quant stood and held her hand out again. "Well, thank you, Jonah. I look forward to seeing you rise inexorably through the NCA."

"Thank you, ma'am." Dismissed, Pennance left.

Forty Three

Pennance was the last to arrive. He squeezed in at a table next to Hoskins, his leg pushed up against McAlaney's opposite. "Sorry."

"Vance's choice," said Meacham.

McAlaney and Hoskins had cocktails in front of them, Meacham just a glass of water.

"I thought it appropriate, sitting here opposite MI5, being all clandestine," said Hoskins. The building which housed the UK's counter-intelligence and security service hulked on the opposite bank of the Thames, the bleached stone façade bright in the sun.

"But a boat."

"A floating bar and restaurant to be accurate. And far enough away from the office to be discrete."

A waitress – bright orange, several piercings in ears and nose and black painted fingernails – came over. "Can I get you anything, sir? It's happy hour, docktails are half price."

"Docktails?"

"It's a boat and it's docked, Jonah," said Hoskins. "So, a docktail."

"Oh. Flat white, then."

"You're no fun."

"Anything to eat?" asked the waitress.

"Pizzas are good," said Hoskins.

"We're fine, thanks," said Meacham.

Hoskins poked out his bottom lip.

"Okey-dokey." The waitress retreated.

THE BLUE CODE

"Well?" Meacham leaned on elbows. "How did it go with Quant?"

"Quickly," said Pennance. "She said thanks, job well done, posed some questions, I played dumb and left."

"You can definitely do dumb." McAlaney high-fived with Hoskins.

"She asked about the hard drive. I told her it's still missing."

"Which is true at least," said Meacham.

"But I didn't say we had the data anyway."

The waitress returned then with Pennance's coffee. "Here you go."

"I'll forever feel guilt over Logan's murder," said Meacham.

"You weren't to know he was under Quant's eye." Pennance took a sip. "It's the Director's fault, not yours."

"I'm just glad Elliott shared some of the programme with me beforehand."

"How are you doing with the encryption?" asked Pennance.

"Between me and Ava, we're making progress," said Hoskins.

"I can give you all the technical details if you want?" said McAlaney.

"Not necessary." Meacham held up her hands.

"Quant suspects then?" asked Hoskins.

"The Director suspects everyone, all the time," said Meacham. "That's how she got to where she is now. So we find ourselves in a Mexican stand-off. A position of mutual destruction. If either one of us talks, our careers are over."

"I can get a job anytime," said McAlaney.

"Good to know we're all in it together, Ava," said Hoskins.

McAlaney raised her glass. "You're welcome."

"What about CINN itself?" asked Pennance.

"For now, Obsidian has shelved the development, but I suspect that's temporary," said Meacham. "The opportunity is just too great, so Quant is biding her time. Meanwhile, Naughton infiltrates as many government departments as possible, spreading the tentacles of his system. And once there's another problem, another surge in crime rates, then Quant and CINN will be wheeled out all over again."

"Have the Carnforths been tracked down?" asked Pennance.

"Remind me who they are?"

"They viewed the two properties owned by Mercer where the bodies were found," said Hoskins. "We haven't found them yet, and I suspect we never will. Latest theory is they were hired by Mercer to leave us a trail of breadcrumbs to blindly follow."

"Quant also asked about O'Shea," said Pennance.

"He'll never see the inside of a cell," said Meacham. "Not while the NCA are paying him to clear up their mess."

"So, what do we do now?" asked McAlaney.

"Nothing," said Pennance. "We just have to wait it out."

"Jonah's right," said Meacham. "Quant will be watching our every move. The slightest slip and we're in trouble. From now on we only trust each other. Not even Simone, Jonah. Understood?"

"I don't like it, but yes."

"Vance, Ava?"

Hoskins and McAlaney nodded.

"I don't know about you, but I could do with a drink." Meacham raised a hand, beckoned the waitress. "You too, Jonah."

"No argument from me this time," said Pennance.

"Sex on the Beach all round," said Meacham.

"Now we're talking!" Hoskins rubbed his hands together like Crosse had.

"Coming right up," said the waitress.

"Pizza, too?"

Meacham rolled her eyes. "Why not."

"See, I did know what I was doing when I picked this place!" said Hoskins.

When the docktails arrived Meacham raised her glass in a toast. "To us," she said. "We stick together."

They clinked glasses. Pennance sat back. Declined the offer of a slice when the pizza arrived and smiled when Hoskins took both his own and Pennance's portions.

Pennance had spent a lifetime keeping secrets, even from those closest to him. So what was one more?

The people around the table, these were his family now.

About The Author

Keith Nixon is a British born writer of crime and historical fiction novels. Originally, he trained as a chemist, before holding various senior commercial roles at high-tech businesses. Keith recently took the opportunity to become a full-time author.

Keith currently lives with his family in the North West of England. Readers can connect with him on various social media platforms:

Web: http://www.keithnixon.co.uk
Twitter: @knntom
Facebook: Keithnixonauthor
Blog: www.keithnixon.co.uk/blog